MURDER IN THE EVENING

A lone howl punctuated the night. When it didn't end, but merely seemed to pause before escalating, Sarah realized the sound wasn't coming from the mouth of a dog. It was the cry of a person.

Followed by Harlan and Chief Gerard, Sarah ran out the restaurant's back door toward the singular human cry. She stopped midstep. The two men barely avoided running into her. A few parking spaces to the left of the door, Jane stood frozen, screaming. Her gaze seemed fixed on the garbage bin area shared with the veterinarian's office. The hairs on the back of Sarah's neck prickled as she turned in that direction.

Jacob, his knees resting on the ground, was bent over Riley. Her long, light hair, tinged coppery dark in spots, spread in all directions. As Chief Gerard struggled to get around Sarah to check for a pulse, the pallor of Riley's face and the angle of her neck belied the fact that Riley's vibrancy was extinguished without the need for Jacob's hoarse whisper, "She's dead . . ."

Books by Debra H. Goldstein

ONE TASTE TOO MANY

TWO BITES TOO MANY

THREE TREATS TOO MANY

Published by Kensington Publishing Corporation

THREE TREATS TOO MANY

A Sarah Blair Mystery

Debra H. Goldstein

KENSINGTON BOOKS
www.kensingtonbooks.com

KENSINGTON BOOKS are published by

Kensington Publishing Corp.
119 West 40th Street
New York, NY 10018

All Kensington titles, imprints, and distributed lines are available at special quantity discounts for bulk purchases for sales promotion, premiums, fund-raising, and educational or institutional use.

Special book excerpts or customized printings can also be created to fit specific needs. For details, write or phone the office of the Kensington Sales Manager: Kensington Publishing Corp., 119 West 40th Street, New York, NY 10018. Attn.: Sales Department. Phone: 1-800-221-2647.

First Kensington Books Mass Market Paperback Printing: September 2020
ISBN-13: 978-1-4967-1949-2
ISBN-10: 1-4967-1949-2

ISBN-13: 978-1-4967-1952-2 (ebook)
ISBN-10: 1-4967-1952-2 (ebook)

10 9 8 7 6 5 4 3 2 1

Printed in the United States of America

To Hayden, Hannah, Abby, and Eliza

CHAPTER ONE

Sarah Blair took a deep breath before entering the main dining room of Jane's Place. Attending the grand opening of her greatest nemesis's restaurant was the last thing she wanted to do, but she had no choice. Sarah was there to check out the competition. Her misery was only made worse because the opening of Southwind, the white-tablecloth restaurant across the street that she partially owned, was mired in red-tape delay by Wheaton's building inspector.

Looking around Jane's Place, Sarah didn't see either of her Southwind partners, but she immediately spotted the bottle-tinted flaming red hair of Jane's Place's namesake. Jane Clark stood near a small bar in the room's far corner, conversing with the chief of police and two city councilwomen. Sarah turned in the opposite direction.

Emily and Marcus, Southwind's co-owners, stood a few feet away, talking to one of their frequent catering customers, Deborah Holt. From their relaxed expressions, Sarah assumed her twin sister and Emily's boyfriend were turning the charm on to keep Mrs. Holt loyal to Southwind, no matter how good the food at Jane's Place was. Observing the three talking, Sarah decided her presence was not only unneeded but might be problematic. Mrs. Holt liked perfectly prepared catered food served in her own bowls, so her guests would think she cooked all day. That was exactly the opposite of Sarah's few efforts in the kitchen, which normally consisted of bringing in take-out or throwing together something simple using premade ingredients.

Peering beyond them, Sarah was pleased there were enough other people crammed into the canary-yellow painted dining room that Sarah could avoid Jane, her late ex-husband's bimbo, for most, if not all, of the time needed to survey the restaurant. Even if Sarah didn't stay long enough to have an opportunity to sample and form an opinion of all the available dishes, she was confident her partners, Chefs Emily and Marcus, with their more discerning palates, would.

Sarah took a quick inventory of the restaurant's setup for tonight. It appeared she was in the room where the main buffet was. Most of the two- and four-top tables were pushed back against two of the room's walls, leaving the center of the room clear for guests to mill around. Directly across from the dining room's main entryway was the buffet tasting table. A long line of people reminding her of vultures stood perched for a chance to sample Jane's Alabama farm-to-table food and her specially advertised vegan dishes.

Skipping an offered glass of pinot grigio that might

have helped make the next hour bearable, Sarah fell into the food line behind two of the three veterinarians from the practice that cared for her Siamese cat, RahRah. Without their identical white coats, the doctors, who in the clinic went by their first names, seemed as much a contrast to each other as Sarah and her twin sister were.

"Quite a line." Sarah pointed at the waiting patrons. "I can't imagine what possessed Jane to put the buffet table flat against the wall."

Dr. Tonya Putnam, RahRah's favorite vet, rolled her eyes. "Don't ask. Who knows with Jane? Considering how much food she put out, having only one side available for serving is a real pain."

"Hopefully, the wait will be worth it," Sarah said as they inched forward.

The other doctor, Vera Hong, poked her heart-shaped face around the taller Dr. Tonya. "Because our clinic and Jane's Place share the same parking lot, we saw the flow of people attending the past two weeks of soft openings. All our patients who told us about eating here raved about the food—especially the dishes made by Jane's sous chef, Riley Miller. That's why we couldn't resist trying everything for ourselves tonight."

Dr. Tonya leaned over conspiratorially to Sarah. "Besides, it's a free dinner."

Sarah laughed, but she silently prayed, for Southwind's sake, everything wasn't that good. Unfortunately, she'd heard the same thing about Riley's food from the grapevine—her mother.

Even though her mother lived fifteen minutes away in Birmingham, she always seemed to know everything going on in Wheaton, Alabama, before Sarah did. Sarah had originally planned to let Emily and Marcus attend the grand opening alone, but when her mother reported the over-the-top praise she'd heard about Riley's dishes, Sarah's curiosity won out.

The moment she'd walked into Jane's Place, her feelings had completely changed. The desire to taste Riley's food was gone. Instead, she wished she could go back out the front door, cross Main Street, and walk down the driveway beside the big house, where the new Southwind was, until she reached the carriage house behind it. Sarah owned the big house, but the carriage house where she lived was where she felt comfortable and safe. Playing at home with RahRah would be a lot more fun than making small talk or having to congratulate Jane if the food really was as good as everyone said.

Thinking of how RahRah, her alpha cat, was probably exerting control throughout the carriage house over Fluffy, Sarah's recently adopted dog, made her smile. It also reminded her she needed to make a vaccination appointment for Fluffy with either Dr. Tonya or Dr. Vera. Sarah had been so busy accidentally finding herself in the midst of a flurry of murders in Wheaton that taking Fluffy to the vet had completely slipped her mind. With their clinic located in the remodeled house next door to Jane's Place, she had no excuse for not running Fluffy by for her shot.

"Hate to interrupt your checked-out moment, but you need to move up," a voice behind Sarah said.

Flustered at being caught daydreaming, Sarah muttered, "Sorry." She glanced over her shoulder while she closed the gap in the line.

Her friend Jacob Hightower grinned at her with a smile that not only sat on his lips but reached his blue eyes. Having not seen much of him since the fire that temporarily put his job as a line cook at the original Southwind strip center location on hold, she was glad to run into him tonight.

"I didn't see you get in line."

"You were zoned out." He glanced around the room. "Whew. Jane's got some crowd. I bet most of Wheaton is here tonight."

Sarah frowned. "You might be right. People always like to try the new place in town—especially when they can do it for free."

"That's true. My shift at the Southwind Pub was dead tonight. I was somewhat surprised when I ran into Emily and Marcus eating in the other room, but considering your history with Jane, this is the last place I expected to see you."

Shoving her hands into her pockets, Sarah whispered a sheepish confession. "Call it self-protection. Emily, Marcus, and I came to try out our competitor's food. We've heard some of Jane's menu items are out of this world."

"Jane's food is no different than ever. Fine, but nothing special. It's Riley's dishes that are delicious."

"That's what I heard, but vegan dishes?" Sarah didn't notice how loud her voice was until the person behind Jacob shot her a dirty look. Her attempt at apologizing drew stares from more people until she realized

she was standing in front of the plates and they
wanted her to get on with making her selections.

She took two clear plastic plates from the pile at
the end of the table and handed one to Jacob. As she
served herself, she realized another reason the line
was moving so slowly. Riley Miller stood at the mid-
point of the long buffet table, explaining to each
group of guests what they were about to taste. Sarah
couldn't help but stare at her. Riley's ease and sense
of assurance reminded her of how Emily effortlessly
worked crowds when she did food demonstrations.

Watching the way Riley's blond ponytail bobbed
and how she accentuated her words with her ever-
moving hands, there was something about Riley that
made Sarah think the young chef might fly away at
any moment. It wasn't that Riley resembled a butterfly, but she radiated more of a sprite vibe. That was it.
She reminded Sarah of Tinker Bell, the fairy in *Peter
Pan*. Clad in a short green chiffon dress, Riley was
small, athletic, and had an engaging smile.

Sarah presumed Riley was quite the salesperson
from the amount of food Drs. Tonya and Vera had
piled on their plates while Sarah was daydreaming.
As she reached Riley's part of the buffet table, Sarah,
having heard and observed Emily in action, wondered how similar Riley's patter was.

"Hi. I'm Riley Miller."

"Sarah Blair."

"Oh, I know who you are."

Sarah cringed. She knew something like "You're
the one who helped solve that murder recently" was
probably coming.

"You're Chef Emily's sister. You know my friend Grace, Chef Emily's sous chef? She raves about Emily."

So much for letting her little bit of success unraveling a few murders go to her head. At least Sarah agreed with Grace. As much as Emily and she were polar opposites in everything from height to temperament, each was the other's strongest supporter. "Grace is right. Emily's not only great in the kitchen, but, if I say so myself, my sister's a pretty good egg. I'll have to tell her what Grace said."

"Oh, no. Please don't. I mean, it's what Grace said, but Grace would be so embarrassed for Chef Emily to know she gushes about her."

Sarah held up her hands to slow the torrent of words. "Whoa! Don't worry, Riley. It will be our secret." Sarah began spooning some type of casserole onto her plate. "Why don't you tell me about your food? Did you make all of these dishes?"

"Yes. My recipes, which are all vegan, are inspired by my love of nature. The one you're serving yourself is one of my favorites. It—oh, I'm sorry. Jane is signaling me. Time for the Jane and Riley dog-and-pony show."

Sarah followed Riley's gaze to the center of the room. Jane was indeed waving for Riley to join her. With a little shrug, Riley did. While Jane expressed her gratitude for everyone coming and supporting the opening of Jane's Place, Sarah, content to listen with one ear, focused on picking items to taste from the remainder of the buffet. Her plate was almost full when her attention was caught by Jane's explanation that her motivation for opening a farm-to-table, fine-dining restaurant on Main Street was to fulfill a dream she'd had with Bill Blair.

Sarah, her body tensing, stepped away from the serving table. Not only did she feel Jane's remarks were over-the-top, but the mention of Sarah's late ex-husband reminded her of the two things she most disliked about Jane. First, Jane was the bimbo who broke up Sarah's marriage almost two years ago, turning Sarah into a twenty-eight-year-old divorcée. And second, Jane had put Sarah through the wringer, trying to take her beloved cat, RahRah, from her after Bill died.

Sarah turned back toward Jacob, who still was filling his plate. She kept her voice low so only Jacob could hear her. "I swear the only reason Jane bought this house for her restaurant was because it's directly across the street from where Emily, Marcus, and I are opening Southwind."

Jacob nodded. "Probably true, but it won't hurt having two good restaurants to spur activity in Wheaton's entertainment district. Southwind and Jane's Place will help build our reputation as a foodie destination. Hopefully, that will convince people to drive the fifteen minutes from Birmingham."

From the perspective of enhancing traffic, Sarah couldn't disagree with Jacob. She knew he understood what he was talking about. After all, he'd quit working as a line cook for Marcus in San Francisco to return to Wheaton to be part of a group hoping to develop Main Street into an entertainment district. Because of his prior relationship with Marcus, Jacob was the one who convinced Marcus to move to

Wheaton to be an owner/chef of the original strip center Southwind location.

After a fire destroyed the first Southwind, Marcus and Emily had the restaurant remodeled to be the casual Southwind Pub. Although they had recently opened the doors of the Southwind Pub, their passion, with Sarah as a partner, was to launch a more formal dining establishment in Sarah's big house.

It was one thing to have a mostly local crowd frequent the chefs' Southwind Pub, but the survival of upper-end white-tablecloth restaurants like Southwind and Jane's Place needed local and neighboring customers. Even if Jacob was right that the proximity of the restaurants would prove beneficial, Sarah couldn't help wishing the competition across the street was owned by someone other than Jane.

"Come on. Let's see if there's someplace else we can eat." Jacob guided Sarah to a smaller room adjacent to the main dining area. From the looks of it, it had once been the house's formal parlor, but Jane was using it for a more intimate dining experience. There were only six tables, each set for four people. Jacob picked one and motioned Sarah to the seat across from him.

She looked at the food piled on her plate while she slid into her seat. It was way more than she should eat. "Jacob, you made it sound like you've tried a lot of the dishes served here. How? If I heard Jane right, tonight is the first time she's put everything on her menu out at one time."

"I came to all the soft openings."

Sarah was about to ask why when she remembered

she'd heard that Jacob had a thing for Riley. For a moment, Sarah tried to remember the source of the rumor. When it came to her that it was Emily's copper-skinned sous chef, Grace Winston, who mentioned it in passing, she knew from Riley's comments about Emily and Grace that Grace's info hadn't been idle gossip.

Rather than tease Jacob about having a crush on Riley, she feigned surprise at how many tastings he'd attended. "All of them?"

"Yup. Jane's food hasn't changed, but customers are going to line up out the restaurant's door for Riley's."

"I can't see anyone lining up to order any vegan option on a menu."

He pointed to the right corner of Sarah's plate. "In the past, I'd have agreed with you, but Riley's food is delicious. Try a bite of that."

She followed his direction. Her taking another taste was enough to show how much she'd enjoyed the first one. "What is this?"

"A tofu-based dish."

"Tofu? That's not something I usually eat, but this is different." She took another forkful.

He gave her a thumbs-up. "Mark my words, Riley is going to put Jane's Place on the map. We'll definitely see foodies from Birmingham lining up to eat here, which can only be good for Southwind, too."

Sarah frowned. From observing Emily and Marcus's efforts with the original Southwind restaurant before the fire, she knew it wasn't easy to convince people to drive from Birmingham to Wheaton. Much as a success for Jane galled her, Sarah guessed if Southwind and Jane's Place could help each other increase traffic to their respective restaurants, it would be okay.

In silence, they sampled the rest of the food on their plates. Everything Sarah tasted was so good she couldn't decide which dish she liked best. Sadly, Jane's Place was going to be stiff competition for Southwind.

Feeling stuffed, despite the portions being only tasting size, Sarah thought it was time to give Jacob a bit of a hard time. "Jacob, could there have been another reason you attended every opening event?"

An out of character redness made Jacob's cheeks flush. Seeing Jacob blush, Sarah was again struck by how handsome he was. When they met, she wrote him off as a rich boy temporarily slumming as a line cook in Southwind's kitchen to annoy his real estate mogul father. Slowly, she discovered that, despite being the son of one of the wealthiest families in town and having been blessed with the best looks in the Hightower family, he was a good guy.

Observing his discomfort, Sarah couldn't resist pulling his leg a bit more. "I never thought you would give up meat and potatoes. When did you develop such an interest in vegan cooking? Or is it vegan cooks?"

The serious look that crossed Jacob's face made Sarah stop her kidding.

He put down his fork and pushed his plate away. "Neither anymore, but that doesn't take away from the fact Riley's food is delicious. Speaking of delicious food, do you have any idea when Southwind will open?"

"That depends on Louis Botts. We've been waiting for him to come by and do the final city inspection for two weeks."

Jacob grimaced. "With Botts that doesn't surprise me. What does our mutual friend Cliff say about Botts and the time it's taking to get an inspection?"

Now it was Sarah's turn to be in the hot seat. Cliff was not only the contractor overseeing the construction and remodeling for Jane's Place, the Southwind Pub, Southwind, and the vet clinic next to Jane's Place, but he was also a close friend of Jacob's and a maybe boyfriend of Sarah's. Should she tell Jacob that when they were out sailing on his boat last weekend, Cliff admitted he thought something smelled fishy about how long it was taking to get a final inspection? No, she decided. Cliff's livelihood required him staying on good terms with Botts, and if she told Jacob what Cliff thought, it could make things worse.

It wasn't that long ago that Cliff dismissed Marcus's repeated complaints about how the town's only building inspector was or wasn't doing his job. But now, even Cliff couldn't understand why so much time had elapsed without the final inspection taking place. Renovations for the Southwind Pub had sailed through. The same was true for the remodeling of Jane's Place.

In retrospect, it seemed like Jane barely closed on the property before her restaurant was ready for soft openings. Southwind's Main Street location was an entirely different story. Anything to do with permitting, equipment deliveries, and inspections, especially the final one, seemed stuck in the mud if not sinking in quicksand.

Rather than answering Jacob's question about Cliff's opinion, she reached with her fork over to the food still on his plate. "I think I missed this one." She barely snagged a taste, but she took her time chewing and swallowing it. "Wow. This is delicious, too."

"Told you." He cocked his ear toward the dining room. "Sounds like Riley is talking. Want to go back in?"

"Sure."

They left their dishes on the table and returned to the dining room. Riley, surrounded on three sides by Jane and her guests, was addressing the importance of healthy eating and how one accomplished that through a vegan diet. Once she explained the healthy premise of her cooking, she segued into the specific vegan menu items available at Jane's Place.

As she listened, Sarah sorted through the different rumors she'd heard about Riley since Jane's Place began opening events two weeks ago. Sarah wasn't big on gossip, but the talented sous chef and her food probably were the hottest topics in town. While some of the talk addressed her skill as a chef, quite a bit focused on her personal life and romantic attachments. If what was being said was true, Riley was a heartbreaker who dated everyone and anyone, but no one in particular. Jacob's name was linked with Riley's by Grace, but seeing his reaction to the mention of Louis Botts, she wondered if Botts was the man of the moment while Jacob had been pushed out in the cold. She wasn't about to ask Jacob. Even if she did, she doubted he would answer her.

When Riley finished speaking, the crowd broke up. Some people, including the veterinarians and a few of the city VIPs, left immediately. It was as if common courtesy had dictated that in exchange for their free dinners, they wait until Jane and Riley spoke before fleeing. Those who remained made their way back to the bar or tasting table.

Leaving her side, Jacob made a beeline toward Riley. At the same time, from the other side of the room, a tall man purposely broke through the remaining groups of people apparently intent on doing the same thing. Because of his comb-over and leather motorcycle jacket, which, underneath its embellishments, was the same slick shade of black as his hair, she recognized Louis Botts. She'd met him when he inspected the Southwind Pub. Sarah also saw him occasionally when she walked Fluffy. His ever-present unique jacket, as he gunned his motorcycle onto Main Street from the driveway the animal clinic and Jane's Place shared, was a dead giveaway.

Before Botts could reach Riley, a beefy hand caught his sleeve and stopped his forward movement dead cold. Although the individual attached to the hand wore a plaid suit that reminded Sarah of a checkered picnic blanket, instead of his usual chef's white jacket, balloon pants, and orange clogs, Sarah immediately recognized Emily's boyfriend, Chef Marcus. She could see from his stance that he was in a confrontational mode.

"Botts, if I ran my restaurant with the 'I'll get around to it when I can' attitude you have, I'd be out of business within a month."

"I'm sorry, Marcus. There's only one of me. Remember, besides the renovation and building inspections for Wheaton's new entertainment district, I'm still handling every other city commercial and residential inspection. If you want to complain to someone, go talk to those city council folks over by the bar. See if you can get them to loosen their purse strings enough to hire another inspector. Believe me, I've tried."

As Marcus and Botts's voices escalated above the ruckus of the party, Sarah looked around but didn't see her sister or, for that matter, Jane anywhere. Scared as to what might happen next, Sarah hurried toward Botts and Marcus. Just as she reached Marcus's side, he pushed himself into Botts's personal space.

While Botts explained something about the delivery and construction delays dropping Southwind to the bottom of his schedule, it was Marcus's partially raised arm, with its closed fist, that concerned her. She grabbed his arm and exerted as much pressure as her full 128 pounds would allow. Either surprised or reacting to her weight, Marcus relaxed his fighter's stance. He dropped his unclenched fist even with his thighs.

Botts grabbed a glass of champagne from the tray of a passing waiter. He downed it in two gulps and wiped his mouth with the back of his hand. "Marcus, be careful with those mitts of yours. You don't want to take on someone who's been trained to use his hands. Besides, you're going to need them for mincing and mixing whenever you get your fancy restaurant open."

Sarah tensed, half expecting to feel Marcus tighten his muscles again to throw a punch. When he didn't, she released her grip on his arm.

"And when will that be, Botts? We've been waiting for your inspection for almost two weeks."

Botts held up his well-manicured hands while he moved out of the uncomfortable circle of closeness Marcus and he shared. "I honestly don't know. How many times do I have to tell you and your contractor if things for this job had been timely, like at your Southwind Pub or any of the places around you here on Main Street, we wouldn't be having this discussion?"

"But it's been two weeks!"

"I'm doing the best I can, but there's only one of me."

"One too many," Marcus muttered.

Sarah flinched. Considering the disruption of sleepy Wheaton by murder only a few months ago, she assumed people might be a little jumpy at anything that sounded like a threat.

Botts must have heard what Marcus said. He lost his smile and thrust his jaw forward. "What did you say?"

Sarah decided, before Marcus dug himself in deeper, a Sarah Blair intervention was necessary. "We understand Wheaton only employs one of you to do all its local inspections, but having had so many delays, you can understand why everyone involved with Southwind is frustrated." She waved her hand randomly around the room. "It's never a good feeling having your competitors get a few weeks jump on you."

From the corner of her eye, Sarah caught sight of her twin, Emily, flanking Marcus's other side and slipping her arm into his. Sarah ignored her sister, concentrating her milk-and-honey attention on the city inspector. "Watching the vet clinic and this restaurant, right across the street from Southwind, not to mention the Southwind Pub, sail through their remodeling has been unsettling."

"Nothing I can do about that."

"We understand everything you're faced with."

Marcus stirred next to her.

By his continued silence, she assumed Emily had a good grasp on him. "But I certainly hope you can squeeze us in this week for our last inspection."

Botts threw his hands up in a way Sarah interpreted as a sign of futility or giving up. "Sarah, the best I can say is I'll try."

"That's all I'm asking."

The lines in Botts's forehead relaxed as did the timbre of his voice. "Honestly, I don't like this delay any more than all of you. It's not my fault there's a process I've got to follow. I understand your concern is your restaurant, but everyone is concerned about their own buildings. Like I said, there's only one of me, and I've been backed up for weeks. Remember, I'm not only handling the approved entertainment district, the restricted area where restaurants like yours that serve alcohol are, but I'm also responsible for the wider zoned parts of Wheaton that include residential, industrial, and commercial projects. I've gotten to telling people, 'Take a number.' "

"If only we could," Marcus said.

Botts frowned again but then forcibly relaxed his mouth into a thin smile. "Maybe I should get one of those automatic number dispensers."

Marcus shook Emily off his arm. "The question as

I see it is how much you'd charge per number, or do you prefer a sliding scale?"

Now Botts moved into Marcus's space. Heads almost butting, the two circled each other. "You're out of line, Marcus."

"Am I? I'm only speaking the truth. Ask anyone."

Sarah pushed herself between the two men. She gave Marcus a cold stare before focusing her gaze on Botts. "Come on, guys. This is a tough enough situation for both of you. Let's not say anything we don't mean."

A new voice, Riley's, joined the mix, almost pleading. "Especially tonight."

Sarah and Emily exchanged a glance.

Emily tugged on Marcus's arm. "I'm sure Louis will try to get us on his schedule as soon as possible." Marcus opened his mouth to say something, but Emily beat him to the punch. "In the meantime, let's go check out the dessert table, Marcus. Remember, this is Jane and Riley's night."

Although she knew he still had to be angry at Botts, Sarah watched the gentle giant melt.

Without another word, he let Emily lead him away from her and Botts. Sarah was, as always, struck by how Marcus dwarfed Emily. A hug from him enveloped her diminutive twin, yet Sarah had the feeling size didn't matter in their relationship.

Why the contrast between the two surprised her, Sarah didn't know. After all, how many times had she heard that opposites attract? Besides, she'd given up counting how often people refused to believe Emily and she were twins or asked if they were identical when anyone could see Emily was the blond cheerleader type while Sarah was a willowy brunette. She was about to try another dose of her sister's Southern charm on Botts and Riley when Riley laid her hand on Botts's arm.

He shook it off.

Riley pleaded. "Louis?"

"Not now. I've got to get out of here. I'm going to take a ride to clear my head."

"Let me get my jacket and I'll go with you."

"No. Stay here. Enjoy your night." He turned away so abruptly his swinging arm grazed the side of Riley's, almost knocking her over. Riley staggered for a second but regained her balance. Looking to Sarah like she was doing anything but enjoying her night, Riley repeated his name, but he didn't stop. Considering he was already halfway out the restaurant's back entrance, Sarah doubted he heard her. Riley must have concluded the same thing because she immediately followed his path to the rear parking lot.

The way Riley trailed Botts made Sarah think of the devotion with which Fluffy shadowed RahRah throughout the house. Catching sight of the furry puppy following the haughty Siamese cat always made her laugh, but there had been nothing amusing about this scene. Sarah glanced around the room, wondering if anyone else had observed the exchange between Botts and Riley.

At first, she didn't think so, but then she saw Jacob cross the room, headed toward the exit. From where Sarah first saw him, she surmised he'd made his way to Riley's side while Marcus and Botts were having their standoff but then had been deserted by her. The combination of his quick pace and scowling face made Sarah fear another possible confrontation. Without consciously thinking, Sarah planted herself directly in his path. He slowed and tried to go around her.

"Jacob?"

"Not now, Sarah. I'm in a hurry."

She ignored his urgency and lightened her tone, while remaining in his way. "Jacob, I just want to tell you that, to my dismay, you were right. Everything of Riley's I tasted was delicious. I understand why you said everyone is dying for her food."

The loud rev of a motorcycle outside the building, followed by a bevy of dogs barking, almost drowned out Jacob's reply. "Yeah, it's murderous."

CHAPTER TWO

Before Sarah could respond, Wheaton's acting police chief, Dwayne Gerard, and Sarah's boss, attorney Harlan Endicott, joined them. Harlan immediately greeted Sarah and Jacob and commented on the evening's success while Chief Gerard swallowed the last bite of a black and white cookie.

With a sweep of the outside of his hand, the chief flicked away the crumbs clinging to the mustache he'd grown in the past month. "Black and whites were my favorite kind of cookies when I was a boy, but I rarely find good ones anymore. If Jane keeps them on her menu, she'll have me as a regular customer. Great food, don't you think?"

"Couldn't agree more. Some of the best in town." Harlan patted his stomach.

Sarah stared at him. Admittedly, he handled the legal work for Jane's Place and Southwind, but didn't he owe the Southwind crew a bit more loyalty? After all, she was *his* receptionist/secretary. Not to mention his only employee. And what was with his budding bromance with the chief? The way the two sparred a few months ago over whether Sarah's mother was guilty of murder, Sarah couldn't understand how they could suddenly be so chummy. Harlan often said, "Keep your friends close, and your enemies closer," but seeing the two men side by side, nothing indicated they were frenemies.

Chief Gerard rubbed his hand against the side of his mustache. "Sarah, it sure tastes like Emily and Marcus are going to have some real competition on Main Street."

"Now, Chief, don't you think you should wait to pass judgment until Southwind opens? I bet they'll run circles around Jane," Sarah said.

Harlan laughed. He took a quick look around him before quietly speaking. "That won't be hard when it comes to Jane's dishes. She apparently did get something out of the time she worked for Southwind. In fact, I think she tweaked a few of Marcus and Emily's original recipes and is claiming them as hers, but none of hers holds a candle to theirs."

Sarah exchanged a glance with Jacob. Having worked with Jane, Marcus, and Emily, especially during the Food Expo, Jacob had personal knowledge of Jane's limitations in the kitchen. He didn't respond or even appear to be listening to what Harlan was continuing to say.

"It's Riley's food that has all of us on the edge of our chairs. None of us knew vegan dishes could be this good. Do you know if Southwind will offer any vegan specialties?"

Sarah admitted she didn't.

Chief Gerard kissed his fingertips. "I don't know how Riley makes everything taste so light and creamy and still be vegan. Mark my words, she'll have a huge following. Maybe Marcus and Emily should consider stealing her away from Jane in time for Southwind's grand opening?" He laughed at his little joke.

Sarah bristled. Considering the time and training Marcus and Emily had put into their chosen field, which was far more than that of the amateurly trained Jane or new culinary school graduate Riley, Sarah was stung by the police chief's comments. She wondered how many more people who attended the soft openings for Jane's Place harbored similar feelings.

Much as she thought she hid her conflicted emotions, she obviously failed, or at least Harlan picked up on them. "He's only teasing, Sarah. If you knit your brows any closer together, you'll have a sweater the perfect size for RahRah by morning."

The image of anyone trying to squeeze her cat into a sweater did the trick of easing her black mood. "I might be able to knit the sweater, but fat chance of getting RahRah into it."

She looked for the telltale signs of whether Harlan was going to continue their RahRah banter. From the twinkle of his hazel eyes showing through the lenses of his glasses and the lines deepening around his mouth, she knew he was playing the joke out in his mind. If there was one thing she'd learned working for him during the past year, it was that he was very serious when it came to the law and his clients, but he took great pleasure when he came up with a funny—even if no one else laughed.

To her dismay, Chief Gerard chuckled and played along with Harlan. "Are you sure? What if it was a one-of-a-kind Sarah Blair designer number?"

Sarah didn't give Harlan a chance to get off another one-liner. "Not going to happen. RahRah has a mind of his own. Besides, crafts, like cooking, aren't my thing. You can be sure if you ever see RahRah in a sweater, it's store-bought."

She looked at Jacob, hoping he would introduce a new topic. When she caught sight of his scrunched nose and lowered brows, she immediately realized she should have let Harlan continue with his one-liners. "Are you okay, Jacob?"

"I'm fine, but considering what we just saw, I'd think you'd be able to come up with more than a string of bad jokes."

Sarah heard rather than saw Chief Gerard's intake of breath as he moved from being a party guest into his more official role. "What did you see, Jacob?"

Instead of answering immediately, Jacob locked gazes with Sarah. He was the first to break their link. Angling himself to face Chief Gerard, Jacob averted his gaze from Sarah's face. "We saw Botts manhandle Riley Miller. You know what a master he is when it comes to charming people, especially the opposite sex, and then taking advantage of them."

"I don't think I understand," Chief Gerard said.

Before things got out of hand, Sarah interrupted. "That wasn't exactly what we saw."

Still keeping his shoulder turned as if shunning her, Jacob cut Sarah off. "He hit her."

"No, he didn't. Riley came up behind him while

Botts was pivoting abruptly. His arm bumped into her, but it wasn't intentional. He didn't . . ." She glanced at Harlan, hoping he could come up with the word she was seeking.

Harlan picked up on her need for help and prompted her. "He didn't hit her willfully?"

"That's right. He was being rude and moving quickly, but I saw and heard everything. He didn't intentionally strike or threaten Riley in any way. In fact, when Botts left, she offered to go with him, but he told her no. He told her this was her night and she should enjoy it, but he needed to take a ride to clear his head."

The chief queried Jacob. "Did you see it that way, too?"

Jacob's gaze dropped to his shoes. "Maybe. Sarah was closer to Botts and Riley than I was, but anyone could see he was short with her."

"He left abruptly," Sarah admitted. "In fact, he was out the door before Riley followed him. I heard the rev of a motorcycle, but I don't know if she caught up to him or not."

She stopped for a breath. This time, Jacob didn't interrupt her, but his red face and pressed lips were telltale signs of how agitated he was. In all the times she'd observed him involved in a crisis at Southwind or during one of the heated battles relating to the entertainment district at city hall meetings, he always kept his cool. Often, he was the one who came up with the solution everyone agreed to.

"Chief Gerard," Sarah continued, "I didn't like a lot of what I saw from Botts tonight with Riley, or anyone else, for that matter, but his behavior wasn't an act of violence or I would have said or done something immediately."

Jacob forced himself into the chief's line of sight. "Maybe Botts making contact with Riley wasn't intentional, but we all know he's as bad and dishonest as they come. I'm surprised you haven't checked him out professionally, or did the city council or some of the other political bigwigs tell you to leave him alone? Perhaps they hinted you should look the other way if you want the permanent appointment?"

Harlan put his hands up, seemingly to shush Jacob, but it didn't work.

"You can keep your heads in the sand, but the proof is out there about Botts. It's only a matter of time until the rest comes out."

"That's more than enough, Jacob. Why don't you go home and cool off?" The chief kept his voice even, but he moved his hand to rest on the top of his holstered gun.

Jacob shook his head one more time as he stared at Chief Gerard. Making a sound of disgust, he pivoted away from them. Without stopping, he left the restaurant through the rear door, slamming it behind him.

Even though Sarah had seen the door flying closed, she still jumped when it banged. She turned to see how Chief Gerard was reacting to Jacob's accusations. She wasn't expecting much. She'd known Chief Gerard for almost a year now, since before he became the acting chief of police, and more times than not he'd bumbled things—some involving her own family. Still, making mistakes during an investigation was a far cry from intentionally overlooking criminal behavior.

Sarah understood the tenuous position he was in as acting chief of police. Any scent or accusation of impropriety could ruin his chances for the actual appointment. She hoped the chief would let Jacob's words roll off his back. As the chief stared at her, Sarah silently held her breath.

"You're sure Botts didn't do anything out of line?"

"Not that I know of. He was rude and quick to leave, but he wasn't violent, at least not here at the party."

The chief rested his hand on the bottom of his face. With his forefinger, he rubbed the edge of his mustache before using a movie-like Southern drawl. "Sounds to me like we might have a little bit of rivalry going on here. I think we'll just let everybody, especially that young 'un, cool down a bit."

Sarah breathed a sigh of relief on Jacob's behalf. She couldn't go after him now, but she'd call or try to see him tomorrow. Hopefully, he'd have cooled down by then. If not, she might have to give him a big sister-like lecture about going overboard. In the meantime, she needed to focus on the moment.

Harlan looked as though he might try to tell another joke, so Sarah was relieved when all he said was, "Sounds like a plan. Speaking of which, Sarah brace yourself. Here comes Jane."

Sarah peered behind her. Not only was Jane zeroing in on them, but they were about the last guests left in the dining room. With her back to the main part of the room, she hadn't realized everyone, except the city council members talking near the bar and a few people taking a last pass at the food table, were gone. Maybe the reason they'd been lucky Jane hadn't come over during the earlier altercations was because she'd been busy with departing guests.

Working around the stragglers, the servers were already clearing things away. For a moment, Sarah considered fleeing through tonight's revolving back door, but gauging Jane's velocity, there was no escaping the redheaded dynamo about to attack them.

"I'm so glad the three of you came to my little ol' opening tonight. Wasn't it divine? Sarah, such a shame Emily and Marcus disappeared before I could talk to them. I wanted to tell them I certainly hope when you get Southwind open you can have as nice a night as this. Maybe you should suggest they hold your grand opening on a Monday night, when we're closed. That way we won't be siphoning off any of the crowd who might come to your opening. I'm sure that would help you get some extra folks glad for the free food."

"Like you did?"

Jane gave her a floppy wave. "Bless your heart, dear. Haven't you heard how busy we've been the past two weeks?"

"It was a lovely evening, Jane." Harlan effectively cut Sarah off while drawing Jane's attention to him. "You must be very proud of how well your staff performed and how well received Riley's dishes were."

"Oh, I am. And did you get a chance to sample any of my new soups?"

"Just a little bit," Sarah said. "I tried your butternut squash soup."

"I love that soup. Maybe not as much as my chilled zucchini soup, but it's so comforting."

Still annoyed at Jane's earlier remarks, Sarah couldn't resist jabbing her. "It reminded me a lot of an easy one Emily makes in a Crock-Pot. You've had it, haven't you?"

"Yes." Jane batted her eyes at Harlan and Chief Gerard. "Our recipes are quite similar, but mine has more taste because Emily's is gluten-free. It's a shame so many of those gluten-free recipes, like Emily's, taste like cardboard."

"If anyone knows how to make food that tastes like cardboard, it's you," Sarah muttered under her breath.

"What did you say?" Jane narrowed her eyes.

Sarah, realizing the futility of arguing any further with Jane, decided to change the context of their conversation. "Vegan dishes were the last thing I expected to see on your menu."

At the change in subject, Jane flashed them all a giant smile. "The decision was easy. When I judged one of Carleton Junior Community College's student culinary competition evenings, I tasted Riley's entries. I was hooked after the first bite. I knew Wheaton would be, too. The timing of opening my restaurant and her graduation couldn't have been better. I think hiring Riley as my sous chef, instead of trying again to lure Emily's Grace Winston from Southwind, was one of the smartest decisions I made. Don't you agree, Sarah?"

Mercifully, Sarah's need to answer was blocked out by the sound of barking and whining dogs. A motorcycle roar only agitated the animals into a louder frenzy.

"Chief," Jane said. When he didn't answer, she yelled his name until he heard her above the din. "You've got to do something! Between the dogs and Harleys, my customers can't eat in peace. Aren't those veterinarians and their friends in violation of some city noise ordinance?"

"Not that I know of. Besides, they aren't all Harleys out there. Last time I looked, some of the bikes are Hondas, Yamahas, or Suzukis. There's even one or two BMWs."

Jane rolled her eyes and turned away from Chief Gerard. "Harlan, can I sue them?"

"For what?"

"Trying to ruin my business. The noise is terrible when they let the animals out in the runs, but it's especially bad during my dinner rush. I bought this house thinking I was buying a quiet Main Street property. I was excited when they suggested taking advantage of our adjacent driveways and putting our separate dumpsters near each other to create more available parking between their place and my restaurant. I thought it would be perfect for evening overflow parking. They never mentioned they planned to put their animal runs practically on top of my main dining room or to let that community motorcycle gang hold meetings and park at their place. I swear, if it isn't the dogs yowling, it's one of those doctors or their motorcyclist friends zooming in or out on their Harleys at all hours. So, can I sue them?"

"The zoning for these houses lets every owner use their own property as desired."

"But isn't the noise a nuisance or something? Their privacy fence is meaningless. Whenever anyone parks on the motorcycle parking pad, the animals staying with them go crazy. It's even worse when someone leaves."

"Wheaton doesn't have a noise ordinance. If they use their property as it's zoned, their guests are allowed to make noise consistent with their mission."

Jane's cheeks now matched her hair. "By that logic, my diners are entitled to a pleasant dining experience because feeding them in peace and quiet is my mission."

"And I thought your mission was making money or undercutting Emily and Marcus," Sarah muttered.

"What did you say?"

"Now, now." Chief Gerard raised his hands so the palms were aimed in Sarah and Jane's respective directions, seemingly signaling "enough." Once he had their attention, he continued to use his hands almost in a tomahawk chopping manner to emphasize his words. "Jane, tomorrow I'll talk to the doctors and see if I can work out a better schedule for their animals to be outside so your guests can enjoy a quiet experience during your core dining hours. Okay?"

Apparently not fully satisfied, Jane pouted. "What about the riders and the noise they make?"

"That I may not be able to help you with, but I'll look into it."

"Thank you, Chief Gerard." Jane flashed a big smile at him. "You're a peach."

Not exactly the words Sarah would use to describe him. Her pondering of what might be more descriptive of Chief Gerard was interrupted by Jane.

Flashing a toothy grin at them, Jane piled on the Southern charm by using an exaggerated drawl. "Gotta run, but I can't thank y'all enough for attending the opening of Jane's Place. The three of you are so special."

Once Jane was out of earshot, Harlan turned toward Chief Gerard. "I don't think this is the last you're going to hear from her about the noise and her neighbors."

"Not by a long shot, but I am going to have to figure out something to keep the peace. The vets next door aren't going to put up with Jane's shenanigans."

"I know at least two of the doctors ride hogs. Are you going to tell them they can't park their motorcycles in their own parking spots because they make too much noise crossing the open lot? Or, for that matter, their club can't congregate at their place?"

"Of course not. Baby steps, Harlan. Baby steps. If I can get them to keep the boarding animals in during Jane's core dining hours, that will give her something to be happy about. The last thing we need on Main Street is owners yipping, if you'll forgive the pun, at each other."

While the chief laughed at his own wit, Harlan and Sarah exchanged a look between themselves. Jane had given in too easily. Knowing her like they did, Sarah and Harlan agreed Jane's polite capitulation probably meant she wasn't going to wait for Chief Gerard to do something tomorrow.

Sarah glanced around the room. There was no sign of Jane's red mane. If Sarah was a betting person, she would lay odds Jane already was taking matters into her own hands. Remembering how vindictive Jane was in the past, Sarah hated to think what might be said between the neighbors in the next few minutes.

A lone howl punctuated the night. When it didn't end, but merely seemed to pause before escalating, Sarah realized the sound wasn't coming from the mouth of a dog. It was the cry of a person.

Followed by Harlan and Chief Gerard, Sarah ran out the restaurant's back door toward the singular human cry. She stopped midstep. The two men barely avoided running into her. A few parking spaces to the left of the door, Jane stood frozen, screaming. Her gaze seemed fixed on the dumpster area shared with the veterinarian's office. The hairs on the back of Sarah's neck prickled as she turned in that direction.

Jacob, his knees resting on the ground, was bent over Riley. Her long, light hair, tinged coppery dark in spots, spread in all directions. As Chief Gerard struggled to get around Sarah to check for a pulse, the pallor of Riley's face and the angle of her neck belied the fact that Riley's vibrancy was extinguished without the need for Jacob's hoarse whisper "She's dead."

CHAPTER THREE

"Murderer! Just because you couldn't have her, you killed her!" Apparently spurred by Jacob's words while Sarah had involuntarily looked away, Jane had regained her mobility and now stood toe to toe with a standing Jacob. Her face was thrust forward, even with Jacob's. She was straining so hard as she screamed at him her vocal cords stood out in the tight skin of her neck. "You couldn't leave her alone. I swear, I'll see to it that they put you away for the rest of your life."

Jacob flinched but didn't try to defend himself. He simply stood, shoulders sagging, head down, hands at his side. Sarah couldn't decide if he was stunned, in shock, or acknowledging the truth of what Jane was yelling. Could Jacob have done something this horrible? Was it possible her dear friend, who would do anything for anyone, was somehow a killer? Surely not. Admittedly, other than Riley, only Jacob and Jane were outside when the others responded, but someone else had to have done this.

Not Jacob. She couldn't tell from the expression on his face. It was as if his handsome features were as devoid of life as Riley was.

Sarah waited for Chief Gerard to quiet Jane or at least say something. He had immediately rushed to Riley, ignoring Jane's tirade. After reaching her side, the chief slowed his motions as he peered down at her. Sarah took it as a bad sign when he didn't check for a pulse or shout for someone to call an ambulance.

When he looked back to where Harlan and Sarah still stood, Sarah knew from the anguished look on his face that there was no disputing Jacob's words. Riley's twinkling energy was gone. Harlan and she started toward Riley and Chief Gerard, but the chief put his hand up. "Please. Please stay where you are. Don't come any closer."

He turned toward Jane and Jacob. Jacob still stood silent, while Jane continued spewing accusations at him. Chief Gerard curtly cut her off. She closed her mouth midsentence.

Having quieted her, the chief began barking orders. "Harlan, go inside and tell everyone there's a problem and they're going to have to stay put for a while. If anyone gives you any grief, explain it isn't a request."

Harlan left her side. She wondered if he'd get any resistance from those still in the dining room, considering most of them were the city's type A politicos. Her thoughts also wandered to whether her sister and Marcus were still inside or had left. She hadn't seen them again after Emily dragged him away to check out the dessert table.

Chief Gerard's mention of Sarah's name cut off her personal thoughts. "I'd appreciate it if you would stand on the left over there until we can take your statement. Jane," he added, "if you'd go stand on the right of the parking pad, please." He pointed toward the privacy fence that separated the parking lot from the dog runs and the cement pad at its end where a group of motorcycles were parked.

Sarah immediately did as he asked. Jane took a couple of steps in tandem with her but stopped and turned around. Curious, Sarah looked to see what she was doing. Jane had returned to her spot near Jacob, where she stood, hands on her hips, giving Chief Gerard a piece of her mind.

"Dwayne Gerard, I'm not going to be ordered around. You have the murderer right in front of you— why don't you arrest him?"

Chief Gerard, with his thumbs hooked into his belt loops, wasn't smiling. "There's a way to do this, Jane. Please go where I asked."

In the face of his firmness, Jane frowned. With her lips clasped tightly, she slowly walked away from him until she stood several feet away from Sarah. Jacob didn't move.

Still ignoring Jacob, Chief Gerard pulled his cell phone from his pocket. Sarah strained to hear what he was saying. When she heard "backup," she surmised he was calling the dispatcher for additional help. It wasn't as if he could expect a big response. With Chief Gerard being in the interim position, there were only two other members of the Wheaton police force.

Officer Alvin Robinson, whom Sarah had gotten to

know during the last murder investigation she was involved with, had been on Wheaton's payroll for only the past six months. His college-linebacker physique was helpful when he patrolled, but that, combined with his ability to tell tales of his playing days, had made him an instant favorite as Wheaton's school resource officer. If Chief Gerard used him in the same capacity he had while investigating the last Wheaton murder, Officer Robinson would be handling crowd control and taking statements with the chief.

Five-year police force veteran Dr. David Smith's youthful look gave the impression he should be a Wheaton High student. As the town's coroner and the police department's sole detective, Dr. Smith, Sarah was certain, would be responsible for Riley's body, autopsy, and any forensic work related to the crime scene.

Whether Chief Gerard had called one or both in, Sarah knew it wouldn't be long before they arrived. In Wheaton, unlike sprawling Birmingham, it never took long to go from point A to B. Still, Sarah hoped they hurried. As warm as it was when she left the house for the opening, she hadn't thought about being outside long enough after the sun had set to need a light jacket.

Rubbing the goose pimples on her arms, Sarah watched the chief examine the crime scene in more depth. Because he hadn't immediately strung the area off with yellow crime tape, she assumed he must not have any with him. Looking around, though, she was impressed when she realized the way he'd placed everyone essentially cordoned off the crime scene and separated the main witnesses. She also noticed that while he was making observations from all angles, he wasn't getting close enough to disturb anything.

Sarah's attention was caught by the sound of the restaurant's back door being flung open. City Councilor Anne Hightower barreled through it, trailed by Harlan. Her target wasn't Chief Gerard, but her brother, Jacob. Sarah marveled at how, despite the urgency of her mission, there wasn't a hair out of place on Anne's carefully coiffured head. If it had been Sarah, not only would her hair be flying in all directions, but she would be a walking mess. Not Anne. She remained immaculately put together in a navy dress accented by a red scarf. It was the perfect look for a councilor running for mayor. The pièce de résistance, though, was Anne's three-inch red heels, which alternately clicked across the asphalt.

Before she reached her brother, the chief blocked her path. "I'm sorry, Councilor. You'll have to wait to talk to him. Please stand over there with Harlan until we sort things out."

"You don't understand. Jacob is my brother."

"I know that, but he's also someone I need to talk to about what's happened here."

"But I'm a member of the city council."

"And I'm the chief of police."

"Acting."

He grimaced. "Acting. But this is my crime scene. If you can't stay out of my way and let me do my job, you'll have to go inside and wait with the others." He pointed to where Harlan stood.

Anne clamped her mouth shut and joined Harlan, shooting a menacing look in the chief's direction.

There was no question in Sarah's mind that Anne had Jane beat in the if-looks-could-kill department. The interim chief had surely lost Anne's support to give him the job permanently, but he'd gone up two notches in Sarah's opinion.

Anne and Harlan weren't close enough to where Sarah and Jane stood for either group to talk to each other without shouting, but Jane's continued mutterings were coming in loud and clear. Sarah almost bit her tongue in amusement when Officer Robinson and Dr. Smith pulled into the parking lot and Jane observed, "The cavalry has arrived."

Dr. Smith, camera around his neck, placed his black leather satchel on the ground. From inside the bag, he removed booties and gloves for himself, Officer Robinson, and Chief Gerard. The three donned their protective gear and went right to work.

While Dr. Smith took pictures in a wide circle before approaching Riley's body, Chief Gerard and Officer Robinson restricted the area with a roll of yellow crime tape that Sarah saw Dr. Smith hand the chief. From the chief's careful actions, Sarah knew this time no one would be able to accuse him of contaminating the crime scene. He not only seemed more knowledgeable, but he had an air of confidence about him. Doubting he'd obtained either one from reading books, she made a mental note to ask Harlan, the chief's best bro, what course Chief Gerard attended.

Sarah, to avoid the horror she felt looking at Riley, focused on counting the motorcycles parked on the cement pad next to the veterinarian clinic while the police worked. She counted at least twelve bikes.

Sarah's attention was drawn back to the scene of the crime by Anne's voice.

Because Anne and the chief were standing across from each other, Sarah could see only Anne's face as she confronted Chief Gerard outside the secured zone, her arms crossed. "I want Harlan to represent Jacob."

"There's no need for a lawyer. It's standard procedure to take statements from all of you at the scene in a case like this."

With a look of utter disdain, Anne turned from the chief and, with her back ramrod straight, purposefully strutted over to where Harlan stood. She grabbed his arm and pulled him toward Jacob, causing Harlan to misstep. As he stumbled, Anne braced him while yelling, "Jacob! You need representation. Now!"

At his sister's voice, Jacob raised his head. He stared in the direction where Harlan, having regained his footing, and Anne were. Sarah wasn't sure from Jacob's expressionless face how much he was comprehending even when he echoed Anne. "Representation."

Was he making his own request or simply parroting Anne? Sarah had read about situations where a person who experienced something awful went into a form of shock where only familiar voices filtered through. Anne and he might be on opposite sides when it came to business, especially regarding their position on developing Main Street into an entertainment district, but as Sarah had found with her mother and Emily, even in the most challenging situations, their blood bond proved to be the proverbial "thicker than water." She wasn't sure if Jacob was responding to Anne from deep in a fog or if the sound of her voice had brought him back to reality.

When Anne started calling to Jacob again, Sarah realized Anne wasn't sure, either. To Sarah, Anne's insistence on Harlan as his attorney seemed almost illogical considering how many times Harlan had represented Southwind and other parties with predevelopment interests before the council. As such, Anne and Harlan had often squared off against each other.

There also was no question Anne knew that taking statements of everyone who'd been in the restaurant or parking lot when Riley was probably killed was, as Chief Gerard explained, standard procedure. Sarah wasn't a lawyer, but she was aware of that much from watching *Perry Mason* reruns. No, something else had to be motivating Anne's continued insistence on bringing Harlan into the picture now. Could she also fear her brother was a murderer?

"Jacob, look over here. At Harlan," Anne called.

Jacob did as he was told. "Harlan. Help me."

"You want me to be your lawyer in this matter?" Harlan moved toward Jacob's side.

"What is this? A new form of ambulance chasing?" Although his words sounded harsh to her ears, Sarah noticed Chief Gerard didn't stop Harlan. Instead, the chief stood still, his lips held in a way that made his mustache appear almost flat.

When Jacob replied "Yes" to Harlan's question, Sarah could have sworn Chief Gerard's mustache line straightened even more. She didn't care. From experience, she knew having Harlan on the case could make all the difference in the world.

CHAPTER FOUR

Chief Gerard and Officer Robinson worked efficiently, taking statements in the main dining room and its adjacent parlor, but it still was two hours before Officer Robinson got to Sarah. She was relieved Officer Robinson was the one taking her statement. They'd become friends when her mother was accused of murdering the president of Wheaton's largest bank. There was no chance Officer Robinson would put words in her mouth or try to twist her into saying something she didn't mean.

"By now I'm not sure there is anything I can add to what you've already heard."

"That's okay. I always say, 'Save the best for last.' Sit down, and we'll go through this quickly." He motioned for her to take the seat she'd sat in a few hours earlier when she ate with Jacob.

Based on his questions, she gathered Officer Robinson thought the same thing about what she could contribute, because he didn't spend much time asking what she saw outside. Instead, his main emphasis was having her help him reconstruct a list of guests in attendance at the grand opening event. He also wanted to know what she recalled hearing or over-hearing during the evening.

Sarah consciously didn't plan to mention the incident between Botts and Marcus, but Officer Robinson brought it up. From the way he framed his questions, she realized he was only having her confirm what he already knew. She was sure the same was true when he inquired about the discussion between Botts and Riley and the one involving Chief Gerard, Harlan, Jacob, and her. Concerned her answers might put Marcus or Jacob in a bad light, Sarah also threw Jane's irritation with the noise from the animal clinic next door into the mix and asked whether he'd heard the gossip about Riley playing the field.

"Yes, we know she was a heartbreaker." Officer Robinson looked around as if to see if anyone was listening. He asked his next question so quietly Sarah could barely hear it. "Are you familiar with any other incidents involving Jacob and Ms. Miller?"

"I think they went out and I know he attended all of the soft openings, but I don't know anything else about their relationship."

He rested his pen on the pad on which he'd written her statement, but didn't add Sarah's last comment to the page.

"Are you suggesting something happened while they were dating?"

Officer Robinson shrugged. "I'm not suggesting anything, but if Harlan is representing Jacob, he better make sure he dots all the i's and crosses the t's."

Officer Robinson stood. The interview was over. "Thanks for your time, Sarah. You're free to leave now."

She stared at his retreating figure, wishing she knew what he was hinting at. Perhaps Emily, Marcus, or Grace knew something more about Riley. Sarah glanced at her watch. It was only nine. Time to take Fluffy for a walk and still give RahRah some quality playtime before turning in for the night.

Even though she was closer to the back door, Sarah decided to save herself a few steps by using the restaurant's front door. That way, all she'd have to do was cross Main Street and walk up the big house's drive to the carriage house.

Jane's Place's front door opened onto a wrap-around porch. Stepping onto it, she was surprised how much the temperature had dropped.

Feeling the chill in the air, she wanted to hurry home but paused to take in how Jane had set up the porch for customers waiting for their tables. She'd interspersed rocking chairs, a two-person swing, and a few tables with chess and checkerboard tops to keep people from becoming bored or irritated until their table was ready. Sarah had to admit it was well thought-out. Southwind needed a similar customer overflow area, but its limited porch space made it trickier.

Instead of a wide-open area, Southwind boasted marble stairs leading to a pillared stoop. Cliff already had designed and installed a handicapped ramp to reach the stoop from one side, but she didn't know if her sister and Marcus had given any thought, other than Southwind's bar, for handling waiting guests.

Sarah's concentration on what she hoped would

be a simple logistical problem was interrupted by the sound of dogs hysterically barking as a motorcycle revved up. She jerked her head in the direction of the animal clinic next door in time to catch a glimpse of a leather-jacketed rider zooming out of the driveway. The biker barely hesitated before turning onto Main Street. Although she could see colored patches on the person's jacket, the rider sped away too quickly for her to see a face or what the patches said.

Listening to the ruckus the dogs continued to make, even though the motorcycle was gone, Sarah understood why Jane was so upset. Feeling a bit wicked and that lightning might strike her any minute, Sarah smiled as she continued down Jane's walkway. Southwind was far enough away from the dog runs that her diners were guaranteed a much quieter experience.

A few steps ahead of her, Sarah spotted a woman who'd had the sense to plan ahead for the cooler night weather. She wore a Burberry raincoat over her dress. Sarah instantly recognized her mother and Sarah's own dear friend Eloise from her beehive hairstyle. Of late, neither Sarah nor her mother, Maybelle, had seen much of Eloise because of the new responsibilities associated with Eloise filling a vacant spot on the city council.

"Eloise?" Sarah hurried to catch up to her. "I thought Chief Gerard finished with the political dignitaries hours ago."

"He did, but I didn't want Anne to have to wait alone. I'm so glad to run into you. There's something Anne and I are hoping you will do for us."

Sarah shot Eloise a skeptical look. Although Anne Hightower and Eloise occasionally found some common ground on the council, most of their views were 180 degrees apart. For them to agree on something involving her piqued her curiosity, but so did Eloise's not leaving when her interview was finished.

"You stayed all this time to keep Anne company? I don't understand. Weren't you two of the first people interviewed?"

"Yes. We were. Officer Robinson took my statement while Chief Gerard spoke with Anne. They both finished with us quickly. Anne thought Chief Gerard was going to question Jacob next, but that wasn't his plan."

"Chief Gerard had a plan?"

The older woman peeked over the rim of her glasses. A quick snicker belied the reproving tone of her voice. "Now, Sarah. You don't give our police chief enough credit. He wanted Jacob to stew before taking him to the station to record his confession."

"He told you that?"

"Of course not. In front of Anne and me, he said that although he appreciated Jacob agreeing to talk with him, he preferred recording his statement at the station. He apologized to Jacob for the delay, making sure Anne and I heard, but said it couldn't be helped because he's down a man. When we didn't bite, he wrapped up by reiterating how sorry he was Jacob would have to wait while Officer Robinson and he interviewed the other witnesses."

Sarah's stomach tensed. She pushed away the memory of how her sister had almost been railroaded last summer when she offered a voluntary statement. "Why didn't Jacob simply tell him he'd either give his statement right then or offer to meet him at a set time at the station? That's what Emily did last summer."

"Exactly what Harlan and Anne suggested. Chief Gerard sidestepped them by again assuring them the wait wouldn't be too long."

Sarah frowned. "It sounds to me like the chief was playing some sort of mind game with Jacob. Why didn't Harlan object?"

"Harlan did scoff at him for insisting Jacob hang around Jane's Place when they could just as easily go to the station later or tomorrow morning, but Chief Gerard gave him a wounded look and said the sooner they let him finish the other interviews, the sooner Jacob and he would be able to go to the station. Harlan let it go at that."

"I'm surprised. Harlan is usually a bulldog when it comes to standing up for his clients."

"I agree, but this time I think he thought it was more strategic to let Chief Gerard get back to taking witness statements while he calmed Jacob down. We're all upset about poor Riley's death, but Jacob is shattered."

Sarah shuddered, thinking of Riley lying in the parking lot. "What happened tonight is horrible. You know, I was one of the people who responded to Jane's scream after she went outside?"

Eloise nodded.

"Seeing Riley lying there keeps playing over and over in my mind. I can only imagine what's going on in Jacob's head. As upset as he must be, I can't understand why Harlan didn't insist on delaying the statement or at least taking Jacob to a more neutral place, like his office or even my house, to talk."

"You forget, Harlan also had to deal with Anne. At that point, I'm not sure if she was more furious with Chief Gerard or Harlan, but she was on the warpath. Harlan made her see reason by explaining that while he'd prefer to leave, the most important thing was ensuring Chief Gerard didn't interview Jacob while he was in this state. He and Jacob went outside on this porch to talk while I babysat Anne."

Sarah laughed at the image of the woman running for mayor needing a babysitter. Thinking about Anne's mayoral candidacy, Sarah had an idea flit through her mind. "Eloise, why were you doing the babysitting? Now that she's officially running for mayor, doesn't she have one or two eager-beaver campaign people usually accompanying her everywhere? Couldn't they have babysat her?"

"One was here when the open house began but left quickly to make a presentation at some meeting. I guess because this wasn't a fund-raiser or political gathering, but a more down-home feel-good event, Anne felt she could and probably should work the restaurant alone. It's too bad. After Chief Gerard said he wanted to interview Jacob at the station, we could have used one of her campaign staff to take her outside and calm her down. She was making verbal threats about taking away the chief's interim appointment."

"Again? For a politician who insists people play by the book, saying things like that is crazy."

"Not really. I seem to remember a person who didn't let anything get in her way when her mother was accused of something she didn't do."

Sarah chuckled and exchanged a look with Eloise. "Bull's-eye."

In her regal way, Eloise grinned. "Anne and I may not be bosom buddies, but I thought no one should hear her say something that might come back to bite her. More importantly, Harlan needed one-on-one time with Jacob. The only way I saw that happening was for me to stay with Anne until Chief Gerard was ready to take Jacob to the station."

Now, Sarah understood Eloise's ulterior motive for babysitting Anne was Eloise's absolute confidence in Jacob's innocence. She knew they had gotten to know each other while Eloise worked at the bank and he was a front man for the group developing the strip center area and hoping to make Main Street a designated entertainment district. Recently, it was Eloise's vote, after her appointment to a vacancy on the city council, that cleared the way for the mixed use zoning Jacob needed for the different elements of his Main Street project. Even if Jacob and Eloise had been on different sides of the development issue, like Jacob and Anne, Sarah knew Eloise's support of Jacob wasn't political. It was solely tied to her belief in his basic integrity.

There was no question in Sarah's mind that Eloise had wanted Harlan to have as much time as possible to mentally prepare Jacob for any games Chief Gerard might be trying to play. Considering how, until a few months ago, Eloise spent years as the bank president's executive assistant, Sarah knew her friend had observed and mastered more than her fair share of mind games.

Being aware of this side of Eloise, Sarah was even more intrigued as to what Anne and Eloise could possibly want from her. "If you're not in a rush, why don't you come back to the carriage house for coffee and a piece of pie and tell me what it is Anne and you want? Emily played with some new dessert recipes this afternoon, and I was the benefactor of her baking attempts. She sent me home with a pumpkin pie I can't possibly eat by myself."

Eloise hesitated, as if weighing her words. She ignored the extended invitation. "We want you to quietly investigate and find out who killed Riley. Anne and I know it wasn't Jacob."

Sarah took a step backward. "Excuse me? In case you've forgotten, there are professionals doing that."

"We don't trust them. If anyone can understand that, it's you. Sarah, you know Jacob like we do. He wouldn't hurt anyone, especially someone he cared about as much as Riley. Anne and I know, from what you've done in the past, you'll go beyond the target we're afraid Chief Gerard has painted on Jacob's back."

"I wish I had the skills you think I have, but solving those other crimes was accidental."

Eloise crossed her arms and shook her head. "Don't be so modest. If it hadn't been for you . . ."

Sarah cut her off. "Look, if Anne and you don't trust Chief Gerard, talk to Harlan. He's Jacob's lawyer and he'll leave no stone unturned defending him. Besides, Harlan can access things from the police I can't."

"I already told Anne to trust Harlan, but we feel we also need you on the case for Jacob's sake." Eloise leaned closer to Sarah. "Between you and me, one of the reasons I fully agree with Anne that we need you to investigate is Chief Gerard gave me a bad feeling when he interviewed me. I don't know what it is, but I think Harlan is going to have his hands full protecting Jacob."

Eloise's comment made Sarah think about the inference Officer Robinson made when he questioned her. She still couldn't decide if his questions were perfunctory or if he was looking for a suspect other than Jacob. "What makes you say that? Have you heard of any conflict between Jacob and Riley?"

"No, did you?"

Sarah shook her head. She didn't personally know of any specific conflict between the two, but thinking of how Jacob indicated Riley and he weren't seeing each other anymore and his reaction to Botts, Sarah could almost bet someone that something unpleasant had gone down between the two.

Despite the misgivings Sarah had from talking with Officer Robinson, she didn't think this was the moment to share them with Eloise. Thinking of Chief Gerard and Officer Robinson's comments, though, created a sensation of butterflies fluttering in Sarah's stomach. She prayed the professionals would take the time to develop suspects other than Jacob.

Sarah put her hand on Eloise's arm. "Right now, there isn't a case against Jacob. Let's hope one never materializes."

CHAPTER FIVE

Eloise and Sarah continued their discussion as they walked toward the carriage house, tucked beyond the property's main house. They paused for a moment in front of the big building, their attention caught by how the shadows cast by tonight's moonlight and the huge magnolia trees played against its facade. Even without the lights planned for when the restaurant opened illuminating the structure's entry area, there was no question the house's Southern architectural bones were sound.

At one time, the big house had been an impressive Main Street home, but a string of owners neglected it. When Sarah's ex, Bill, shopped for a property that would allow them to have their privacy while providing room for his mother, he'd zeroed in on how they could live close to his mother in the big house, while the carriage house would provide a perfect separation for him from his mother and RahRah.

After they bought the property, Bill had plans created to bring the big house back to its glorious heyday. In the years they'd lived there, he never quite got around to doing more than talking about whether to paint the exterior back to its original white. When they were married, Sarah thought his hesitancy was caused by his obsessive desire to pick just the right furnishings and make decisions in keeping with the style of this kind of house, but now she wondered if it was tied to what he would have done if the rezoning proposal was approved. Knowing the rat, Sarah was convinced Bill probably planned to sell the property for a profit and tell her after the fact.

Taking in the quiet majesty of the house, Sarah understood why Marcus and Emily were eager to get their restaurant off the ground and the reverent way Cliff spoke about bringing back the beauty of the home's natural oak stairwells and crown moldings.

"Sarah, it is a beautiful home. I can't wait to see how you've remodeled the interior."

"Except for our final inspection, the restaurant is ready to open. I can't wait for you to see it, either. Cliff and his workmen did a great job renovating the house. It exudes Southern charm. All we need are the magnolia trees in the yard to bloom for it to look like we stepped out of the *Gone with the Wind* era."

"Have you thought about renting the main house out as a movie set? Alabama has become a real go-to state for making movies."

"That hasn't even crossed our minds. We've been too busy trying to get Botts to do our last inspection so we can open to the public."

Sarah thought she heard Eloise snort but was confused when Eloise continued speaking. "You should consider it. This house would make a perfect . . ."

Eloise stopped midsentence when Sarah grabbed her arm and whispered, "Hush."

"Sarah, what is it?"

Sarah pointed to the rear of the house. "There's a light on in the kitchen."

"Maybe a workman left it on."

"No. Emily and Marcus got dressed here, but when I came to pick them up, Marcus was in such a foul mood about Jane's opening, I suggested they go on without me. I told them I'd meet them there after I turned off the lights and locked up."

"Perhaps you missed one."

"Absolutely not. I double-checked myself. Someone is in the house."

"It could be Emily or Marcus."

"No. If they went anyplace other than home after the opening, they'd have gone to the Southwind Pub."

Sarah motioned Eloise to stay put. Slowly, stepping to the side of the third step, which she knew creaked, she inched up the back stairs to peek into the kitchen window.

"Sarah, come back here. I'm calling the police. Let them handle this."

Sarah ignored Eloise. This was her house and she needed to know who was in there. She crouched low and slunk toward the window, avoiding getting too close to the back door. Keeping her head below the windowsill, Sarah glanced back at Eloise, who, thanks to the moonlight, Sarah could see was punching numbers on her cell phone. Making eye contact with Eloise, Sarah slashed her finger across her throat. She watched Eloise until she was satisfied she'd stopped making the call, even though Eloise remained poised with her finger over her touch screen.

"Come back."

Instead of creeping back to Eloise, Sarah peered above the window sash, stood, and tapped on the window.

"What are you doing, Sarah?" Eloise called to her. "Are you crazy?"

"It's okay. Come on up here, Eloise." She rapped on the window harder. This time she was rewarded by Emily's face appearing in it. She gave her sister a little wave. "Apparently, I was wrong. It's Emily, Marcus, Grace, and someone else. Let's see what's going on."

By the time Eloise had come up the few steps to where Sarah was, Emily held the back door open. "What are you two doing here?"

"That's the same question Eloise and I were going to ask you. We were on the way to my place for some of your pumpkin pie when we saw a light shining through the kitchen window. I knew I'd turned off all the lights and locked up, so we were investigating."

Eloise cleared her throat. "Your sister was investigating. I was calling the police." She pointedly gazed at Sarah. "They're the ones who should handle investigations of intruders, instead of private citizens who act without thinking."

Sarah and Emily both grinned and gave Eloise a double side hug.

"Aw, you care," Sarah said. "We didn't know."

When Eloise shot them each a look that Sarah interpreted as exasperated, the twins both laughed.

Sarah laughed harder, reflecting on how, only a little while ago, Eloise had been begging her to try to find a murderer. She guessed there was a difference between sleuthing and encountering a possibly armed burglar.

Their laughter provoked a schoolmarm reaction of crossed arms and a frown from Eloise until they finally quieted down. "Sarah, it isn't funny. You're a grown woman who should think before you act."

Stifling another giggle, Sarah put her hand in front of her mouth. That she wasn't successful was underscored by the intensification of Eloise's scowl.

"Your impetuous behavior already has gotten you into trouble in the past. What if it hadn't been Emily and Marcus? What if some desperate person or trigger-happy kid was stealing copper or vandalizing the kitchen? You could have been shot."

Sarah hung her head. Eloise was right. She had to admit some of her past impulsive acts hadn't had the best results.

Emily cut Eloise's admonition and Sarah's penance short. "Come on in, you two. We were discussing the impact Riley's food might have on Southwind." Emily crossed her arms over herself and shivered as she ushered them into the kitchen. "I tell you, as crazy as our weather has been, one day I'm worrying about hurrying inside before the flies beat me in, and the next day, I'm freezing to death the minute the sun goes down."

"It doesn't seem that cold to me." Eloise exchanged a look with Sarah.

Sarah didn't move. It didn't take a mind reader to know she and Eloise were thinking the same thing:

Emily didn't know Riley was dead. "Em, when did Marcus and you leave Jane's Place?"

Emily glanced over her shoulder, back into the kitchen, apparently checking if Marcus was within earshot. "We left shortly after Marcus and Botts got into it. I dragged him over to the dessert table, where we ran into Grace and Mandy. Turns out they came to the opening with the same goal of tasting Riley's food as we did. We knew Jane made all the desserts and we've had those countless times, so the four of us decided not to subject ourselves to being at Jane's Place any longer. Instead, we went to the Southwind Pub for some good dessert. Apparently, most of the guests at Jane's Place had the same idea. Southwind Pub was jumping. Rather than taking up a paying table, we came back here to talk about Riley's food and how it might affect us."

Sarah glanced from Eloise to Emily. "I think the four of you better lock up and come over to the carriage house. We can share your pumpkin pie while Eloise and I bring you up to date before the police do."

Emily shivered again. "What are you talking about?"

"Riley's dead, Em, and it looks like Chief Gerard has decided to pin the murder on Jacob."

CHAPTER SIX

Fifteen minutes later, with Fluffy walked and a new pot of coffee brewed, Sarah, RahRah, and Fluffy sat on the patch of rug in her kitchen that RahRah usually claimed as his alone. So far, as long as she stroked him, he didn't seem to mind sharing. Emily, Eloise, Marcus, Grace, and Grace's newly introduced friend, Mandy, filled the seats at Sarah's mini table and kitchen bar, eating pie.

"I'm amazed they're letting you pet them both at the same time," Grace said. "I would have thought they'd be jealous of each other."

Sarah gave RahRah a little extra squeeze. "There was a little skittishness between them in the beginning, but my alpha cat made it clear he was the boss. Fluffy, being the sweetheart she is, immediately decided that was okay by her. Now, it's fun to watch the two of them." She nodded toward RahRah. "Whenever this one deigns to allow it, they play together, nap together, and basically are inseparable. I even have to put their food down at the same time, but Fluffy won't touch hers until he nibbles on his."

Grace laughed. "Well, it's nice to know RahRah didn't relinquish his place in your pet pecking order."

"Never. He's my number one man." Sarah bent her head near Fluffy's silky head and whispered, "But you're my number one woman." The dog leaned her head back and placed a sloppy wet kiss on Sarah's cheek. As if he were watching the show going on next to him with a tad of disdain, RahRah flattened his stomach and stretched his paws straight out. When Sarah reached to rub his head and neck again, he moved out of her reach. Fluffy gave a glance back at Sarah and followed suit.

"Oh, that hurts," Sarah said to the dog.

Fluffy wagged her tail but didn't leave her play-mate's side.

It was Marcus's turn to let out a deep belly laugh. "Guess you've been deserted."

Sarah uncrossed her legs and partially rose. She reached her arm above her head and retrieved her pie from the counter before settling onto the floor again. "Guess so, but it gives me a chance to eat my dessert."

Putting her lanky legs out in front of her, Sarah rested her back on the kitchen cabinets, then took her first bite of Emily's pumpkin pie. She let the bite roll around in her mouth, trying to decide what the extra kick she tasted was. "This is delicious, Em. What's the secret ingredient?"

"Love, of course." Emily chuckled while she reached back and redid her blond ponytail. "This is one of the recipes I've decided to go with for our fall South-wind dessert menu."

"It's definitely a winner," Sarah said. "Jane won't be able to touch it with a ten-foot pole."

Emily beamed at the praise, but her buoyant mood quickly disappeared. She shuddered and retrieved her hoodie from the back of her chair. "I can't get over the fact we were just eating Riley's food and now she's gone. She barely had time to . . ." Emily choked up. It took her a few seconds to compose herself. "Sarah, there were so many people at tonight's opening or who could have been in the parking lot. What makes you so sure Chief Gerard already thinks Jacob did it? Anyone who knows Jacob knows he doesn't have a mean bone in his body."

"That's not exactly true when it came to things involving Riley."

Startled, everyone stared at Grace.

"What do you mean?" Sarah asked.

"Before we graduated and she moved, Mandy and I had the apartment next door to Riley's. The three of us hung out together a lot. That was before Riley and Jacob started dating for the first time."

Sarah wondered if this was what Officer Robinson wanted Harlan to know. "They dated more than once?"

"On and off."

"Jacob was head over heels in love with her," Mandy added.

Eloise put her fork down on the table. "How could you possibly have known that?"

"By how Jacob showed up at all hours with gifts, candy, flowers, and the dumbest look."

Marcus put his hand over Emily's. "A lot of us do that kind of thing when we're in a serious relationship."

They smiled at each other.

Grace shook her head. "Yes, but this one was more one-sided, sort of like RahRah and Fluffy. Jacob adored her. Even when Riley made no bones about wanting and actually seeing other guys, he didn't move on. He refused to accept the situation for what it was."

Emily turned away from Marcus and focused her attention on Grace. "That doesn't make sense, Grace. You've worked around Jacob long enough to know he's unusually perceptive. From what you're saying, how did he miss getting Riley's message?"

Grace stared at her fingernails as if examining them for a hangnail. She placed her hands on the table and shifted her gaze back to her tablemates and Sarah. "Look, I don't mean this to sound snarky, but she played him like a spider. Once Riley caught anyone in her web, watch out. But with Jacob it was different. She played up to Jacob, but if someone offered her something she preferred, she dropped him like a hot potato until the benefit of the week was used up. Then, she'd reel Jacob in again."

"How do you know that?" Sarah challenged.

Grace opened her eyes wide and stared at Sarah. "Remember, at that time, Mandy and I lived next door to Riley. We saw her go out with him for a while, and then there were other guys hanging around, and eventually we saw her back with Jacob."

Both Grace and Mandy exchanged a look, before Mandy picked up the story. "Jacob tried to act like he didn't care, but it was obvious he did. He dropped by to say hi, even when they weren't dating. If she was out with someone else, instead of leaving he either came by our apartment or stayed in the building's lobby until the apartment manager, Daniel, or one of us assured him she was out for the evening."

"I still don't get it." Sarah stood and pushed a strand of her dark hair out of her face. She leaned against the gray granite-topped counter. "To me, maybe because he's a Hightower and he's so involved with developing the entertainment district, I've always thought of Jacob as being a man about town. You make him sound like a lovesick puppy."

"That's exactly how it was." Mandy punctuated the air with a pointed forefinger. "He may have been older than Riley, but, may she rest in peace, she ran the show. Whether it was Jacob or one of the other guys who could give her weekend rides, she had them wrapped around her pinkie."

Sarah wasn't sure how dating and rides fit together. "What do you mean? Rides?"

"Motorcycle rides," Grace said. "Riley didn't have her own bike, so most weekends she wheedled a ride with someone else. Sarah, the thing about Riley is she never hid what she was doing or what she wanted from any of us. In fact, she boasted about how she took some fabulous trips because her rides provided the transportation and often picked up her tab."

"That they did," Eloise said.

Sarah jerked her head in Eloise's direction. Her tone was anything but warm, especially considering she was talking about a recently deceased young woman. Maybe it was Eloise's loyalty to Jacob, but it sounded like more than that. "What makes you say that?"

She waited for Eloise to answer, surprised to see the usually inviting facial facade that had served her well at the bank and now as a member of the council replaced, but for a moment, with a hardened jaw and narrowed eyes. In that instant of transition, it dawned on Sarah how Eloise had formed her opinion of Riley. "Eloise, are you in the motorcycle gang? Did you ride with Riley?"

"I am and I did. And we're not a gang."

Eloise, chin jutted forward, faced Sarah, almost daring her to step over an imaginary line. "Motorcycle riders get bad raps from the movies and television. Sure, there are some gangs of roughriders, but just because we wear leather jackets for protection and against the wind doesn't make us all rappers and gangsters. Our group, the Wheaton Wildcats, is a community club that lets people come together for a fun social activity. When we're on our bikes, age, gender, sex, or any other label is immaterial."

Sarah shook her head. "I had no idea."

"Most people don't. I started riding a Vespa in high school when I couldn't afford a car. When, I got a car, I sold my scooter. It's only been in the last year, since I left the bank, that I decided to get a larger motorcycle and join the Wildcats."

Elbows on the table, Emily leaned forward and rested her chin in her hands while voicing the question Sarah had. "I know Wheaton's high school sports teams are called the Wheaton Wildcats, but I've never heard of a motorcycle club associated with the high school."

"There isn't. The Wildcat name for our riding group is an inside joke. Our founder was the history teacher and coach at the high school for thirty years."

"Mr. Peabody? He started your gang?"

Eloise resumed speaking in the voice she'd used in the bank. "Sam, Mr. Peabody, didn't start a gang. When he retired, Sam let everyone know he planned to travel. His current and former players collected enough money to present him with a used bike. He didn't want to ride alone, so he created a riding group to have friends share his love of travel and culture. Giving a nod to his past history, the group adopted the Wheaton Wildcats as its name. Every summer, Sam takes a long trip with other teachers and members of the group, but during the school year, he plans Sunday outings to different parts of Alabama that anyone can participate in. Those were the trips Riley usually tagged along on as a rider whose name begins with 'B' and rhymes with witch."

Sarah immediately guessed the word Eloise was referring to, but she couldn't quite understand how it fit the situation. "Why that word?"

"It's the slang term some motorcyclists use for people who ride on the back of their bikes. There's one group who thinks it's so funny that whether they have a rider or not, they go out on the highway with signs pinned on the back of their jackets saying 'if you can read this sign, the _itch fell off.' In the beginning, Riley jumped rides a lot, but eventually she settled into what we all took as being a thing with Jacob. At least, that is, until Botts showed up with his bigger and more outrageous bike gear. Riley took a fancy to the man and his machine, and even though he wasn't happy about it, Jacob was back to riding solo."

"Seeing his rival at the Wildcat rides couldn't have been easy for Jacob," Marcus said. "But it had to be even worse because of how many of the economic development projects brought Jacob and Botts together. I don't think I could keep it together if I constantly crossed paths with my rival."

"Most people, from what I saw during my years at the bank, couldn't. There was tension there, and Riley did nothing to ease it. As sweet as she could be, she seemed to enjoy stirring people up."

Involuntarily, Sarah's investigative antennae went up. "Eloise, who were some of the other Wheaton Wildcats, besides Jacob, who might have reacted to something Riley said or did?"

"We all liked her, but, at some point in time, you could have put almost anyone in our motorcycle group on a list of people annoyed by her. Behind his back, she mocked Sam for his fuddy-duddy attention to detail, made fun of me for being too old and prissy, derided Cliff for being a Goody Two-shoes, made jokes about the vets and their past military experience, and I could go on.

"For that matter, Grace and I could be at the top of any list you make. We used to hang out with Riley, until suddenly we became personae non gratae. Riley preached tolerance but didn't know how to demonstrate it. There are also lots of folks you might consider who weren't Wheaton Wildcats."

"Mandy! Hush. Let's not speak ill of the dead." Grace held her hands up, fingers splayed as if trying to hold back Mandy's words. Her efforts had no impact on the auburn-haired woman, whose green eyes flashed like a light on go.

. "Grace, let's be honest." She ignored Grace's continued efforts to quiet her and instead spoke to the others in the kitchen. "Riley used the innuendo and scare techniques of her narrow viewpoint to try to keep Grace from being hired instead of her when they graduated. You know, they were the top students, and a number of different restaurateurs, including Jane, made overtures to both."

"Enough, Mandy. There's no need to rehash the past, especially with what happened to Riley. I ended up in the kitchen of the restaurant exactly where I belong."

Mandy ignored Grace's efforts to cut the conversation off. "No thanks to Riley. I'm sorry she's dead, but she was a snake whose actions bothered a lot of people—especially Jacob."

"What makes you so sure of that?" Sarah waited for Mandy to elaborate.

"He showed up at our building a few months ago, having had a bit too much to drink. He must have rung her doorbell and gotten no answer, so he stood in our lobby, demanding to see Riley. When Daniel, the resident manager, told Jacob that Riley wasn't there and he should go home, Jacob got belligerent and refused to leave. Said he would wait in the lobby until whatever time she got home. Daniel told him he couldn't, and they got into a shouting match. He finally called the police to deal with Jacob."

Sarah didn't remember reading anything about

the incident in the paper or even hearing anything from her mother. "Was Jacob arrested?"

"No. When Officer Robinson responded to the call, Daniel alleged Jacob pushed him, but no one else could confirm what he said. The only thing we agreed upon was that there was a lot of noise. Based on our statements and probably what he observed, Officer Robinson took Jacob outside, let him sober up a bit, and, I think, took him home. I'm not really certain about that, but I think Jacob was lucky it was Officer Robinson rather than Chief Gerard who responded."

Knowing how rude Jacob had been to Chief Gerard earlier in the evening, but how the chief only chalked it up to youth, Sarah wondered if it really would have mattered who responded to the call that night. The one thing she was positive of was that the chief and Officer Robinson remembered the incident, which might be another reason the chief wasn't cutting Jacob any slack now.

With a list of suspects as long as her arm, Sarah decided, while she had everyone present, it was a good idea to find out whom, besides Botts and Jacob, Riley had tagged along with as a rider. "Eloise, did Riley ever ride with you?"

"No. My bike is a Honda Gold Wing. It can only hold one person, but a number of people like Jacob, Botts, Cliff, and the veterinarians from across the street have much bigger Harleys or BMWs that can easily carry a passenger."

Sarah opened her eyes wide. "Are you telling us petite Dr. Vera rides a motorcycle?"

"One of the biggest. Dr. Glenn got all the vets and another friend a good deal by going to the Harley dealership and offering to buy four at once for cash. At about sixteen thousand each, the dealer was willing to shave a little off the price and throw in some aftermarket accessory discounts to sweeten the deal."

Marcus whistled. "At that price, I think I'd have thrown in a year's worth of free gas, too. I must live in my own world. I had no idea so many people in Wheaton are involved with your group."

Eloise smiled. "Under our helmets, we're the best kept secret. You probably know all of us, but you'll easily become more familiar with different members of the group now that many of us, who pretty much only ride on Sundays, accepted Dr. Glenn's kind offer to park our bikes in the shed or on the parking pad on his property. He's one of the club's officers, and his place is where we meet to start our trips, so parking there works perfectly for those of us who don't have garages."

"I can imagine that does work well with people like you." Sarah didn't say she couldn't imagine Eloise in a suit, heels, and safety helmet, whipping into her parking spot at city hall on a motorcycle. Instead, she pointed to the last piece of pie sitting in the middle of the table. "Anyone want the old maid piece?"

No one responded until Marcus raised his hand and patted his ample stomach. He didn't look at Emily when she teasingly said his name. Instead, he pulled the pie plate closer.

CHAPTER SEVEN

As she watched Marcus dig into his pie, Sarah couldn't imagine enjoying anything with as much gusto as he did. "What's going to happen to Riley's dishes that were going to be on Jane's menu?"

Marcus finished the last smidgen of his pie. "Jane will try making them. I'm sure she has all of Riley's recipes."

"But following a recipe isn't all that goes into making a good dish," Emily said. "Chefs tinker with basic recipes. I doubt Jane will be able to do any of Riley's recipes justice, which should be good for Southwind."

"But if she does succeed in pulling off Riley's dishes, what we tasted tonight was pretty darn good. That means we could have a tough competitor."

Emily bit her lip. "Don't worry, Marcus. We may both be farm-to-table restaurants, but we know our food is better than Jane's."

"Jane's without Riley's recipes."

Eloise cleared her throat. "I know I'm not in the chef business, but I'm a foodie and I've had some experience with business competition and a touch of politics. On the council, I may want to please all my constituents, but the reality is I can't, so I must find what is good for the majority and follow that route. Of course, that means I'm not going to get everyone's vote next time, any more than you or Jane are going to get every customer. The key is to get the majority to approve of what you're doing."

"I'll buy that," Marcus said. "But you only need the voters to come out every few years. If we're going to survive, diners must want to eat our food a few times a month and tell their friends how much they like us. Word of mouth is big in our business."

Emily covered one of his paws with her delicately boned hand. "We'll simply have to give better food and service than Jane. Making sure our waitstaff is well trained will be important."

"And maybe you can come up with a gimmick," Grace suggested. "A specialty day or some kind of discount?"

"Absolutely not. Emily and I create restaurants that stand on their own merits. Southwind isn't going to be an exception. There will be no gimmicks."

Emily patted his hand but spoke to Grace. "Marcus is a purist, but if you have any marketing or menu ideas to counter Riley's dishes, even he will be willing to listen."

"I'll give it some thought."

"Please do. Of course, nothing can happen until Botts performs our final inspection and we open."

Marcus pulled his beefy mitt back from Emily. "All I can say is that for the sake of his continued good health, Botts better schedule us in the next few days."

CHAPTER EIGHT

Blinking open one eye, Sarah peered over the edge of her blanket. She had to get up and go to work soon, but for now she lay still rather than taking the chance of disturbing RahRah. Cuddled against the back of her knees, he was curled into his usual mini ball. The pressure of his little body, even if only for a few more moments, was comforting to her after the events of last night.

She still couldn't believe Riley was dead. It was always depressing when an older person died, but at least Sarah could take solace in telling herself the person lived a long life and that death was part of the natural cycle. That wasn't the case with Riley. She might have been a flirt and chance taker, but she should have had so much more time. There were so many opportunities and choices still in front of her. More importantly, her death wasn't part of the cycle of life.

There was no doubt based on the angle of Riley's neck that her death was anything but natural. Sarah only hoped Chief Gerard would widen his search for suspects beyond Jacob—and that there wasn't any reason for the chief to limit his findings to him.

Her open eye rested on where Fluffy lay in the corner of the room on her doggy bed. Sheer willpower and being unsure of how her alpha-male cat would react kept Sarah from bringing her second pet into bed with her. Perhaps it was just as well. As tightly as RahRah tucked into a small spot on Sarah's bed, Fluffy stretched out in a comical way. Her head drooped over one side of the dog bed while her body twisted almost backward until her legs were braced against the bed's opposite side. How Fluffy found this position comfortable was something Sarah couldn't fathom.

As she watched, Fluffy, still asleep, jerked slightly and waved two legs in the air. Sarah wasn't sure if the dog was having a dream or a nightmare, but what seemed to be a funny grin on the pup's face implied a happy mood. Whether all dogs smiled or frowned might be questionable, but there was no question in Sarah's mind that her sweet and loving Fluffy did.

It seemed like an eternity since RahRah had come into her life. Together, they'd weathered such storms of distrust and hatred, she couldn't imagine herself without him. Fluffy had come into Sarah's life when her owner moved to an independent living facility. In the few months they'd been together, Fluffy hadn't had time to make as large an indentation in Sarah's heart, but she was getting there.

Moving slowly, to avoid waking RahRah abruptly, Sarah glanced at her charging phone. It was almost seven thirty. She'd overslept. Time wasn't going to be her friend if she was going to dress, eat, walk and feed

Fluffy, and get to the office as close to eight thirty as possible. Breakfast and makeup would have to wait to be done at the office. Some things, like walking Fluffy, had to take precedence before she left for work.

Sarah sighed. It would be nice if she could let Fluffy out by herself while she got ready for work, but that wasn't possible now. Unless she fenced her yard, which wasn't in her budget anytime soon, her only solution was setting her alarm earlier. Sarah wasn't sure which was more distasteful, waking early or spending money she really didn't have. At least, for now, walking Fluffy a few times a day was a necessity, but the good thing was it was putting some extra exercise into Sarah's schedule.

RahRah stirred. As he stretched, shaking off the night's sleep, Sarah reached her hand toward him. Oh, well, she was already late. She stroked him as he lay fully extended on her bed. Apparently satisfied with her loving on him, he pulled his paws closer to his stomach, stood, and gave one final shake before jumping from the bed and making a beeline toward Fluffy. In an almost identical move, Sarah swept away the last remnant of the blanket covering her and jumped out of bed.

RahRah didn't touch Fluffy. Instead, he gently pawed her bed a few times before wandering away. It wouldn't be long before Fluffy woke and needed to go out. There was something to be said about cats and their litter boxes. Although Fluffy was getting better at not needing to be taken outside immediately or as often, Sarah still slept in sweatpants and a T-shirt. Sarah slid her feet into the loafers she'd dropped next to the bed as Fluffy, sitting on her haunches in her doggy bed, seemingly adjusted to the new day.

Sarah grabbed her cell phone. "Ready to go out? Come on."

With Fluffy following at her heels, Sarah walked to the front door, grabbed her windbreaker, and picked up her keys from the bowl she left them in whenever she came into the carriage house. Fluffy waited patiently until Sarah hooked a red leash to her collar. Once leashed, Fluffy pulled against it until Sarah opened the door and let the puppy run out ahead of her. The two strolled toward Main Street, with Fluffy stopping to smell and mark the various trees and bushes that lined the winding driveway.

It was, Sarah reflected, a truly perfect fall morning. Many leaves had already changed colors, but there were still plenty on the old oak and maple trees. The next good rainstorm would probably knock the remainder to the ground, revealing many of the sprawling Main Street houses they shielded. In the meantime, they were a pretty contrast to the clear blue sky.

She was glad she'd brought her windbreaker. It wasn't cold enough for a heavy coat but more than crisp enough for her to wear her jacket. Reaching Main Street, Sarah caught sight of the yellow crime tape blocking the entrance to Jane's Place. She shuddered. The garish yellow and black marred the street's fall color palette.

In addition to the crime tape, there was something else out of place on Main Street for this early in the morning. An empty truck she didn't recognize was parked in front of the big house near where the formal Southwind restaurant entrance was.

Perplexed, Sarah gently tugged Fluffy from the bush she was nosing and hurried around to the front of her property. She reached the sidewalk in front of the house just as Botts walked down the steps. He paused and waved when he saw her.

Sarah waved back. She let an eager Fluffy lead her to the steps. "What are you doing here so early?"

He pointed to the sky. "It's not that early. Unlike you white-collar office folks, construction crews start working when the sun comes up."

She nodded, knowing how early Cliff was at his different construction sites. When he was in the midst of remodeling the Southwind Pub and this restaurant, his crew and he were always on the job by seven. "But I thought inspectors were government employees—eight to five."

For a second, she thought she saw a flicker of irritation in his eyes, but she dismissed the thought. It didn't square with how relaxed his features were.

"Officially, yes, but I work a flex schedule that more closely matches the ones Wheaton construction crews keep. Working the same hours as the contractors helps me get in more inspections in a day."

His answer made sense in terms of efficiency to Sarah, but considering no one was still working on Southwind, coming this early seemed like a waste of energy. She decided in the same vein as the night before to throw him an olive branch to remove any distaste his disagreement with Marcus might have generated. "It must be difficult with you being the only inspector and having such a backlog of inspections."

He cast his eyes to the ground before looking up. The motion reminded Sarah of someone, but she couldn't remember who.

Eyes raised, he didn't quite meet her gaze. "It is, Sarah. Especially knowing no matter how hard I try or how much I do, someone is going to be mad."

Sarah made a noise in agreement, hoping it would be enough to keep him talking.

It was. "Marcus may be an annoyance, but what you said got to me last night. I really appreciated you not only understanding my situation but sharing your concerns with me civilly instead of attacking me."

Now it was his turn, waiting to see how she would react. Botts let their stalemate of silence go on for only a few seconds when she didn't immediately jump at his bait. "Anyway, because of you, I thought I'd slip Southwind into my inspection schedule today. Unfortunately, no one is here. Without an owner or the contractor, I can't do the inspection. Guess it will have to wait for when it comes up on my schedule."

Sarah reined in her pulling dog. "Oh, no. You don't have a problem with doing the inspection now. You must have forgotten. I'm an owner." She pulled her key chain from the pocket of her windbreaker. Keeping Fluffy's leash looped around her arm, she went through the keys until she found the right one. "Come on. I'll let you in to do the inspection, and I'll call Marcus and Cliff. I'm sure one of them can whip over here in a minute to answer any questions you might have that I can't."

Without waiting for Botts to answer, she bounded up the steps and unlocked the door. With a flourish of her arm, she motioned for him to enter. A glance at his face as he did helped her remember who his expressions reminded her of—her sly as a fox late ex-husband, the rat.

Sarah pulled her phone from her pocket. She sent a text to Cliff, who she hoped was working in the vicinity, and punched in the Pub's number. Marcus and Emily should already be there doing prep work. When Marcus answered after the first ring, she didn't give him time for pleasantries before saying, "Marcus, I'm at the big house with Botts. You better get over here now. He's doing the inspection, and I need to go to work."

CHAPTER NINE

Ending the call, Sarah thought it wise to follow Botts around the house until Cliff or Marcus arrived. Besides, it would give her uninterrupted time to ask the inspector a few questions about his relationship with Riley and where he went when he left Jane's Place. Before she crossed the Southwind threshold, Sarah bent and scooped Fluffy up in her arms lest the excited puppy have an accident or find Botts a person of interest for biting.

"Botts?"

"I'm in the kitchen."

Sarah joined him there. He was holding a spiral notebook opened to a page on which she could see he'd drawn a diagram of the kitchen. Although she could see some words on the page, they were too small for her to read. "Thank you again for coming today. It means a lot to us."

When he merely nodded but kept moving along with his inspection, she decided she better slow him down until one of her partners arrived. "I'm still having trouble dealing with last night. I can't believe Riley is dead. You knew her pretty well, didn't you?"

He stopped examining the venting system long enough to dart a gaze at Sarah. "Yes, we were friends. But you already knew that. What is it you're after?"

Sarah shifted Fluffy from under her arm to in front of her. "Silly grapevine—my mother gave me the impression you two were dating. I'm sorry if I came across as sounding like I was prying. I simply wanted to offer my sympathy and give you a chance to talk, if you wanted. As much as Riley's death has upset me, I thought, because you knew her so much better, you might need an ear, too."

Botts put his notebook on the counter and walked toward her. Although he seemed less intense than earlier, when he reached his hand out, Sarah tried not to flinch. She felt silly a moment later when she realized his intent was to pet Fluffy.

"I guess I got the wrong impression last night. Maybe you don't remember? Riley joined us right after your run-in with Marcus. When you said something about wanting to take a ride to clear your head, she offered to come with you. You told her to stay and enjoy her night and then quickly left."

"So?"

"Riley followed you outside. Her attitude and the fact she left her big night to hurry out the door behind you made it seem like more than a friendship."

Botts continued petting Fluffy. "Sarah, Riley and I were friends. She was a sweet kid, but our connection was limited to a few dinners and lots of rides on the back of my motorcycle."

"Well, based on that, I wonder why she was so agitated and insistent on following you outside?"

"The police asked me the same question, and I didn't have any better answer than I'm giving you."

"What did you tell them?"

"The truth. I never saw her after I walked out of Jane's Place. I went straight to where I keep my motorcycle, got on it, and left the parking lot."

"Did you see anyone else while you were getting your bike?"

"I didn't notice anyone, but I really wasn't looking. I was mad at Marcus for calling me out in front of the crowd in Jane's Place and at everyone from the mayor to the city council for not hiring another inspector."

Hearing someone coming in the door, Sarah made a noise with her mouth that she hoped sounded supportive and understanding to Botts as opposed to being relieved her replacement had arrived.

CHAPTER TEN

Sarah made it into the office a few minutes to nine. Makeup and eating had gone by the wayside, and her outfit was the first pair of black pants and sweater she grabbed from her closet. As she hung her jacket, she heard Harlan in the refreshment nook, putting water into the coffee machine.

Normally, she made coffee before he arrived. Unlike some bosses who insisted coffee making was a secretarial task, Harlan didn't. It wasn't an assigned responsibility that made her normally rush to put the coffee on but rather a matter of her personal need for a jolt of java to start the day, coupled with her belief that beating him in by a few minutes and already having the coffee going made her look more efficient. As weak as she'd felt in so many areas of her job when she began a little more than a year ago, anything that provided an appearance of efficiency and competency had seemed important. And it still did, though Sarah felt better about her skills and was no longer nervous Harlan might fire her at any moment.

Thank goodness. Today she felt entirely discombobulated.

She stashed her purse in her desk drawer and popped her head into the coffee nook.

Harlan acknowledged her and handed her an empty mug. "Coffee should be ready in a few minutes."

"No problem. What a morning it's been so far."

Harlan raised his brows. "What happened?"

"Botts showed up before eight this morning to do the inspection. If I hadn't been walking Fluffy, he would have come and gone. No telling when he would have managed to put us on his schedule again. As it was, he thought he had an out because there wasn't an owner or contractor on the premises."

"Sneaky."

"Very. I think that's why he came when he did. I swear when I reminded Botts I'm an owner, too, so he could do the inspection with me, he looked annoyed. If he could have thought of an excuse or called himself on his cell phone with an emergency, I think he would have."

"Why didn't he?"

"Because I didn't let him out of my sight. He had no choice but to do the inspection when I pulled out my key and unlocked the door."

"How did it come out?"

"I don't know. The minute I let him in, I texted Cliff, hoping he was working somewhere in the vicinity, and called Marcus and Emily, so one of them could come over and help with the inspection."

"And you left Botts there alone?"

"No. Because I don't know anything about kitchen stuff and didn't want him to take advantage of me, I stalled by asking him questions about his relationship with Riley."

Harlan chuckled. "What was it you said about not investigating?"

Sarah held up her hand as if saying "stop." "I wasn't investigating. I was protecting our business investment until Marcus, Emily, or Cliff got there."

"A likely story."

"Harlan, that's not what's important. Botts swore Riley and he were only friends. He claimed that except for going out for some meals and giving her lots of rides on the back of his motorcycle, there wasn't anything else going on between them."

Harlan scratched his head. "That definitely isn't the impression I've gotten from anyone I've talked to."

"Me either. Do you think she could have been stoking Jacob's jealousy to keep him in her pocket? And he fell for it?"

"Anything's possible. Did you try to press the issue more?"

"The window of opportunity closed. Marcus and Cliff arrived almost simultaneously, so I left Botts with them and rushed home to get ready for work."

"And here you are." He lifted the full coffeepot and offered her some. She held out her mug. Harlan filled it before pouring himself a cup. He took a long sip. "Jacob and Anne are coming in this morning. I'd like you to sit in and listen. Take notes if you want."

Sarah opened her eyes wide and stared at him. He

normally conducted client meetings privately and insisted on making his own notes. Her office functions were primarily to be the receptionist, handle the filing, and type letters, pleadings, or anything else he needed typed. Harlan had few shortcomings, but he couldn't type. "Did I miss something here? You know I don't know shorthand."

"No, I'm simply interested in your reaction to what Jacob and Anne say. Let's see if your memories from last night are the same or differ significantly."

"I thought the police are supposed to keep witnesses separate."

"I'm not the police. Besides," he quickly added, "all of you already gave formal, signed statements."

Before Sarah could reflect too much on Harlan's motivation for having her sit in, the front door buzzer sounded. While Harlan took his coffee and went into his office, she hurried to her desk. After checking the monitor to see who was at the front door, she buzzed Jacob and Anne in. "Good morning."

Jacob nodded a greeting. Unlike his sister, who radiated "powerful mayoral candidate" in a tailored brown suit with a pink blouse and brown pumps, Jacob was a disheveled mess. He had on the same blue shirt and khaki pants, albeit more wrinkled, from last night. A shadow of a beard on his normally clean-shaven face made Sarah question if he ever went home. Based on Anne's picture-perfect look and the fact Harlan was wearing clean clothing, she knew none of them stayed at the station all night.

That meant Jacob should have had time to go home, sleep, and change clothes before this meeting.

Sarah wondered what he did instead after he left the police station, but she knew, at least here in the office, it wasn't her place to ask. She hoped Harlan would.

CHAPTER ELEVEN

Sarah grabbed a legal pad and pen, then came around the wall that separated her desk from the waiting room. "Harlan's waiting for you. Please come this way."

After she held the door to Harlan's private office open for Anne and Jacob, she waited for them to get settled before following them in and closing the door. Harlan greeted them from where he stood by the side of his large well-polished oak desk.

Rather than choosing to sit in the conversational area where Harlan had two chairs and a couch surrounding a low coffee table, they opted for the two guest chairs facing his desk. Harlan went around his desk and took the seat across from them, while Sarah quietly sat on the couch. She wished she could see Jacob and Anne's faces rather than trying to figure out things from their body language.

"Harlan, I didn't like how Chief Gerard treated Jacob last night. It was like he found him guilty before he even interviewed him."

"I think he's better than that, but he did give that impression."

"What are you going to do about it?"

From the way Anne sat stiffly upright, Sarah feared whether Harlan would be able to keep her calm today. She kept her gaze focused on Anne's back when her boss replied he didn't plan to do anything. Anne stirred in her seat, but Sarah was pleased that, while Anne grasped her chair's arms, Anne didn't attempt to take control of the meeting.

"Anything we would do now would bring more attention to Jacob and subject him to more questions." Harlan turned his gaze toward Jacob. "I need you to go over everything again that happened last night."

"But I've already told you and Chief Gerard whatever I can remember."

"I know, but sometimes details we've ignored flit across our minds. Please."

Sarah listened carefully while Harlan let Jacob run on in his retelling of last night. Although Jacob seemed to relax during his narrative, he didn't mention anything different from what she remembered. The only major addition was what happened after Jacob had crossed the room to listen to Riley talk about her vegan dishes. Even that was pretty much what Sarah had surmised. He'd listened to Riley's formal explanation, but before he could talk to her one-on-one, others had gotten between the two of them. When he'd almost reached her side, she'd left the crowd gathered around her and crossed the room to where Botts was speaking with Marcus and Sarah.

Harlan leaned back in his oversized chair and

touched his fingertips together. From an incident of surreptitiously looking for things in Harlan's desk, Sarah knew the chair was cranked up in height, making him appear nearly as tall as her five ten rather than his normal height of five six. With his hands together, almost obscuring his face, she was sure something in Jacob's recitation caught his attention.

"Jacob, you told us you saw Riley when you went outside, but what made you look in the direction she was lying instead of straight ahead?"

"I don't know."

"Did you hear anything?"

"Do you mean besides dogs and motorcycles?" Anne asked.

Harlan dropped his hands but didn't answer Anne.

Jacob cocked his head. He ran his hand over his right ear and rubbed his hair into the nape of his neck. He turned toward his sister. "You know, that's the funny thing. I don't remember any dogs barking or motorcycles revving when I went outside. I heard those sounds repeatedly during the evening, whenever I was near the back of the restaurant, but when I walked outside, it was silent. The subsequent 'vroom' of a motorcycle a few seconds later is what caught my attention. That's when I looked in the direction of the parking area and dumpster and saw a silver Harley ripping out of the parking lot."

"Did you recognize who was on the motorcycle?" Anne leaned across the opening between their two chairs.

"No. I only saw the back of the rider's helmet and

jacket. He or she was gone before anything really registered with me." His voice rose with excitement. "I'd forgotten. The noise of the cycle is what made me look in the direction where I spotted Riley."

"And what did you do then?"

"Once I realized there was a person on the ground near the dumpster, I ran to help. I don't think it registered at first that it was Riley, but when I got closer and saw her lying there, I stopped dead in my tracks."

"Why?" Harlan asked. "Why didn't you try to help her?"

From the way his voice cracked, Sarah felt sure he was holding back tears. "It wouldn't have done any good. Her face was so white and . . ."

Sarah saw him swallow. She assumed he was struggling to maintain control of himself.

"It was obvious from the angle of her neck that it was too late for me to help her. I should have tried or called for help, but I just stood there doing nothing." His shoulders slumped.

Keeping his voice low, Harlan interrupted whatever emotional flashback Jacob was having. "Do you know how long you stood there?"

"I have no idea. When people talk about time standing still, I think that's what happened. Maybe I was in shock, but I couldn't move. If it hadn't been for the red splayed out on the ground below her head and coloring her hair, I would have sworn she was sleeping like a fairy-tale princess who can't be disturbed except by her prince."

Considering what Grace and Mandy had said about Jacob's adoration of Riley, Sarah hoped he wasn't somehow still lost in a fantasy. What happened to Riley was as far removed from a fairy tale as she could imagine.

"Harlan, the more I think about it," Jacob said, "the more I'm sure there weren't any dogs barking. Except for the motorcycle, everything was silent until Jane screamed."

Standing to interject herself into the conversation, Sarah dropped her pad on the couch. The whack of it hitting the leather caused Anne and Jacob to jump. Either they'd forgotten she was seated behind them or hadn't noticed her following them into the office. She felt them stare at her as she moved from the couch to where they sat.

"He's right, Harlan. Don't you remember when we came outside? Jane was screaming, but otherwise it was quiet. There must not have been any animals in the runs, because if there were, they would have reacted not only to the motorcycle Jacob saw but to Jane's screaming or the noise the rest of us made."

Harlan nodded and looked beyond Anne and Jacob to the couch. Interpreting his glance as an instruction to return to the couch and be silent, she did so as Harlan moved on to another topic. "Jacob, tell me about the motorcycle again. Did you recognize the rider?"

"I only caught a glimpse of the tail end of the bike, but I know it was someone in our club. We all have the same Wildcat insignia on our bikes."

"Jacob Hightower! I knew you had one of those disgusting motorcycles, but are you telling me my brother belongs to a motorcycle gang?"

"It's not a gang." From the tone of his voice, Sarah guessed Jacob had rolled his eyes. "It's a club of cyclists about eighty strong. We all enjoy different types of riding—off-road, sightseeing, or stunts. What we do as a unified group is charity work. We've built wheelchair ramps, held toy drives for the children's hospital, and done a lot of other things for the good of Wheaton without making a big deal of it. Just because we wear helmets and leather jackets doesn't make us all hoodlums. Anne, you'd be surprised who some of us are."

Picking up a pen from his desk, Harlan twirled it between his fingers. "Like who? Jacob, tell me about the makeup of the group. Is everyone like you, or are there some riders that fit the image your sister has of a gang member?"

"From what I've seen, almost everyone is a nice person, but we do fall into some different groups, and that's who we ride with." Jacob glanced at Anne. "I'll admit there is a small group whose image meets what you described. Big bellies, tattoos, and trying to give off an image of being a blue-collar outlaw. Most of that group, who I call the hardcore types, are scary looking but actual pussycats. They do some of the best national charity rides on their Harleys."

From the way Jacob leaned forward toward Harlan, Sarah concluded he was beginning to warm to his topic or at least to not talking or thinking about Riley.

"The next group are the posers. Most of them are doctors, lawyers, dentists, or other professionals who can afford big bikes and spend a fortune on after-market stuff."

Harlan stopped playing with his pen. "What's aftermarket stuff?"

"That's things like pants, accessories, saddlebags, special helmets, badges, and jewelry. The ones I'm labeling the posers have every kind of clothing or personal accessory you can think of, plus they buy extra accessories, like tassels for their handlebars, to jazz up their cycles. Most of them ride Harleys and BMWs. Other than a few of the same insignias or badges, their bikes and jackets tend to be different from each other."

Sarah glanced at Harlan. He was doodling on his pad but not taking notes on what Jacob said. Either he knew what Jacob was telling him, he didn't value it, or he was simply giving Jacob an opportunity to ramble and relax.

When Jacob paused, Harlan inquired if these were all the categories of riders Jacob could think of.

"No, there are the retirees who tend to go sight-seeing on Sundays, but the biggest group of our riders are veterans and people who have law enforcement backgrounds. I don't know if it gives them a thrill, helps clear their heads, or what, but they're the back-bone of the Wildcats' activities. When we do a charity project or ride, this is the group who usually organizes everything. For years, before we were the Wild-cats, a group of them rode in Rolling Thunder."

"What's that?"

"It's a seven-mile ride from the Pentagon to the Vietnam Memorial Wall. The event commemorates the vets still missing in action. About three hundred fifty thousand riders participate in Rolling Thunder, but the event brings about five hundred thousand people to DC."

"That's quite impressive."

Jacob agreed with him. "Last year, because they've talked about discontinuing Rolling Thunder, some of those who'd done it in the past handled the logistics for the Wildcats to take part in the event."

Harlan put down his pen. "So, Jacob, which group do you classify yourself in?"

Jacob stood and walked to Harlan's window. With his back to everyone in the room, he stared outside. "I cross over a lot of groups, but, for the most part, I hang out with the veterans, especially when we have charitable projects. Because of my schedule, I only occasionally ride with them. Usually, on Sundays, I join the retirees."

Sarah was surprised to hear Jacob hung with the vets. She wondered how he worked his way into that group.

His next comment was as if she had asked her question out loud. "I don't consider myself a veteran like most of the Wildcats who served our nation, but they include me because I served six months on active duty and am in the reserves."

This was news to Sarah. In all the time she'd known Jacob, she couldn't recall anyone ever mentioning Jacob was a reservist.

Harlan glanced at the pad on which he'd doodled. He turned to the next page. From her position on the couch, Sarah thought there were words rather than doodles on the page. That would make sense as she knew whenever Harlan was going to court, he always wrote his comments or questions beginning on the second page of a legal pad. When Harlan posed his next question without looking up from the pad, she was sure she was correct. She also was sure he was about to get into the meat of this meeting. "How did Riley become your rider?"

Jacob lowered his body back into his chair. "Riley riding with me wasn't a big deal."

For some reason, his attitude now seemed almost too nonchalant. In fact, his entire body language seemed more relaxed than when he stood by the window. It didn't make sense to Sarah. Considering the discussion was centered on Riley, she was surprised his demeanor was less tense than when he talked about the veterans.

"That wasn't what I asked you. I want to know how she became your regular passenger."

Jacob let out a sigh. "Riley didn't have her own hog, but she loved them. From what I gathered, she grew up with a dad who was one of the more hardcore types, so she'd been around Harleys a lot as a kid. She easily knew more about them than most of the guys. Quite a few of us have bikes that can take a passenger, but most of the Sunday riders aren't comfortable having someone on the back. It's harder to control a bike with more weight, especially keeping balanced in turns. Riley bummed a lot of rides, and one Sunday—I can't remember when—she asked me for a ride, and I gave it to her. She showed up again the following Sunday while we were mounting our bikes and asked again. After that, it became a routine. She'd ride with me, and we'd either get a bite to eat afterward or she'd invite me over for an omelet. Cooking was her way of paying me back for the ride."

"And then you started dating?"

"Yes."

"What happened?"

Jacob shifted in his seat. Where seconds earlier he sat forward, engaged in his discussion with Harlan, Jacob now slumped backward.

Harlan pressed him. "Well?"

"We were together until Botts joined the club three months ago. He started out riding with the veterans, but then claimed, because he was so busy at work, that he needed to shift between groups to give himself more flexibility. Riley went with him so she could stay his rider."

"Was she seeing him, then?"

"Not when she first moved to his bike."

"Did she say why she wanted to ride with him?"

"Yeah, her reason was his Harley was bigger, faster, and had a more comfortable seat than mine. They became a couple shortly after that."

"How did that make you feel?"

"I'd love to tell you it didn't bother me, but it did. Enough people know some of the stupid things I did after she stopped riding with me, so I'm not going to lie to you now. I did some idiotic things, but the one thing I didn't do was kill Riley."

Harlan picked up a clean legal pad from the corner of his desk and held it and the pen he'd been writing with out to Jacob. "Let's see if we can beat Chief Gerard to the punch. Make a list of every Wildcat you can think of and mark the ones who might have observed any of your interactions with Riley or Botts. Also, note any of them who Riley had negative interactions with."

Jacob looked around, as if hoping to find an escape route, before he took the pad and pen from Harlan. For the next few minutes, nobody spoke while

Jacob worked on his list. When he finally finished and went to give the pad back to Harlan, Anne put her hand out for it. Jacob relinquished it to her.

Anne glanced over the names before handing it to Harlan. "Harlan, I gather if we can agree Jacob and those of us in this room are innocent, someone on this legal pad committed murder."

"There's a strong probability that might be the case."

CHAPTER TWELVE

Sarah couldn't help but think about the pad filled with names that Harlan now held. The possibilities seemed endless. Unfortunately, if Chief Gerard held true to form in terms of his past laziness, it would be a lot easier for him to build a case against Jacob rather than check out the motive of everyone on the list. Besides, as Harlan made clear to Anne, it was a probability, as opposed to a certainty, the murderer's name was on the list. In fact, the odds were almost as good it wasn't. When Harlan cleared his throat and began asking another question, Sarah gathered his thinking was on the same wavelength as hers.

"Jacob, there's one more thing the police are going to be interested in."

"What's that?"

"Your background in martial arts."

"You and all of Wheaton are familiar with that."

"Refresh my recollection."

Jacob leaned forward. "My father started me study-ing Taekwondo when I was in second grade, but I wasn't a particularly good student. By the time I was in junior high, I'd only made it to the blue/purple belt stage. He let me stop going when I took up wrestling. I wrestled through high school. During college, I got seriously interested in Taekwondo again, and even though I started back at the beginning, I went through a number of belts . . ."

"What belt do you have?" Harlan interrupted.

"I'm a black belt."

Sarah forgot she was supposed to sit quietly in the background. "Wow!"

Turning toward her, Jacob laughed. "It isn't as impressive as it sounds. There are ten levels of black belt. Nine are achievable before one dies. I'm only at level two."

"Still . . ."

The sound of Harlan drumming his fingers on his desk stopped her from saying anything more. It also drew Jacob's attention back to Harlan.

"Is that all of your involvement with martial arts?"

"No. During college I also took a few courses in judo and jujitsu, and during basic training we had a section they call 'combatives.' They're hand-to-hand techniques more specifically geared to how to use your body and your weapons in close-quarter fighting than some of the other martial arts training. But, Harlan, other than in a classroom setting, I've never used any of this. In fact, during the time I was in California, my hours at the different restaurants were so crazy I didn't take classes or perfect any techniques. When I came back here, I started going to the Studio once or twice a week to work out and taught a few sessions in basic skills and holds at the Boys Club."

"Including neck holds?" Harlan asked.

Aah. This explained Chief Gerard's fixation on Jacob. Only someone who knew what they were doing could have killed Riley so quickly and quietly.

Jacob jumped out of his seat. He pressed his hands palm down on Harlan's desk as he leaned over it almost in Harlan's face. "You've been at the Boys Club when I taught my class. Surely, you've heard how I always make it clear to the kids that our hands and feet are weapons and we must be careful how and when we use them. I always stress temper can never control actions and that force should only be used when absolutely necessary. A clear mind and good intentions are basic to martial arts."

"In theory, that sounds good, Jacob, but Chief Gerard isn't going to be satisfied with the words you teach. He'll want to know if that is the same philosophy you had when you were on active duty."

Jacob glanced around the room, fixing his gaze on the door. Before he could bolt, Anne placed her hand on his arm. He allowed her to guide him back into his chair. For a moment Jacob didn't move, but then he dropped his face into his hands.

When he finally spoke, Sarah strained to hear the words he barely croaked from between his hands. "Yes and no. As a basic premise, yes, but being on duty we were taught to act quickly and use anything and everything to survive. Our platoon's motto was 'Go for the jugular because there might not be a second chance.' It's different in civilian life. Civilians always have an obligation to think and act accordingly."

"Fine, but Chief Gerard will push you. He'll ask if sometimes human emotions overtake that analytical obligation you just defined." Harlan waited until Jacob looked up. "Whichever way you answer, he'll then go for the jugular by bringing up other instances where you acted out."

"You probably know I got into some trouble with Daniel, the manager at Riley's apartment, who, by the way, also liked her. Anyway, I had a little too much to drink and got the brilliant idea to go over to her place and straighten things out face-to-face. I knew she was dating around, but I was hoping to make her see I was the right one for her."

"And?"

Jacob threw his hands up in the air. "When the manager told me Riley was out for the evening with Botts, I don't know what got into me. Maybe it was the alcohol talking or my frustration at everything with my family and their opposition to an entertainment district." He paused and scowled at his sister.

"Instead of handling myself like I normally would, I got into it with Daniel. He shouted at me to leave. I refused, yelling some choice words back at him. He called the police, and when they came, he accused me of shoving him. I hadn't."

"You realize it will be your word against his—and you were drunk."

"I may have been drinking, but I know I didn't shove him."

"With as much as you had to drink, how would you even know?"

Harlan was again goading Jacob, probably to see how he reacted under pressure when discussing Riley. This time, Jacob didn't bite.

"Look, Harlan, I'm not denying I was belligerent and vocal about not leaving, but I kept my hands to myself. In the end, nothing came of it."

"Not exactly what I heard. Anne?"

Anne turned her head away from Harlan toward her brother. From her vantage point on the couch, Sarah could see only Anne's profile. She was convinced from Anne's tightened jawline Anne was back in fighter mode. "Harlan, it really wasn't a big deal."

"No, then tell me about it."

"The reality is my little brother is a sloppy drunk. When the apartment manager called the police to make Jacob leave, Officer Robinson responded. He got Jacob out of there and brought him to the station to sober up."

"Should I presume Chief Gerard, rather than Officer Robinson, called you?"

Anne nodded.

"Why?"

From the way Anne tilted her face toward Harlan, Sarah could tell she was either angry or on the defensive. "It was simply a courtesy call because I'm on the council."

"Did you get those kind of calls from the last police chief?"

"No, but in this case, Dwayne had only recently been appointed as interim police chief, and he knew I was acting president of the council. I guess he wanted to make sure he did everything by the book."

Sarah wondered what book Anne was referring to. She'd never seen one that said the police chief should selectively call the town's politicians.

Apparently, Harlan hadn't seen one, either. "Does he still call you when he takes someone into custody?"

"No." She shifted in her chair. "It was only that one time."

"I see. When he called you, what did you do?"

"I thanked him for his call and instructed Chief Gerard to handle the matter as if he were the duly appointed police chief. We hung up, and to my knowledge he took my advice and followed established protocol. That's all there was to it."

"Did he investigate?"

"Of course he did. The manager alleged there had been some shoving, but nobody else confirmed that. After poking around a bit more, Chief Gerard learned the manager was another one of Riley's castoffs. Based upon his investigation, he concluded men will be boys when it comes to matters of the heart. Consequently, the chief informed Jacob and me he didn't see any reason to pursue the matter. Jacob made a fool of himself, but nobody got hurt, so the case was closed."

"And in your mind, everyone forgot about it."

"Yes." She looked in her brother's direction again. "I hoped the shame of the incident would be enough to get Riley out of Jacob's system. Apparently, I was wrong."

The silence that followed Anne's statement was heavy until Jacob banged his fist on Harlan's desk. "Look, how many times do I have to tell you. I may have been a fool, and I may still be one, but I didn't kill Riley. When I found her, she was lying the way the rest of you saw her—already dead."

Harlan didn't respond directly to Jacob's outburst. Instead, he flipped the pages of the pad until the doodles were back on top. "I think that's enough for today."

He stood. Without a word, Anne followed suit. As Harlan came around his desk, Jacob slowly rose from his chair. Sarah took his movement as her cue to open Harlan's office door and hustle to her own desk. Harlan followed, escorting Anne and Jacob through the waiting room.

Sarah waited for Anne and Jacob to leave and reach the bottom of the cement walkway before speaking to Harlan. "Do you think Jacob understands what an uphill battle you're going to have to fight?"

"I'm not sure he does, but Anne's silence tells me she got the message."

"They both should have. You certainly made body contact with your gloves today."

Harlan frowned. "We were only sparring. Wait until the gloves come off in the next few days. I hope Jacob has the fortitude to survive until we figure this mess out."

CHAPTER THIRTEEN

Without another word, Harlan went into his office and closed the door. Sarah glanced at her cell phone to see if she'd missed any calls. There was a text and a missed call from Emily. She opened the text. If she hadn't been at work, she would have done a jig: Southwind had passed its inspection. She tried calling Emily back, but her call went straight to voice mail.

After leaving her sister a congratulatory message, Sarah was busy the rest of the morning, typing a pleading and filing. Somehow, no matter how much she promised herself she would stay on top of it, her filing always seemed to need catching up. At noon, she knocked on Harlan's door and told him she was going home for lunch. "Do you want me to put the answering machine on?"

"No, I'll be staying put. Just make sure the doors are locked."

She saluted him. "Aye, aye, sir. I'll check them on my way out."

As Sarah double-checked the locks, she wondered if Harlan would ever recognize she'd finally learned her lesson on that score. After the events a few months ago, her sister and his admonishments to always lock the doors were firmly stuck in her head.

Finished, Sarah hurried home. One good thing about living within two blocks of the office was not having to worry about RahRah and Fluffy being alone all day. She walked briskly not because of the crisp chill under the cloudless blue sky but knowing she had only a finite amount of time to play with RahRah, take Fluffy for a walk, and feed them. Rounding the driveway's bend to where the carriage house sat, she was surprised to see her mother's car parked outside her front door. Because there was no one sitting in the car, Sarah steeled herself for what she might find inside. Her mother, Maybelle Johnson, was a one-of-a-kind piece of work.

There was no telling what her mother, who had a key to the carriage house, might do or want. Furniture could be rearranged, artwork could be moved, or her mother could simply be sitting on a couch, lying in wait for Sarah's return. In the time since Sarah's dad died, different people had used words like "eccentric," "quirky," and "deceptive" to describe her mother. Depending upon the day, any of these descriptions might apply, but underneath her exterior, her mother was as sly as a fox and, as she recently had had the opportunity to learn, one of the bravest people she knew.

Squeezing the door handle, Sarah found it locked. As she rummaged through her purse looking for her key, the door was opened by a small bow-tied man wearing a pince-nez. He clutched Fluffy to him cheek to cheek. Sarah was taken aback at having George Rogers, Cliff's uncle and her former neighbor, whose house Jane now owned, standing in front of her. "Mr. Rogers, I wasn't expecting you, but how nice to see you."

She peered around her entryway to the part of the living room she could see, while managing to pet Fluffy and plant a kiss on Mr. Rogers's unoccupied cheek. "Is Mother here, too?"

"Of course. It's Wednesday. Come on. She's in the kitchen." He lowered his voice. "Don't forget, she wants you to call her 'Maybelle.' "

"Will do." *That is until I slip up for the millionth time.* Until nine months ago, when her mother came home from a stay at a new age spa in Mexico, declaring "Maybelle" had a better energy around it than any of the other ways people referenced her, she'd been "Mom" or "Mother." At the time, Sarah thought her mother's idea that using her proper name increased her psychic energy would fade the way of so many of the other fads her mother previously adopted, but it didn't.

Sarah followed Mr. Rogers to the kitchen, trying to figure out why her mother was in there instead of one of the more comfortable rooms and what it being Wednesday meant. Seeing tuna cans stacked on the kitchen island and her mother in one of Sarah's EAT AT YOUR OWN RISK aprons, she knew what her mother was doing in the kitchen.

"Hello, honey." Her mother angled her cheek for a kiss. "I thought I'd whip up a little lunch for the three of us. I've already fed those two."

Sarah stared at her mother. Had she heard her correctly? Her mother, who rarely came into the carriage house because she swore she was allergic to animals, had fed Fluffy and RahRah? And was her mother really batting her eyelashes at Mr. Rogers? They'd been friends a long time and hung out together a lot while he recovered from an injury that necessitated surgery, but could their friendship have moved to a different level?

"Actually, George fed Fluffy and RahRah. Once I found their food, he knew exactly how much to give each one."

"It was nothing." Mr. Rogers was still hugging Fluffy. He pointed across the kitchen to where RahRah slept stretched out in a patch of sunlight. "After all, Fluffy and I lived together long enough for me to know what to feed her. I sort of guessed on RahRah, but he ate all the tuna I put down for him."

Observing the sleeping cat and the opened cans of white tuna in water on her island, she wondered how much tuna her little pig had devoured. No question more than she would have given him. Ever since Dr. Vera said RahRah was getting a little heavy, Sarah used only real tuna as a topper to the cat food his vet recommended. "I'm sure you fed him just fine. RahRah looks very content."

Mr. Rogers gave Fluffy another hug before he put her on the ground. He picked up his cane from the back of one of the kitchen chairs. "And this little gal will be, too, once I walk her. Is her leash still by the front door?" When Sarah replied in the affirmative, he turned to the dog, who was glued to his side. "Come on, Fluffy."

Fluffy trotted from the kitchen behind him, without even a glance at Sarah.

After Mr. Rogers and Fluffy left the kitchen, Sarah peered around her mother into the big bowl she had on the island. "George seems to be doing quite well."

Her mother, who was mixing mayonnaise with the other ingredients in the bowl, agreed.

From the number of empty tuna cans, Sarah presumed tuna also was one of the ingredients for the humans' meal.

"You don't really have a lot of food in the house."

"I eat out a lot."

"That can get expensive. It's better to eat in more."

Sarah bit her tongue rather than thank or challenge her mother for the unsolicited advice. For the sake of this surprise lunch, Sarah felt it better to remain silent.

"I made tuna salad for the three of us. Why don't you wash up for lunch?"

Obeying her mother, Sarah washed her hands at the kitchen sink, while Maybelle carried the bowl to the table set for three. Hands wet, Sarah grabbed a clean towel from the drawer next to the sink. "Mother, how did you know I'd be coming home for lunch today?"

Her mother portioned out the tuna salad onto the plates she'd set. "It's Maybelle, remember dear. Is this enough?"

Sarah nodded.

"Good. And I knew because it's Wednesday."

"What's the significance of it being Wednesday? Mr. Rogers mentioned it, and now you have."

"Why, dear, you know I normally have lunch with George on Wednesdays at his new place."

Sarah acknowledged what her mother said. She knew the two had become dear friends earlier in the summer, after the incident Sarah avoided thinking about. Right afterward, Sarah had thought her mother spent time with Mr. Rogers out of guilt or empathy, but now she wondered . . . Could it be more? "But why did you two come here today during my working hours?"

"Well, I've noticed that when I talk to you on Wednesdays and you tell me what you did during the day, you always say you went home for lunch. I figured you either aren't too busy at the office on Wednesdays or subconsciously you think you don't have to worry about me dropping by during lunch on Wednesdays because I eat with George."

Sarah didn't even want to try to untangle her mother's logic. "But you're here on a Wednesday?"

Maybelle shrugged. "George wanted to visit Fluffy." She dropped her voice to a stage whisper. "He also wanted to see what's been going on with his house. I figured you could fill him in."

"Why not ask his nephew instead of me? After all, Cliff remodeled his house into Jane's Place."

"Oh, honey. George thinks it upsets Cliff when he brings up the circumstances that made him move. Typical men. It's a touchy subject for them. You know, we were going to come to the opening of Jane's Place to see for ourselves last night."

"Jane invited you?"

Maybelle flung her hair back the same way Emily did. The only difference was when Emily did it, it was blond, rather than almost entirely gray. Maybelle's hair flicked up before settling back on her shoulders. "Of course. We planned to attend, but at the last minute George didn't want to be part of the hoopla over what Jane did with his house. We went to a movie instead."

"What did you see?"

"The new one with that cute guy star everyone's talking about."

Sarah choked back a laugh. She knew her mother had no idea who starred in the movie she'd seen last night. "How was it?"

"It was okay. From the crime scene tape we saw them taking down, we figured you saw more action at Jane's Place than we did at the movies. What happened?"

Sarah started to tell her, but her mother interrupted and called for George, who was just bringing Fluffy back in, to come for lunch. Maybelle grabbed a bowl of crackers from the counter. "Tell me while we're eating so you only have to tell the story once."

At the table, Sarah quickly filled Mr. Rogers and her mother in on the events of the night before.

When she finished, Mr. Rogers blinked and peered at her over the top of his glasses. "Riley? I can't believe it? She was so excited about everything that was happening to her."

"You knew her?"

"Yes. Cliff went out with her a few times. He brought her by on his motorbike to help when he was setting the internet up at my new place."

Sarah didn't know what to say. She knew, besides his boats, Cliff had lots of toys. Consequently, it didn't surprise her that one was a motorcycle or that he hadn't mentioned it. What bothered her was the inference he'd dated Riley at the same time they were going out. Their relationship was new, but Sarah had thought it was exclusive. Sarah wanted to ask him more about Cliff dating Riley, but she didn't think she could control her voice in front of her mother. Instead, she focused on the motorcycle club. "Are you telling me Cliff belongs to the Wheaton Wildcats?"

"Why yes, he does."

"I never realized how many people in Wheaton belong to the Wildcats. If either of you tell me you're members, too, I'm going to pass out."

"Not us," her mother said. "Those things scare me even when I see one on the road. I'm always afraid it's going to wipe out and end up under my car. Eloise belongs, though. She keeps telling me I'm being silly and that if I come out for a ride just once, I'll change my tune."

"Though Cliff is a member, I'm with your mother on this one." George reached over and put his hand over her mother's.

Her mother didn't pull away immediately. When she did, she did it by throwing her hands up in surprise after glancing at the kitchen clock. "My, look at the time. Don't you need to get back to work, Sarah?"

"I do. I didn't realize what time it was." Sarah hustled to help her mother clear the dishes and toss the empty tuna cans into a garbage bag. When they finished, Maybelle handed the full garbage bag to George to take out.

Once George left, but before Sarah could gather

up her things to go, she felt, almost more than she saw, her mother shooting her a mother-knows-best look. "I'm so glad George and I came today. I just don't hear from you enough."

Rather than getting into it with her mother, Sarah broached a different topic. "What's going on between the two of you?"

"George and I are friends."

"Now, Mom, I saw him take your hand and I didn't see you stop him. I doth think you protest too much."

"There really isn't anything to it. We're special friends. I eat lunch with him every Wednesday when they have Guest Day at his place. The food is pretty good. We've also started going to the five-dollar movies on Tuesdays together, as well as a few other things here and there, but corny as it sounds, we've both had our true loves. My friendship with him isn't much different than the one I have with Eloise. At my age, it's all about companionship."

"That's true at any age." Sarah leaned over and gave her mother a kiss. "I've got to run. Lock up when you leave. By the way, did you talk to Emily today?"

"No, why?"

"Southwind passed inspection. We're set to have our first soft opening tomorrow."

"So soon?"

"Marcus and Emily have had everything ready to go for the past ten days."

Hurrying back to the office, Sarah thought about her mother and Mr. Rogers. She was convinced, even if they didn't know it, they had the potential to have something special. At least, for now, as her mother said, they offered each other companionship. Maybe, at her mother's age, companionship was enough, but she doubted it. Sarah knew, at her age, even though she'd been scarred by the rat, there had to be more. Only of whom or what, she wasn't sure. Her past track record left something to be desired, and the present wasn't looking too much better.

Harlan was kind and attentive, but she'd made it clear to him a few months ago that with him being her boss, she wouldn't cross that line. He'd never pushed since then. She'd thought Cliff and she had something going, informal as it was, but having just learned he'd been dating Riley at the same time changed things. How much, she'd figure out tonight. Cliff had invited her to his place on the bluff for steaks and a view of the sunset.

Chapter Fourteen

Driving out of town to the bluff on Wednesday evening, Sarah realized she was nervous, but she wasn't sure why. This wasn't the first time she'd been back to Cliff's place since the incident a few months ago. Maybe it was because she wasn't clear, now that she knew he'd gone out with Riley and whoever else at the same time he'd done things with her, if the steaks and sunset tonight were a date or simply two friends getting together. Maybe they were companionship for each other like his uncle and her mother were? She felt torn trying to decide if her feelings for Cliff were tinged with romance or friendship. What were his for her? She knew he still blamed himself for what had happened no matter how many times she told him it wasn't his doing.

Reaching the place where the road leading to Cliff's cabin allowed one an unblocked view of the water, Sarah slowed. For years, while the property had an absentee owner, the bluff was her favorite spot to bike to when she was upset or simply needed a little informal spiritual renewal. It had remained unspoiled because there wasn't a road to follow and few people ventured in this direction, not realizing the bluff over the water existed. Almost two years ago, when No Trespassing signs appeared and a grated dirt road was cut, she stopped coming to her spot. She told herself it wasn't appropriate to trespass on someone else's property, but deep down she knew she'd stopped coming because she couldn't bear the idea of her favorite spot being destroyed by someone randomly plopping a house on the bluff. When Jacob introduced her to Cliff and she discovered he was the owner, she eventually accepted Cliff's invitation to see his cabin and take a boat ride.

To her astonishment, then and now, she marveled at how Cliff had taken pains in designing his cabin to take advantage of the beautiful surroundings. His cabin was perfectly situated so he could sit in his great room or on the porch and enjoy the bluff's natural beauty. What was even more impressive to Sarah was how he routed the road to make sure it didn't ruin the view from any direction. She could sit here midroad and be quite happy, but Cliff was waiting for her.

He must have been listening for her because he came out onto the porch when she pulled up to the cabin. He was in his usual uniform—plaid flannel shirt, blue jeans, and well-worn cowboy boots. To her knowledge, the only time he took this pair of boots off was on a construction site because the law required wearing steel-toed shoes.

Sarah waved at Cliff while she turned off the motor and popped the trunk. She couldn't wait to see Cliff's face when he saw the coconut cake she'd brought for dessert. It was another recipe Emily was trying out for Southwind's dessert menu. Because Cliff loved desserts, she thought getting his opinion tonight would be a good taste test.

She bent into her trunk to retrieve the cake. She'd placed it in an empty grocery box she kept there to prevent objects from sliding around. Carefully, she carried the cake up the cabin's first few steps. From the top step, Cliff bent toward her, kissed the top of her head, and removed the cake box from her hands.

"You didn't have to bring dessert."

"I wanted to."

Cliff stared at the cake. "This is beautiful. It looks homemade." He shot her a quizzical look.

Sarah laughed. "It is homemade, but true confession, Emily made it. She's thinking of putting it on the menu, so I thought we could try it for her."

"Well, I'm rating it a ten on looks. Speaking of which, you look lovely tonight." He carried the cake inside the cabin and put it on the big wooden table he'd made.

She paused for a moment but then followed. Even though she'd been here since he replaced the soiled rug, as well as the glassware and other things that had been broken, she couldn't keep the memories from flooding back. Better to look ahead and make new ones. "Do I get a ten, too?"

Coming back to where she stood, he stopped in front of her and drank her in before repeating, "A ten, too? No, I think you're off the charts."

"Ah, at least an eleven."

Cliff kissed her—a real kiss this time. "At least. Wine?"

"Please."

He walked to the oak and copper bar that matched his dining room table and poured them each a glass of red. "Why don't we drink them on the porch. That way, we can watch the sunset while I prep the coals for our steaks." As she started toward the porch, he walked over to the refrigerator and took out a small plate of cheese and crackers.

Sarah saw he'd cut exactly the right amount of cheese for two. "You were pretty sure on that one, weren't you?"

"Well, I figured if you said no, I could always eat our appetizer as a snack later tonight."

While they both laughed and got comfortable in matching rockers on the porch, she couldn't help the nagging thought of how many times he'd prepped an appetizer before and wondered whether he ever needed to eat it as a midnight snack when he'd been with Riley. Looking at him sipping his wine and offering her a cracker and cheese, she wanted to slap her own face. Cliff wasn't a rat like her ex. He was a nice guy. Still, the devil on her shoulder nagged at her. Remember, it seemed to say, he apparently went out with Riley after Sarah thought she was the only one he was interested in.

"A penny for your thoughts. You look like you're a million miles away. In fact, I'm not even sure you've noticed the sun is starting to set." He pointed to the edge of the bluff, where the sun dipped closer and closer to the water.

Sarah glanced around the porch, uncertain what

to say. "I was thinking how much I love your bar and dining room table and wondering if you made this furniture, too?"

"The answer is no. Some things are better purchased, but surely you weren't that deep in thought over my rocking chairs." He stopped rocking, leaned over, and put his hand on her knee. "Sarah, is there something bothering you? Something I said or did?"

She gazed into the dark pools of his eyes. It was as if he was pulling the words out of her mouth. The warmth of his touch only added to the power of his reach into her soul. Although she hadn't meant to bring it up tonight, the words slipped out, "It's Riley."

He sat back up and began rocking again. His gaze no longer locked with hers. "That was terrible, wasn't it?"

Sarah took a sip from her glass. She didn't think the sour taste in her mouth was from her wine. "Did you know her well?"

"We were friends."

"Like we are?"

He turned his head away from her. She couldn't tell if he was gathering his thoughts or trying to figure out how to let her down gently. When he looked at her again, instead of answering, he repeated her question, "Like we are? What do you mean?"

"I don't know." She swallowed more of her wine. "I heard the two of you dated."

He put his glass on the table next to him. "Who did you hear that from?"

She couldn't tell if he was mad or not. Although she felt guilty for the way she asked the question, Sarah wanted to know the answer. "Your uncle. He and my mother came by the carriage house today. He mentioned you brought Riley by the independent living facility. He thought it was nice that the two of you interrupted a date to help him set up his internet. Your uncle thought she was a sweet girl."

Cliff put his head back and roared. The lines over his brows relaxed, replaced by deep laugh lines at the corners of his eyes. "Leave it to Uncle George to misinterpret the facts."

"I've always known him to be fairly accurate when it comes to facts." She couldn't believe the defensive tone in her voice.

The laugh lines on his face disappeared. "I think this discussion is going to need more wine. I'll be right back." He went into the house.

While he left her sitting alone on the porch, she weighed whether she wanted to continue this discussion or simply leave. His return, carrying the wine bottle, eliminated her moment of escape. He refilled both of their glasses and put the bottle on the table before he dropped into his rocking chair. Fortified by another sip, he ran his hand over his face.

She waited for him to drop a bomb on her. How she could have misread him so badly these past few months amazed her. Then again, with her track record, why should she be surprised?

"Earth to Sarah."

She looked at him.

"I know they say men are like Mars and woman are like Venus, but tonight, for some reason, I think you keep going out of this stratosphere."

"My specialty. I guess I can't walk and chew gum like you."

"I'm not sure what that means, but, Sarah, let me explain about Riley. We did go out to dinner a few times, as well as a movie, but it wasn't a relationship like you and I've been building."

"But you admit you did it at the same time we've been going out?"

"Sure. There's nothing to hide." He opened his mouth and shut it again. "Oh, I get it. It didn't mean anything."

"It must have meant something or you wouldn't have gone out a few times or taken her by your uncle's place."

He stood and walked across the porch. For a moment, he leaned on the railing, staring at the setting sun before turning back toward her. "I shouldn't have to explain myself, but you mean enough to me that I'm going to this one time."

Cliff held up his hand to keep her from saying anything. "Sarah, men and women don't always mean or feel the same thing when they go on a date. I think you and I both feel a real relationship takes time to cultivate, but other people are more spur-of-the-moment. Riley probably fell into that group. I hate to speak ill of the dead, but she was a real flirt."

Sarah nodded. That tied in with what Grace had said about her. "Are you saying she changed you to a more spur-of-the-moment guy?"

The ends of his mouth curled, but she couldn't tell if he was holding back a smile or an angry retort. "Not at all. What I saw in Riley was a little girl in a woman's body. She used the flirting to cover her neediness and a huge sense of loneliness. I felt like I knew her better than she knew herself. I wanted to help her."

"By dating her?" Sarah felt warm. She put her glass of wine on the table. Maybe she'd had too much. She was having trouble keeping her thoughts from getting ahead of what Cliff was saying.

"No. Sarah, you know I'm a member of the Wheaton Wildcats?"

Confused why he was changing the subject, she didn't answer.

Cliff apparently took her silence as a yes.

"Most of the members own their own bikes, but there are a few folks who hang around and bum rides from those of us whose cycles can take a passenger. Riley was one of those. The club joke was that she loved bikes as much as she loved vegan cooking. You see, she brought a different vegan dish whenever we had a potluck. Each was better than the last. When I heard she was going to be making the same dishes for Jane's Place, I bet the restaurant would be a success. I also figured she'd probably use most of her first paychecks to put a deposit on a used bike."

He walked back in her direction, scuffing his boots against the wood floor. "Anyway, that's no longer important, but your question is. Whether by flirting or simply making everyone laugh, she went out of her way to be friendly and helpful. That's why no one complained that she was taking advantage of us when she bummed a ride. It almost became a game to see who she would pair up with during any week. Most of the time her choice was a spur-of-the-moment decision that meant nothing in terms of romance."

"That's not what I heard about her riding with Jacob."

He rubbed the back of his neck while he seemed to contemplate how to word his next comment. "It started with her bumming rides from him, but Jacob was smitten. I don't think she cared about him as much as his bike, but, for a few months, they did have something going. When Botts showed up, she changed her allegiance. From then on, when Botts was there, he was her ride."

"Now I'm confused. From what you've said, you went out with her during this period, too. Was she fickle? Loving the one she was with?"

"Not in my case. One day when neither Botts nor Jacob was there, she bummed a ride with me. When we got back, she offered to whip me up some lunch as her way of saying thanks. I told her it wasn't necessary, but she said she often did that. It was only fair in exchange for the gas I'd used. I thanked her again and said I needed a rain check because I promised to help my uncle get settled in his new place. She responded that her afternoon was free and offered to tag along and help me, and then we could go back to her place for a late lunch."

"And that's what you did?" Sarah said frostily, now standing, too.

Cliff put himself in front of her, blocking the final moments of the sunset. "I shouldn't even answer this, but whatever you're thinking, it's way off. I went back to her place and she made me a late lunch and that was it. Sarah, if she felt like she was paying me back by making me a vegan omelet, I wasn't going to say no. It was a matter of dignity. She couldn't afford her own ride or to pay for our gas, but tofu and hummus and her skill were what she could give most of us in exchange for her rides."

"But . . ."

"I know you and others may have seen her as a real flirt, and that was her style. She may have stirred up some interest in some of the guys, but except for Jacob for a short period of time and then Botts, I don't think she ever got serious with anyone. I tried to be her friend because I felt sorry for her. So, yeah, the few times she rode with me, I let her make me lunch or I took her out for a meal, and once to a movie that had a star we both liked, but all of that was as a friend."

Sarah backed up and sat again. She knew Cliff's background as a lonely child shunted off to schools had resulted in his putting a shell around himself, but it apparently had created a streak of empathy, too.

Cliff knelt beside her. In the darkness his face was illuminated by the limited light coming through the picture window behind them. "Sarah, Riley was too young for me. She may have looked like a woman, but underneath she was a needy kid. The kind I once was. I only offered her a hand of friendship." He took both of Sarah's hands in his. "The kind of relationship I'm looking for has to be based on a mutual friendship, but it needs to share more than that. There must be respect, caring, love, and communication. It's the kind of relationship that takes time to build—especially when both people have things in their past to get over. I know we've been taking things super slow, but that's how I thought you wanted it. I didn't want to rush anything, especially after how we've both been badly burned in the past, but I felt we were building something special. Was I wrong?"

She barely got the word "no" out of her mouth before he kissed her.

CHAPTER FIFTEEN

A rush of adrenaline coursed through her, followed by a fluttering sensation.

Gently, Cliff pulled back and stood. "Now do you understand?"

"Yes." She smiled because she did.

"Well then, I guess I better go put the steaks on. I think the coals have heated up enough. Want to help?"

"Sure." She rose and followed him toward the grill. As she walked across the porch, she stumbled. Instinctively, she cried out.

Cliff turned back. He leaped toward her, barely managing to catch her before she face-planted.

Sarah leaned against him as he steadied her. "Thanks."

When Cliff let go of her, she didn't move from where she stood. Instead, she stared at the floor but saw nothing that could have catapulted her so quickly into falling. She glanced at Cliff. If he hadn't caught her, she hated to think how badly she might have been injured by the velocity of her fall. There was no question she probably would have, at the least, broken her nose. The mental image she had of how she might have landed made her reflect on the way Riley lay when Sarah first saw her.

Like Sarah, Riley's body had fallen forward, but her head and neck weren't at the angle Sarah's would have hit. Instead, it was as if Riley had twisted around to see if someone was behind her.

"Sarah, are you okay?"

"I'm fine, but I just realized from the way I almost landed something about the way Riley was lying."

"What's that?"

"Someone must have grabbed her from behind, and when she tried to look back to see who it was, she was off-balance, so her neck snapped awkwardly as she fell." Sarah shuddered. "Or someone snapped it and twisted it back as they killed her. From what I understand, the autopsy will tell us, but Chief Gerard seems convinced Jacob used a martial arts hold on her from behind."

"Jacob? Our Jacob? No way. I've known Jacob since we were kids. He's a good guy."

"I guess I'm talking out of school, but I thought you knew Jacob was the one who found Riley. And, well, with their history . . ."

Cliff frowned. "Once again, the good chief is jumping to the wrong conclusion."

"I agree with you, but apparently Jacob's known ability to choke someone from behind is a key factor in Chief Gerard's thinking."

"Well, he's barking up the wrong tree when it comes to Jacob. Besides, what you're describing could be accomplished from the front, too. Here, look."

Cliff demonstrated several holds and twists that could be done from the front as well as from the back.

When he finished, Sarah was totally confused. "Where did you learn all those holds?"

"Some I learned in basic training and a few I learned when I was a Boy Scout."

Sarah tried to imagine Cliff dressed as a Boy Scout. She couldn't picture the rugged man he now was shrunk into a tan uniform. "I know everyone takes a combatives course during basic training, but they teach these skills in Boy Scouts, too?"

"Oh, of course." His face took on a pensive expression. "The Boy Scout motto is 'Be Prepared,' and the Scouting program made sure we were prepared in every way possible."

"I guess I thought the Boy Scouts emphasized camping and that kind of stuff." Sarah shook her head. "In Brownies and Girls Scouts, we did a lot with survival skills, math, science, and other things, but never anything like that."

"That's a shame."

He turned away from her, chortling more of a snort than a laugh, but the increased intensity of his body shaking gave him away.

"Cliff!"

Facing her again, he didn't even try to hide his amusement. "You are so gullible! I learned a lot in

Scouting, including many things I could do with a pocketknife, but definitely not choke holds or ways to kill people."

"Thank goodness! I had visions of all these little boys practicing choke holds on their brothers and sisters."

Cliff stopped laughing. "Maybe that idea has some merit to it."

"You don't really mean that."

"No, I don't. Is there something in what we've been talking about that helps figure out who, other than Jacob, might be a suspect?"

"I honestly don't know. I'm relieved I don't have to limit my suspect list to someone who was once a Boy Scout. I think Chief Gerard's fixation on martial arts is valid, but his focus on military training is too narrow. As you noted, the murderer may have learned defensive skills somewhere other than the military. Maybe in law enforcement or self-defense classes?"

"All are good possibilities."

"The murder seems so personal. First, I think if Riley let the killer get close to her, he or she must have been someone Riley knew and felt safe with, but then I wonder if the murderer came up super quietly behind her. Startled, she may have turned funny when she realized someone was there."

"That's possible, but unless the person was very light on their feet, Riley should have heard footsteps on the gravel and cement in that parking area."

What Cliff said made sense. Sarah remembered the clacking sound Anne's heels made. What if it hadn't been as quiet as it was when Anne walked across the lot? "Cliff, what if the dogs were outside and barking? Maybe Riley didn't hear the killer because the dogs yapping masked the sound of footsteps?"

"That makes sense, but if they were outside, how did you hear Jane scream?"

"That's right. If they'd been outside, we wouldn't have heard Jane so clearly from inside the restaurant. So I guess we're back to square one."

"Not quite. In my mind, Riley may have been a flirt, but her background made her wary of trusting people. That would seem to indicate she knew her killer. Right there, the circle of who might have murdered her narrows."

Although Cliff's logic sounded good to Sarah, thinking of Jacob's list of Wildcat members, plus all the people Riley knew from every aspect of her life, Sarah only saw her list of potential suspects growing. There were plenty of people who might not have been inside Jane's Place at any time that evening but who Riley still could have talked to in the parking lot. People she wouldn't have considered strangers.

Contemplating her suspect list, Sarah thought she might be able to strike a few people because of a lack of familiarity with combatives, but talking with Cliff had made her understand the list was far wider than Harlan and she originally thought. If Chief Gerard didn't help cull it, Sarah had a daunting task ahead of her. "I guess I'll be scrutinizing everyone who comes into Southwind this week."

Cliff raised a brow. "This week? I know Botts finally signed off on everything, but don't Marcus and

Emily need a few days before their first soft opening? And, for that matter, they're letting you near the restaurant?"

"Ha ha." Pulling herself up as tall as she could, which was still an inch shorter than Cliff, Sarah jutted out her chin and chest in Cliff's direction. "I'll have you know I'm a valuable member of the Southwind team."

"I didn't mean to say you aren't an essential member of the Southwind team." Tumbling over his words, he hastened to assure her he was only thinking of her professed lack of love or skill in a kitchen.

Sarah let him flounder for a moment, trying to talk his way out of having insulted her. "I'm not going to have an everyday role in the restaurant, but for the soft openings, I'm going to help out at the hostess desk."

"What about Emily? I thought she was going to work front of the house."

"My being a backup will let her also be in the kitchen, when it's necessary. I'm not getting anywhere near there. As for the soft openings, Marcus and Emily had everything ready to go once Southwind passed inspection. Emily and he decided, with Jane having almost a month to get ready and two weeks serving food and building a following before her grand opening, they wouldn't waste time with a lot of days devoted to invited guests or tastings. Two or three days of soft openings to get out any service bugs is all they're going to do. Their plan is to be completely open and advertising for real-life customers by this weekend."

"I'll make sure to stop by and check on how things are going. In the meantime, want to watch me make the steaks?"

"Well . . ."

"I said 'watch.' I want us to be able to eat them."

Sarah stuck her tongue out at Cliff but didn't disagree with him.

CHAPTER SIXTEEN

Despite not having gotten home until late, and only then because she had two pets to take care of, Sarah was at her desk by eight a.m. Knowing she would be working as the backup hostess during the Thursday night dinner rush at Southwind, she hoped if she got everything done, Harlan wouldn't mind if she left a little before five. She figured that would give her time to feed RahRah and Fluffy and change into her one simple black dress.

Marcus and Emily thought that from the moment a guest arrived, they should be met with the ambience of the evening. The usual slacks and sweater she wore to the office wouldn't cut it.

As Sarah typed the last words on a letter Harlan wanted to get out today, the office doorbell rang. She checked the monitor and saw Jacob standing outside the door, holding a folder.

Sarah buzzed him in. "Hi! What are you doing here so early?"

"When Harlan asked me about my martial arts moves yesterday, it got me thinking."

"Thinking is always a good thing to do." After the words left her mouth, she hoped Jacob would take what she'd just said as sister-brother teasing as opposed to being a commentary on his behavior. When he made a quick retort and grinned impishly, like the Jacob she was used to, Sarah was relieved, but the good feeling lasted only a moment as a cloud came over his face again.

"Harlan is in court this morning. Jacob, is there something I can help you with?"

"Actually, yes. My sister told me Eloise and she asked you to investigate to prove my innocence and that you agreed."

"I agreed to help, but I warned them they needed to let the professionals handle things."

Jacob's face tightened as he seemed to suck in the air from the room. "If I do that, we all know how things are going to go."

He laid the folder he clutched on the counter that separated her reception area from the general waiting room. "If you're not willing to help me, will you at least give this to Harlan?"

"Jacob, I didn't say I wouldn't help. I said I'd poke around and see what I could find, but, Jacob, there are lots of things in your case I don't have access to. Plus there are a lot of people out there who had dealings with Riley."

"Well, maybe we can narrow down some of those people. Last night I racked my brain trying to remember who she knew who had some type of martial arts training besides me. I made a list of the people I could think of for Harlan." He tapped on the folder.

"May I see it?"

Jacob slid the folder to Sarah. She opened it and scanned the first page.

Louis Botts
Cliff Rogers
David Smith
Dwayne Gerard
Alvin Robinson
Daniel Howard
Glenn Amos
Tonya Putnam
Vera Hong
Sam Peabody
Mandy Davis
Grace Winston
George Rogers

Instead of turning to the second page, she looked up at Jacob. "How many more names are there?"

"In total, I came up with fifty-seven, including me."

"Are you telling me we have a walking militia in Wheaton?"

"No. I was brainstorming people who have some type of martial training, so I included anyone I knew who was a Wildcat or knew Riley through school or the restaurant. Some of the folks, like Botts, the vets, and me served in the military. Others, like Mandy or Officer Robinson, have law related jobs."

"Officer Robinson is on the Wheaton police force, but Mandy?"

"She's a paralegal for a personal injury law firm and also teaches self-defense classes for women."

Sarah tapped the list. "And the others?"

"Most are people who took classes in self-defense, jujitsu, or something similar. As you can see, there are plenty of names. Not all of them could possibly have killed Riley, but it's a start."

"That it is."

Scanning the first page again, Sarah saw there were a few names she could immediately delete like Cliff and his uncle George. She pointed to George Rogers's name. "Between his surgery and recovery, I think we can safely rule him out. Here's another one like that. Why don't I hold on to this and look over the entire list? I might be able to think of a few more who could be scratched."

"That would be great."

"And don't worry, I'll give the folder to Harlan the minute he comes back from the courthouse."

"Tell him to call me if he wants to talk about any of the other names."

"I will."

CHAPTER SEVENTEEN

After juggling her normal workdays and spending Thursday and Friday evenings as the backup hostess at the newly opened Southwind, Sarah looked forward to sleeping in on Saturday. She didn't have to meet Harlan at the animal shelter for their shift as dog walker volunteers until nine thirty. Unfortunately, Fluffy had a different idea.

Her insistent scratching on the side of the bed at seven didn't end when Sarah patted her head. With a groan, Sarah threw back her comforter, grabbing the edge of it before it smothered RahRah. Because he wasn't cuddled against her, she hadn't realized where her cat lay burrowed in the bed.

He made a guttural sound and raised a tan paw but didn't fully wake when she retrieved a pair of already worn sweatpants from the floor.

"Come on, Fluffy," she whispered. "Let's get your business done so I can go back to bed."

Fluffy wagged her tail while waiting for Sarah to open the bedroom door. Once there was enough room for her to squeeze through, Fluffy twisted by Sarah and trotted straight to the carriage house's entry hall. Sarah proceeded more slowly, amused when Fluffy paused and seemed to look back at her. Apparently convinced Sarah was following her, she went straight to the front door and sat patiently until Sarah clipped the leash to her collar.

Outside, Sarah gave Fluffy the freedom to sniff around while Sarah listened to the quiet surrounding her, broken only by an intermittent birdcall. At least for the moment, there were no cars traveling Main Street, nor did she hear any construction sounds. The latter surprised Sarah until it dawned on her that neither Cliff nor any other contractor had a remodeling or new construction job underway on Main Street. Considering the months of almost nonstop hammering, sawing, and trucks rumbling up and down Main Street, the silence seemed weird.

What was also weird was the lack of customers Southwind had had during the first few days it was open. The Southwind Pub was still doing great business, and now that Jane had reopened, her parking lot was again full every night, but the tables weren't turning at Southwind. Marcus and Emily hadn't been thrilled but weren't overly alarmed when business was slow the first few nights. They hoped it would pick up tonight, now that an article about the new restaurant ran in Friday's entertainment insert and Emily had been on a cooking segment on one of the local morning TV shows. Not content to chance everything on word of mouth, they'd also placed a temporary sign announcing Southwind was open on the grass on the far end of their property, near the well-traveled intersection of Main and Spring Streets that led to the highway.

Sarah was glad Marcus and Emily were being aggressive in their marketing. With Jane's Place as busy as it was, they needed to be seen to not only gain new customers but hopefully attract the overflow crowd waiting on her porch. She wished Chief Gerard would be as aggressive in finding a suspect other than Jacob. Harlan and she had gone over the list Jacob left, but other than a few names they easily struck, nothing jumped out at them.

Hoping Jacob's visit meant something positive for his case, Sarah had commented to Harlan, as they reviewed the list, that she guessed Jacob's not being arrested yet was a good sign. Harlan hadn't shared her feelings. He thought the chief was waiting for the lab results so his case would be open-and-shut. She made a mental note to try to catch Jacob this weekend to see if they could narrow down the suspect list.

A chirp coming from her pocket announced she had a text. She pulled her phone out. The message was from Cliff. **Enjoyed Wednesday eve. Glad we cleared the air. Dinner tonight?**

She quickly texted him back. **Enjoyed, too. Probably have to help at Southwind again. Won't know until later. Let u know then?**

Ok.

Sarah stuffed her phone back into her pocket. At least he was one person with a knowledge of martial arts she could cross off Jacob's and her suspect list.

Realizing Fluffy was pawing at something in the yard rather than taking care of business, Sarah gently redirected her puppy away from the driveway to the far-side flat patch of grass near where they had put the sign. Although most people, like Sarah and the Southwind staff, used the rear entrance from the driveway or the restaurant's front walkway to access Southwind, the partners deliberately positioned the sign, hoping motorists delayed getting onto the highway by the short traffic light would subliminally remember its name. Their goal was to capture the eye of individuals driving in and out of town who didn't necessarily live close to the restaurant.

As Fluffy sniffed near the sign, Sarah was surprised to see it had been vandalized. The black plastic letters used to spell out IS OPEN! were lying on the ground, and someone had pasted a large COMING SOON message below the word SOUTHWIND.

Sarah yanked the paper off the sign. Because she normally didn't pass this intersection, she wondered if part of the lack of customers might be attributable to the vandalism. She glanced at her watch. Emily and Marcus were planning to be at Southwind by eight to prep with Grace before they went over to the Southwind Pub to get things started for its lunch crowd. So much for going back to bed. She would take Fluffy back to the house, feed her and RahRah, and use her key to Southwind to wait for her twin's arrival.

CHAPTER EIGHTEEN

Grace was standing on Southwind's back porch when Sarah returned to the restaurant after taking care of her pets and grabbing a quick shower. As always, Sarah was delighted to see the stately woman, whom she had gotten to know when Emily was accused of killing Sarah's ex. At the time, Sarah had tried to fill in for Emily for a few days. Something she should never have done. Without Grace's help in the kitchen, there might have been two tragedies, because being in the kitchen was a fate worse than death for Sarah and the diners.

"Hi, Grace! Can't you get in?"

"No. Marcus is having an extra key made so I can open and close, but he hasn't given it to me yet. We hoped to get an early start on tonight's prep in case we have a really good Saturday crowd, but Marcus and Emily aren't here yet."

Sarah held up her key. "Not a problem. I can get us in." While she unlocked the door, she handed Grace the COMING SOON sign she'd brought in to show Marcus and Emily. She took it back after she turned off the building's alarm system.

Grace took her pocketbook and jacket to the little area where there was a bank of individual lockers for the employees. In the meantime, Sarah placed the sign, with her coat and purse, on one of the kitchen chairs. She waited in one of the other chairs for Grace's return or Marcus and Emily's arrival. When Grace came back into the kitchen, she went directly to where a small coffeepot was on the counter.

"Sarah, I'm starting the coffee. Do you want some?"

"Please."

Grace plugged in the coffeepot.

"How are you enjoying working full-time?"

Instead of answering her immediately, Grace pulled four mugs out of a cabinet. She put them on the counter near the coffeepot. "It's funny. This week I've been thinking a lot about how things could have turned out if Harlan hadn't helped me when I was running with the wrong crowd and was picked up for being in the wrong place at the wrong time. If Harlan hadn't taken my case pro bono and then taken a personal interest in me, who knows where I'd be today?"

"Knowing the type of person you are, you'd have been fine."

Grace shook her head. "I was going nowhere fast. If Harlan hadn't gotten me interested in the college's culinary arts program and convinced your ex to underwrite my tuition when I got in, things would have been different."

This time, Sarah didn't disagree with Grace.

"When I started culinary school, Harlan told me to enjoy every minute of it—even the annoying or rough parts—because I'd never have the same freedom and lack of responsibilities. Even though he urged me to relax, I couldn't. I knew I had to give it everything I had because my scholarship was my only chance to make something of myself."

"And you did. Plus, beyond school, you took on so many extra things like working for Emily. You exhaust me with your energy. Watching you in action always makes me think of that bunny that keeps on going."

Grace smiled slightly, but it wasn't with her usual intensity. Something was off, but Sarah couldn't put her finger on it. She joined Grace at the counter where Grace stood staring at the coffeepot.

"I don't think you watching the pot that intently is going to make it boil. Tell me why you'd like to be a student again."

"Is it that obvious?"

"Yes." Sarah waited, unsure if Grace would confide in her.

"Because as much as I had to work hard in school, I felt safe there. I didn't take advantage of them, but there were always school advisers who I could turn to for help. Even though I know Mandy always has my back, it's a lot harder sorting things out as a grown-up. Coffee's ready." She pulled the coffeepot from its cradle so quickly the last drops splashed onto the cradle.

Without saying anything, Sarah tore a couple of sheets of paper towel from one of the rolls strategically placed throughout the kitchen and handed them to Grace.

With her full concentration on the droplets of coffee, Grace vigorously wiped them up. "There, that should keep the coffee from staining anything."

Sarah weighed whether to press Grace. She hated to see her friend in such obvious distress. "Grace, what's wrong? You can tell me."

"Nothing." Grace turned her head away from Sarah, but not before Sarah saw a tear slide down her cheek.

Sarah put her arm around Grace and gently used her thumb to wipe away the escaping tear. "What is it?"

Grace met Sarah's gaze. "I don't know. I've felt like there's a hollow place in the pit of my stomach since I found out about Riley. And I don't know why. It's not like we were good friends."

"But you've said there was a time Mandy, Riley, and you all hung out together. Surely the three of you shared some experiences and dreams, right?"

Grace hiccuped but nodded her head in agreement.

"It's always hard when someone dies, especially someone young like us. I think what you're feeling is perfectly normal, but if these feelings don't go away or you feel worse, promise you'll tell me so we can get you some help."

"I promise, but don't worry. I'm sad about Riley, but that's not the worst of it."

"What is?" Sarah prompted.

"Jane called me last night."

Hearing her ex-husband's bimbo's name immediately raised Sarah's dander. "What did she say to upset you?"

"She complimented me on my cooking."

Sarah didn't understand. "Why are you so upset about a compliment?"

"Because in the next breath she offered me a job, and, well, I thought about it." Grace looked miserable.

"What! You're not serious, are you?"

"I am. She offered me the executive chef position at Jane's Place."

"But Jane is the executive chef."

"In confidence, she told me she shared those duties with Riley. She can't handle the everyday operation of her restaurant alone, so she wanted to put me in charge of the kitchen, with any menu I want, and she'll be responsible for the fiscal side."

Sarah blinked. Every muscle in her body tensed at the thought of Jane going behind Emily and Marcus's backs. That poaching witch! It wasn't enough she'd stolen Sarah's husband and tried to take RahRah from her; now Jane blatantly wanted to steal Southwind's sous chef. Outrageous!

Looking at Grace's anguished face, Sarah sighed. She had to admit it would be a step up for Grace, and that position wasn't open at Southwind or the Southwind Pub. Much as Sarah didn't like it, she knew it wouldn't be right to make Grace feel bad for taking advantage of this opportunity.

"Considering Marcus and Emily have those roles for the Southwind restaurants, I guess this is a great offer. I know they'll miss you, though. When do you start?"

"I don't."

"You turned Jane down?" Sarah felt a wave of relief.

"Yeah. There will come a time for me to be an executive chef, but I have a lot more I can learn from Marcus and Emily. That's why I explained I appreciated the offer but wouldn't accept it."

"How did she take it?"

"She told me to think about it some more, but I told her that wasn't necessary. She had my answer."

If Grace wasn't leaving, Sarah didn't understand what could be bothering her. "So why are you so upset?"

"Because, for a minute, I thought about taking the job. Also, it reminded me how I once wished Riley would fall off the face of the earth, but I didn't really mean it."

"What?"

"Thanks to Riley, when we were being interviewed by different restaurants in the placement office at school, Jane, and at least one other restaurant with whom I thought I had an excellent shot, canceled my follow-up interviews because they didn't think I was a good match for their customer base. At that point, I could have killed Riley, but then Emily interviewed me. She and Marcus didn't care. They hired me because they knew I could do the job. How can I be so disloyal to them now?"

Sarah shook her head in disbelief. Knowing Grace hadn't accepted, she could afford to be magnanimous. "You aren't disloyal. You're only human. Anyone would have contemplated a job offer like the one Jane made you."

Before Grace could say anything, she and Sarah heard Marcus and Emily yell a greeting from the front of the restaurant.

Grace wiped her eyes. "Please. Can we keep this between us for now? Emily's been so good to me."

Sarah hated the idea of keeping something from her twin, but, at the same time, she respected Grace's right to privacy. She hoped Grace would tell Emily and Marcus about the offer eventually. It was easier to work together without secrets.

"Of course." Sarah gave Grace a hug. "I may be Emily's twin sister, but I'm here to listen if you need a sounding board, though I can't promise you not to be somewhat biased. In exchange, you'll keep your promise to me if the funk doesn't lift?"

"On my honor." Grace raised three fingers while making her thumb touch her pinkie, in the way Emily and she had done when they were Girl Scouts.

Thinking of how Cliff tricked her with his Boy Scout line flashed through her mind while her mouth was saying different words. "You were a Girl Scout?"

"A Brownie for a year or two, but then we moved out of the project where they had the after-school troop."

"I gather your troop never got into martial arts, then?"

Grace crinkled her brows, narrowing her eyes. "Martial arts? That's not something I normally associate with Scouting."

"Neither do I. I'm just being silly, but have you had any martial arts training?" Sarah hoped it wasn't obvious she was holding her breath, waiting for Grace's answer. Could her friend have wanted Riley's job enough to kill her and then turned it down because she was overwhelmed with guilt? Or was she devious enough to make Jane sweeten the pot to a point where Emily and Marcus would encourage her to take the job?

"When we lived in the project, I took a year of after-school karate, and I've taken and now help Mandy with the weekend self-defense classes she teaches."

A lump rose in Sarah's throat. Much as she liked Grace, she had as strong, if not stronger, motive for killing Riley than Jacob, plus she'd had some defensive arts training. Although she wouldn't reveal everything Grace had told her in confidence, she'd have to tell Harlan part of what she'd learned today if Jacob was arrested.

CHAPTER NINETEEN

Sarah waved at her sister and Marcus when they came into the kitchen.

Marcus waved back, but Emily came over and gave her twin a peck. "What are you doing here now? What are you doing up so early?"

"Fluffy didn't think I needed to sleep in today. Marcus, you, and I have to talk."

"Is something wrong?"

When Sarah nodded, Emily called Marcus over to listen to what Sarah had to say.

"What is it? Don't tell me you're already raising our rent," he said. "We're not doing the kind of business that we can justify an increase."

Sarah picked up the sign and handed it to him.

Marcus glanced at the sign and turned it over. There not being anything on the other side, he flipped it back to where the wording was. "What is this?"

"Our sign outside was vandalized. The person tore off the letters saying we're open and taped this on the sign instead. I hadn't looked at that sign since we put it up. When was the last time either of you checked it?"

In watching them, Sarah was reminded that she'd heard pets and their masters often began to look alike, but seeing how Marcus and Emily simultaneously went from smiling to frowning, she wondered if the same could be said for most long-term couples. Even though their body sizes were dissimilar, there was no question they had taken on some of each other's mannerisms.

With a nod to Emily, Marcus answered, "Neither of us has looked at it since we put it up the night before our soft opening."

"Well, this might explain some of the lack of business. People don't think we're open yet."

Marcus's face reddened. "I bet it was Jane!" He stomped toward the door, but Emily's shout stopped him.

"Wait, Marcus. You don't know that. It could have been kids pulling a prank on us."

"Emily, I doubt that," Sarah said. "Jane might not be the one behind this vandalism, but it was intentional."

"Maybe we should have had a few more soft openings and publicized a big deal grand opening event," Emily suggested.

Marcus came back to the table and sat in the chair Sarah had recently vacated. He ran his hand through his hair. "I think it's more than this sign. That may explain why we're not drawing crowds like Jane, but between our soft opening and actual business nights, we haven't drawn enough people, period. I've been racking my brain trying to think what's wrong. Perhaps our price point is off? Maybe I should have kept everything low, like loss leaders, and raised the prices after we were established. I didn't expect us to be profitable immediately, but we can't bleed like this forever."

Grace stepped forward. "It may have something to do with Jane." Perhaps sensing how Sarah's words fueled Marcus's immediate desire for revenge, Grace hastened to continue. "You know, after work, the servers from Jane's Place and I meet up for a bite or a drink."

"You cross-pollinate?" Sarah wasn't sure why the workers from one restaurant would hang with staff from another.

"Not quite. A lot of us worked together on other jobs or went to school together. We're all too keyed up to go to bed, so we go hang somewhere for a while. From the little bit I've heard from some of Jane's staff, they say customers consistently all think your food is great, but they still can't get enough of Riley's dishes. Remember, Jane kept them on her menu and somehow, people say, while her other food is pretty run-of-the-mill, she seems to have picked up Riley's magic touch for the vegan dishes. To beat Jane, you're going to have to have your own gimmick."

Marcus crossed his arms over his bulging chest. "I told you before. We serve good food, not tricks and gimmicks."

"But, Grace, from what you're saying, we need a hook?" Emily said.

Grace nodded, seemingly grateful Emily had run with the ball.

Marcus scrunched his face up in a way that made Sarah wonder if that was the same expression he had as a child when he dug his heels in over not wanting to go to bed or to eat something healthy. "Having a gimmick may work for some people, but our gimmick is serving quality food. I can't see myself putting a vegan section on our menu."

"That's not what I'm suggesting, Marcus." Grace glanced from Marcus to Emily. "I know Emily and you haven't been thrilled with our dining crowds, and you did tell me to think about it, so I've been giving this a lot of thought. The last thing you want to do is copy Jane, but you both use a farm-to-table concept. I think it's safe to say the idea of you making food without eggs and dairy products isn't going to happen. They're too integral to many of your recipes. As I've thought about it, I personally think you need to stick with what you do well, rather than trying to be something to everyone."

Sarah raised a finger as she picked up the thread of the conversation. "I talked to Eloise the other day. She mentioned she may want to please every constituent, but the reality is she can't, so she has to decide what is good for the majority and go that route. Of course, as she explained, that means she's not going to get everyone's vote next time. Her not getting every vote is comparable to you or Jane never going to get every customer coming back. The key is to get the majority."

"I'll buy that," Marcus said. "But she only needs the voters to come out every few years. If we're going to survive, we need diners to want to eat our food a few times a month."

"Marcus, maybe we should consider highlighting special recipes perhaps through specialty weeks or a specialty day of the week?" Emily's train of thought was interrupted by Grace raising her hand schoolgirl style.

Seeing Grace's raised hand, Sarah formally called on her. "Did you want to add something, Grace? By the way, this is a discussion. You don't have to raise your hand."

Grace giggled like a pigtailed schoolgirl. "Force of habit. I haven't been out of school long enough yet. I do have an idea, though."

"Sure, what is it?" Marcus leaned forward.

"You all know, from what happened a few months ago, I'm diabetic. When I eat out, I'm usually careful what I order, but it means going through the entire menu, figuring out what will work for me. A friend of mine is lactose intolerant. You'd be surprised how many restaurants think that means she simply can't have a glass of milk. They don't understand she can't have any sauce made with milk or dairy or any cheese put on her salads."

"But we already accommodate those challenges and, I hope, do a good job of training our staff to ask the chef about what's in our food if any allergy or other medical problem they don't already know about is raised."

"Marcus, you and Emily do a better job of training everyone who works for you than a lot of other restaurants, but what if instead of trying to be like Jane's Place, you offered a few specialty items each night that fit the dietary needs of different medical conditions? You print your menus daily, so you could put a box on your template that could easily be edited depending on what you're serving that evening. If you opt not to print your menus daily, you could have two or three standard dishes in the box that you rotate whenever you change the menu."

Emily rubbed her chin. "That wouldn't be hard to do. Marcus, we could do something like offering a salad entrée with chicken on top but guarantee up front it doesn't have cheese in it."

Sarah remembered the argument Jane and she had had during the grand opening for Jane's Place over Emily's gluten-free squash soup. "You already offer a gluten-free menu, but you could always feature a gluten-free item. Your squash soup would be perfect." She looked to Grace for further encouragement.

"You could still have the gluten-free menu that a customer can order off of, because so many people who eat gluten-free are used to asking for that kind of menu, but on the main menu in the box would be tonight's treat for those of us who have to be a little more careful."

Marcus let out a low whistle. He rubbed his hands together. "Grace, I love your idea. We can bill ourselves as the restaurant that cares. If someone says they want vegan, gluten-free, diabetic, or any other kind of dish, our waiters can be trained to point them to those menu items, but for the person who doesn't ask, the box would visually reinforce we care about the health of all customers. Moreover, we believe everyone deserves an evening that's a treat."

When Emily held her hands up to approximate the size of a menu, Sarah knew her twin's practical business side was kicking in. "Making sure our wait-staff is well trained will be important, but we also need to be careful to keep the box sized properly for the menu to look balanced. We can't put too many treats in the box. With descriptive language about the dish, I'd keep the number limited to three, maybe four."

"Three. That's what we'll do. Three is a good number. And those three will be three treats too many for Jane's Place." Marcus guffawed at his own joke.

"I think this could be a winning idea," Emily said. "Let's try it next week. Maybe the delay Botts caused us will be to our benefit by giving us an opportunity to size up Jane's strengths and weaknesses."

Marcus's joyous mood abruptly departed at Emily's words. As he often did when something irked him, he punched one of his beefy hands into the other. "That's a person who I would pay to have continue eating at Jane's Place. For the sake of his continued good health, Botts would be smart to stay far away from Southwind."

CHAPTER TWENTY

Surprised that Marcus was still so angry with Botts, but satisfied Emily and he had a plan of action beyond fixing the sign to build interest and attendance at Southwind, Sarah left them discussing possible treats with Grace while prepping for tonight's service. On the way back to the carriage house, she fretted about whether Grace had fully confided in her or if Emily and Marcus had interrupted her sharing something else. Feeling somewhat uneasy, Sarah made a mental note to add finding a time to visit with Grace in the next day or two to the list of people, like Jacob, she wanted to visit with before Monday.

Even with spending time at Southwind, Sarah realized Fluffy's early wake-up call had begun her day at a point that, for once, she wouldn't be running late for her weekly dog walking stint with Harlan at the animal shelter. She was only sorry that, other than feeding RahRah, she hadn't been able to get any quality playtime in with him this morning. No matter what, she'd make it up to him when she got home this afternoon.

When Sarah arrived at the animal shelter, the sound of Harlan's distinctive chuckle told her he'd once again beaten her there. Sarah followed the sound toward the break room, where a woman, whom Sarah didn't know, stood in the doorway, her back to the hall, laughing. Whatever the woman found funny apparently also had amused the break room table's occupants: Harlan, Phyllis, the shelter's new director, and the veterinarians, Drs. Vera and Glenn.

The woman Sarah didn't know turned to leave and almost bumped into her. Acknowledging Sarah's presence with a nod, she slipped by and went down the hall, while Sarah joined the group, who seemed to have been overcome by another round of laughter.

"Now that's a sight. What's so funny?"

Phyllis pointed at Dr. Glenn. "He was describing how, during one of his animal rescue missions, a dog and a cat were rescued from the same house. When they were put in separate cages for their flight to a no-kill shelter, both started going crazy the minute people tried loading them on the plane, so Glenn stopped everything and made nice to both animals. Unfortunately, when he stopped, they freaked out again. Because all the seats, except the pilot's and one for a passenger, were removed for the rescue flight, Glenn had them stack some of the smaller animal carriers on the passenger seat. He contorted his six-foot-two body into the available floor space between the two cages for the flight. It doesn't sound as funny when I tell it as when he acted it out, but you get the idea."

"I do." Sarah turned her attention to the tall veterinarian. Although she knew he owned the building where the clinic was, she'd seen him only in the hallways, as her animals usually saw his associates, Drs. Tonya and Vera. "Dr. Glenn, I didn't know you were involved with rescue missions."

"Yes, ever since Hurricane Katrina, I've tried to help whenever there's a hurricane or natural disaster. Unfortunately, there have been way too many of them."

"Glenn's being modest again. He doesn't volunteer only during disasters," Phyllis said. "He was active with protecting our working animals when he was in Afghanistan, and now his staff helps raise funds and solicit volunteer flights to bring domestic animals from kill to no-kill shelters. They're working out the details for us to be formally recognized as one of those shelters and for them to be fully associated with a national group. Harlan just agreed to handle the legal details for our shelter and the clinic pro bono."

Glancing at Harlan, she saw the flush rising on his neck and knew his little bald spot was also probably blushing with embarrassment. Because of how much work Harlan had done pro bono for her, Emily, and their mother, she knew the animals were in the hands of a dedicated lawyer who would do an excellent job for them. "You couldn't get anyone better to help you, even if you paid them."

At that, everyone laughed again. Sarah didn't laugh as robustly as the others. She was still puzzling over a few things Glenn had said. If he started helping during Hurricane Katrina in 2005, attended vet school, and did a tour of duty in Afghanistan, which could have been any time after 2001, she was confused about his age. The other doctors referred to him as being the senior partner and the old man, but she didn't think he could possibly be much older than thirty-five.

"Is this national organization the same one you worked with during Hurricane Katrina?"

He looked up and met her gaze. She couldn't help but notice his eyes had the clarity of two deep, multifaceted emeralds. Never having seen eyes of such a pretty shade of green, especially on a man, she wondered if he wore contact lenses. Apparently, from the way the skin around his eyes crinkled with laugh lines, there were lots of things that tickled his funny bone.

"I wasn't even aware of the issues involved with animals when Katrina hit. Until the storm rolled in, I was a freshman at Tulane, majoring in partying. My grandparents lived in New Orleans. When word came to evacuate, I piled them and as much of their stuff, including their pets, into my car and drove them to Birmingham. We were able to save their pets, but we saw others stranded on the street we couldn't help. My grandmother was in tears. Through a family friend in Birmingham, she volunteered, basically doing paperwork and phone calls, matching agencies and pets other people went back to New Orleans and rescued. Rather than letting me sit at home distressed at being displaced, she dragged me along with her. As I helped, I found my calling."

"Your grandmother sounds like a special lady."

"She was. Our clinic is in the house she left me while I was in the army." He clicked his fingers. "You own the property across the way. Did you know her?"

"I only know of her. My ex-husband and his mother bought our property shortly before your grandmother moved into Sunshine Village."

His green eyes widened. Glenn seemed surprised Sarah knew his grandmother had moved to the retirement center.

"The only reason I'm aware of where and when she moved is Bill, my ex-husband, wanted a house on Main Street. When he heard through the grapevine she was moving, he checked into whether hers was going on the market. He didn't pursue it, because ours, which already had the carriage house for mother-in-law quarters, went up for sale a few days later."

"Small world. Anyway, that's the story of how I went from being a party animal to becoming a veterinarian who believes in rescue missions, as well as your neighbor."

"It's a fascinating story." More important, it made him younger than her first calculation would have. In fact, they were probably very close in age. Why she cared about his age, Sarah didn't know. She glanced at Harlan. He was staring at her. "I'd love to help, too, if I can. Pro bono, of course."

"Great." Glenn made a note on his cell phone. "Vera, Phyllis, or I will let you know when we schedule our organizational meeting. Looking at the time, Vera and I better get on with what we came to do."

While she nodded at Glenn, Harlan stood and offered his hand to him. "I'll be in touch." Harlan shot her the look, where his eyebrows bunched and his piercing stare seemed like it could bore through a person. "In the meantime, two of us have some dogs to walk."

Irritated and uncertain why he'd shot her the Harlan look, she opted to ignore it as they retrieved their respectively assigned dogs. She hoped his mood would lighten up or it was going to be a long few hours.

"Hey, Buddy," Sarah said to the beautiful black Lab who limped toward her on his three good legs. She bent and rubbed him behind his ears. Sarah let the rheumy-eyed dog smell and nuzzle her before she leashed him. "You're such a sweetie. I was hoping you'd find a home this week. You know I'd take you home if I could, but I'm at full capacity."

She really wished she could take him home, but the carriage house wasn't big enough for a third pet, especially a dog of Buddy's size, with a bad leg and poor vision. Sarah knew Phyllis and several of the volunteers, who had come up with his name when he was found wandering, paid special attention to him. How could they not? He was so gentle and affectionate. Still, Buddy was the longest unadopted pet at the shelter, but at least with its unofficial no-kill policy, he still had a chance to find a forever home.

Spotting Harlan already on the fenced-in walking path, she lowered her head so only Buddy could hear her. "Do you want to catch up to Uncle Harlan and Lady Lassie, or should we let the sourpuss walk alone?" She took Buddy's immediate pull on his leash to be an affirmative answer, though she bet Buddy's interest was in Lady Lassie rather than Uncle Harlan.

"Harlan, wait up! Buddy wants to walk with you." Even as the words came out of her mouth and Harlan stopped to let them catch up, she hoped she wouldn't be struck by lightning for lying.

"Hi there, Buddy." Harlan bent to the dog's level and greeted him by rubbing his head. He held Lady Lassie so Sarah could do the same to her. "Guess we can't keep these two apart."

"No. It's funny, you'd think they were courting."

"Well, we'll give them a good time together today." Harlan circled behind Sarah, untangling the leashes that had crisscrossed in the dogs' happiness to see each other and the humans' efforts to greet them. Situated back on the official Astroturf path, Harlan and Sarah fell into lockstep.

"Harlan, have you talked to Chief Gerard lately?"

"Yes. We had a meeting yesterday." Harlan kept walking, facing the trail ahead of him.

Sarah was surprised by how curt his response was. "Were you able to tell if he's been looking at some of the other possible suspects on Jacob's list?"

"Anyone in particular?"

"Well, yes. Louis Botts. When we talked the other day, Botts told me Riley and he really weren't dating, but from what everyone says, I find that hard to believe. Because the perpetrator in books and on *Perry Mason* often is the boyfriend and Botts acted so harshly the night Riley died, he's at the top of my suspect list. If Chief Gerard hasn't considered him, I'll . . ."

"Darn it, Sarah. How many times do I have to tell

you to leave it to the professionals? Chief Gerard talked to Botts and a lot of the other names, but he thinks it's more likely the murderer is the spurned boyfriend."

Sarah started to disagree, but her attention was diverted when Buddy pulled her to the side of the trail. Instead of trotting ahead, Lady Lassie sat, her eyes focused in Buddy's direction.

Harlan made no effort to disturb Lady Lassie. "You know, people talk about animals not being as smart as humans, but there are times, like this, I don't agree with that. These two seem to have a relationship as strong as any human bond."

"I know what you mean. RahRah and Fluffy are like that. Even though RahRah is a cat and Fluffy a dog, they seem to have made a connection, too. I originally thought I had to keep them apart, but now, except for bedtime, they're each other's best friend. It's so cute. They often nap resting on each other."

"That's nice. Unusual, considering how often cats are agitated by the smell of dogs." Harlan gently tugged Lady Lassie's leash.

When she still refused to budge, he impatiently pulled a little harder. She remained immobile until Buddy and Sarah rejoined them.

"Harlan, what's wrong?" She couldn't think of anything she'd done at the office that would have irked him. Today, he might have been upset by her flirtatious exchange with Glenn, but she doubted it.

"Nothing." He kicked a stone off the path.

"Harlan Endicott, this is our walking time for the

dogs. It isn't good for Buddy or Lady Lassie to feel we're irritated with each other or them. If I did something that bothered you, let's talk about it."

"For the sake of the dogs?"

"That's right." Seeing the slightest hint of Harlan cracking a smile, she pressed on. "We certainly don't want to say or do anything that will upset Buddy or Lady Lassie, do we?"

"Never, Dr. Dog Whisperer."

"Hush. If RahRah even senses you calling me a dog whisperer, he'll get his nose way out of joint."

"And we wouldn't want that either, would we?"

"Absolutely not."

This time, Harlan laughed so loud Lady Lassie jerked her head back in the direction from which the sound exploded. He reached down and patted her head. "It's okay, Lady."

Harlan kept his attention on Lady Lassie but changed the focus of his conversation to Sarah. "I'm not mad at you. I'm frustrated with Jacob. How well do you know him?"

"We're good friends. I met him when I helped Emily out at the Food Expo. You know Jacob worked for Marcus in California until he came home to work for his father's real estate company. By the time I met him, he was back working with Marcus and trying to develop the entertainment district. Why?"

Harlan started to answer, but Lady Lassie caught sight of a bird perched on the fence that marked the end of the dog-walking trail. She excitedly yanked Harlan toward the bird.

By the time Lady Lassie reached the fence, the bird flew off.

As the four turned back toward the shelter, Sarah said, "Harlan, you haven't told me why you're frustrated with Jacob."

"Because he lied to me."

CHAPTER TWENTY-ONE

Sarah's mouth opened, but no words came out. A sudden coldness went right through her that wasn't from the dropping of the temperature since they'd started walking the trail. Finally, her voice returned, but barely above a whisper. "What?"

Harlan petted Lady Lassie. "In talking with Chief Gerard, I discovered the incident at the apartment building wasn't the only one involving Jacob and Riley. It seems that one of the reasons she approached him for Wildcat rides was they knew each other from an earlier period of dating."

"That's the first I've heard about that."

"It was for me, too."

Sarah was surprised Harlan seemed more saddened than angry. He hated being surprised because of untruthful clients. "And I know Chief Gerard is the last person you want feeding you information about your client."

"You're right about that."

"What did he tell you?"

"Enough to understand why Jacob is Chief Gerard's main suspect. Apparently, when Riley and Jacob were both taking a culinary course at Carleton, shortly after Jacob started working for Marcus, they went out for a few weeks. Like this time, Riley broke it off and started dating someone else. Jacob confronted Riley and the new guy, and Jacob took a swing at him. There was a campus incident report filed, but it was the end of the semester and Jacob wasn't coming back, so everyone agreed it was a silly misunderstanding that wouldn't be pursued."

"You make it sound like Jacob has a pattern of having a short fuse."

"A pattern when it comes to Riley. That pattern is exactly what Chief Gerard thinks he can use to tighten the noose around Jacob's neck."

Without thinking, Sarah slowed her steps. Buddy, a little unevenly, matched her unexpected change in their pace.

"Sorry, guy." Frowning, Sarah evened out her stride while reflecting on Harlan's revelation.

She knew, from experience, it didn't take much for Chief Gerard to create a hypothesis, especially if he had any evidence that seemed to support it. If he felt Jacob wasn't forthright or he could establish a pattern for violence, his investigation would become focused only on Jacob.

"Did you ask Jacob about the incident?"

This time it was Harlan who stopped walking. He rubbed the back of his neck with the hand that wasn't holding the leash. "I did. He told me it slipped his mind."

"How?"

"That's exactly what I want to know."

Now Sarah understood why Harlan seemed both angry and like he was burdened by the weight of the world. She could only imagine the agony her boss was going through. The lawyer who left no leaf unturned for clients was questioning Jacob's innocence and trying to balance his obligation to provide topnotch representation against his moral feelings related to Riley's untimely death.

Chapter Twenty-Two

After giving Buddy a final hug, Sarah closed the door to his indoor run. Much as she enjoyed her Saturdays at the shelter, the end of each hour of her shift, when she'd put the dog she'd walked back into its designated cage, was always depressing because she knew the dogs didn't have the ability to leave like she did.

"Goodbye, sweetheart. Maybe they'll find you a forever home next week."

Sarah spent the next three hours walking three other dogs. Finished, she stopped for an extra moment to say goodbye to Buddy again before going to the locker room to retrieve her purse and jacket. No one else was there. She noticed the door of the locker Harlan usually used was ajar. Flipping it open with her hand, she saw it was empty. Had Harlan gone home or back to the office? Knowing how agitated he was, she was sure he was working on ways to help Jacob but was struggling internally with balancing the implications if Jacob was guilty.

As Sarah left the shelter, she was surprised at how much the wind had picked up in the half hour since she'd been outside walking the last dog of her shift. She stuck her ungloved hands deep into her jacket pockets. It was a good thing it hadn't been this brisk earlier. Thinking of Harlan probably back at work, she tried sorting out the images of the Riley she'd seen at Jane's Place.

It was hard contrasting the confidence and vibrancy Riley exhibited while explaining her dishes with her later subservient interaction with Botts. She hadn't seemed to be putting on an act—or was she? And which was real?

Although Sarah tried holding the image from earlier in the evening in her mind's eye, it was her final view of Riley that kept coming back—ashen faced, eyes open, neck angled, and blood-tinged hair splayed around her. Sarah didn't think even having worn her warmer jacket and gloves could take away the chill she felt at this moment.

Distracted by her thoughts, Sarah didn't see there was another woman on the walkway until it was too late to avoid bumping into her. Without focusing on the woman's face, she blurted out an apology.

"It's okay, Sarah."

Hearing her name, Sarah peered at the red-cheeked face surrounded almost into oblivion by a fur-lined hood. Anne. Sarah muttered an apology again and stepped aside to let her pass, but Anne didn't move. In fact, from the hue of her cheeks, Sarah wondered how long Anne had been standing on the walkway.

"Sarah." Anne stopped, almost as if searching for her next words.

Sarah was surprised. Hitting a bull's-eye with her tongue was one of Anne's more finely tuned abilities as a politician. But now, her usual sharpness was missing.

Sensing the other woman's intense discomfort, Sarah debated saying something to ease the moment, but she held back. Anne was one of the few people Sarah often misread. Too many times in the past, when Sarah thought they could work together, Anne had taken advantage of her or twisted the situation to Anne's benefit. Sarah didn't want to give Anne a chance to mock her for mistaking tension when it was something else.

Anne cleared her throat. "Sarah, may I talk to you for a few minutes?"

Afraid talking would result in something to her detriment, Sarah hesitated. She was unable to figure out a way to avoid Anne without lying or appearing rude. "Certainly, but it's cold out here. Would you like to go into the shelter or grab a cup of coffee?" She pointed toward a nearby stand-alone coffee shop.

"I opt for the coffee and I'll buy." Regaining her stride, Anne led the way toward the coffee shop.

Feeling their relationship already returning to its norm, Sarah followed. When both were settled, coats draped over their metal-backed seats, Sarah sipped her favorite white chocolate mocha. Seeing that Anne, even on Saturday, wore a suit, she wondered if Anne ever relaxed. From the way Anne held her black tea in midair, her hands curled tightly around the hot cup, it was obvious she was wound up today.

Anne wasted no time explaining why she was waiting for Sarah. "I'm worried about Jacob."

Before Sarah could get the words out that she
agreed with Anne, Anne declared that she knew
Sarah was worried, too. "I know from the discussion
you had with Eloise that, like us, you've tried figuring
out who, other than Jacob, could have committed
this horrible crime."

Sarah nodded.

"Well, on my end, I'm running into walls and I
need your help."

"I'm not quite sure what I can do for you. Have
you talked to Harlan?"

"Yes, but he keeps telling me to be patient."

"Well, that's not a bad idea. Harlan is on top of
Jacob's case, and he's one of the finest lawyers I
know."

Anne slapped her cup on the table. "He's probably one of the only ones you know."

Sarah leaned back and took a sip of her drink.
Anne's last crack was more typical of what Sarah expected from her. Resting her mouth on the rim of
her cup's cover, Sarah waited, watching Anne fidget
with the long red and blue scarf she wore. Sarah
couldn't help but notice the blue was the exact same
shade of Anne's suit and eyes.

Anne pursed her lips, then opened them enough
to let a sigh escape. "I shouldn't have said that."

"No, you shouldn't have." Sarah couldn't believe
her own retort.

Six months ago, when Anne took over a meeting
at her house or made a negative comment while

Sarah was moonlighting for Emily as an extra server, she forced herself to let whatever Anne said roll off her back, despite it almost always getting under her skin. Pretending to take a longer sip, Sarah hoped her raised cup blocked the smile she couldn't control.

Answering Anne back felt good until Sarah realized her retort hadn't made much of a dent.

"Sarah, I'm a direct person. Whether it's business or personal, I don't beat around the bush."

Sarah took her cup away from her mouth. "And how has that worked for you?"

"Not always that well." Anne laughed, her hat hair flowing backward.

Sarah joined in with her.

"At least I'm honest. I may be a bull in a china shop, but I know it."

They both laughed harder, having finally found something they agreed on.

Anne leaned forward, into Sarah's space, and would have gotten closer but for the table dividing them. "Sarah, I'm desperate. I've tried to prod Harlan to be more aggressive with the chief."

"I can tell you that's not going to work. Harlan is methodical. No one is going to change that."

"So I've found." Anne glanced around the room.

Although the tables were almost on top of each other, no one was sitting at either of the ones next to them.

Anne lowered her head and her voice. "Harlan instructed me not to dare use my office to communicate on this matter with Chief Gerard, but with how some of the reports came back yesterday—"

Sarah cut her off. "How do you know reports came back?"

Anne fidgeted with her coffee holder. "Someone mentioned to me they were back, but Harlan doesn't want to see them now. He said, 'All in good time.'"

"I'd listen to him, Anne. Don't even think about interfering with the police investigation. Believe me, it will only make things worse for Jacob. You hired Harlan. You've got to trust him."

"I'm trying, but something has to be done before Chief Gerard arrests Jacob. That's why I wanted to talk to you. I can't sit back and do nothing. I'm aware that you, not Chief Gerard, resolved the last incidents we had in Wheaton. You've got a real knack for investigating and finding out the truth, no matter how close to home it hits. Like Eloise told you, I need you to help me clear Jacob's name."

"You flatter me, but I didn't figure out those whodunits completely on my own." That wasn't quite true, but Sarah's mother had always taught her not to hog the credit. "If you'd been involved like I was, you could have done it just as easily."

"Don't be so modest. I know the truth."

Not disagreeing, Sarah still demurred. "Believe me, Harlan will view anything I do as interference. The only thing I'd accomplish would be making you number one in his doghouse and getting myself fired."

Anne tightly crossed her arms and pouted. Perhaps it was a surprise to Anne that she wasn't getting her way. "I wouldn't let him fire you."

"You couldn't stop it. Harlan is independent."

Anne scowled. "I didn't mean I'd try to unduly influence him. I simply meant I'd intervene and make sure he understood your efforts were because of me. Believe me, Harlan knows I always take full responsibility for things I'm involved in."

"Like your stance on allowing commercial development on Main Street?"

Crinkling her face in puzzlement, Anne was firm in her answer. "I'm not in favor of it and I've said so repeatedly. It's a main plank of my campaign."

"Why?"

"Why?" Anne raised an eyebrow.

"Yes, what do you have against revitalizing downtown and making Wheaton more of a destination foodie place?"

Anne no longer bent forward. She sat erect and her eyes were blazing. "Nothing, if we do it right and preserve the history and character of Wheaton. That wasn't the goal of your ex-husband or his partners. Their plans were tied solely to the dollar. They didn't care about health, safety, or aesthetic concerns. They didn't want to jump through the hoops necessary for proposing orderly code modifications."

"But they wanted to rezone for an entertainment district."

"Sure, they had a grand vision to make Main Street an entertainment district, after the strip center was developed. You know Jacob was instrumental in attracting Marcus to be part of the center?"

"Yes, with the promise that he'd start Southwind there and later move it into a house in the entertainment district."

"My father didn't know about that promise. His development plan was only tied to the strip center.

When he decided to run for the state senate, he came out against creating an entertainment district."

"Why?"

"Maybe he felt it separated him from the unfeeling real estate stories swirling about him or maybe it was because he has a soft spot for the Main Street of old, but my father also understands there have to be checks and balances when you develop properties. You have to look at whether you're zoning for residential, commercial, industrial or whatever. An entertainment district is a subset of that. Besides, Dad realized the development group had forgotten one main thing."

"What was that?"

"You can't develop property you don't own. They had designs for all the lots, but they owned very few of them. Instead, they planned to use other means, not always aboveboard, to get the lots they needed. That's not my style, nor is it my father's. At least in his lifetime, Dad wants to preserve the Main Street he grew up dreaming to own a house on."

"He certainly accomplished that." The Hightower house was the finest home on Main Street. Set on an angle so it's circular driveway could be reached from two streets, it was a beautifully crafted stone fortress three blocks from Sarah's house, where Main Street began.

Slumping against the metal back of her chair, the rigidity with which Anne held her body, as well as the lines of Anne's face, softened while talking about her father. "Dad knows things will change, but hopefully not without the safeguards I mentioned. He's always going to stay opposed to an entertainment district, but I'm willing to listen when Jacob and his friends come up with a comprehensive plan instead of shooting from the hip."

Having once seen the plans her ex and his cohorts proposed for the Main Street area, Sarah finally understood Anne and her father's negative positions. Although she still wanted to see things go forward with an entertainment district, Sarah remembered how upset she'd been to see her ex's plans included homes like Mr. Rogers's house, long before Mr. Rogers wanted to sell it. The inconsistency of how the first homes on Main Street were developed also had bothered her.

There was a perfect example of what happened without a zoning code in place a few blocks from Sarah, at the beginning of Main Street. Someone had haphazardly subdivided one of the larger elegant homes into apartments by merely slapping up a few walls and sticking a FOR RENT sign in the yard. That house had changed owners at least once, if not twice, in the last three years, and despite neighborhood complaints about its upkeep, there didn't seem to be a way to force the owners to maintain the house or its landscaping to the same level as the houses on Sarah's block.

Knowing she wouldn't be happy if that house was next to her property, it was now clearer to Sarah why Anne and other councilors were so insistent on detailed plans. She wasn't sure if some of the delays, like the ones Southwind encountered dealing with Botts, had the same pure motivation behind them.

"Anyway, we were talking about clearing my brother's name."

"Anne, it's been almost a week and Jacob hasn't

been arrested. I would think every day that passes without an arrest is a good sign."

"Normally, I'd agree with you, but, since his first debacle with your mother, Chief Gerard took some classes. He's only waiting for all the forensic reports because, even without fingerprints, he already thinks he has a sound circumstantial case against Jacob. He's not looking any further, and the evidence he has is getting stale. We've got to act."

"I'm sure Harlan is taking every step he believes is right for the moment. It's simply a matter of patience."

"How? Jacob is my brother. Were you patient when Emily was the prime suspect?"

This time Anne's remark found its target. "No."

"That's why we need to help Harlan. There's no way he can possibly talk to everyone one-on-one who might know something. Besides, Harlan's job is to cast doubt and protect Jacob. He's not really investigating this case. And we know Chief Gerard isn't doing what he should. Surely, if we can get everyone together for a giant brainstorming session, whether Harlan comes or not, we might learn something he can use to help Jacob."

Thoughts of how her mother and sister had almost fared against the local police crowded out Sarah's "Let Harlan handle it" stance. "Well, I guess a get-together couldn't hurt."

Anne put her hand over Sarah's. It was icy to the touch, as if she'd never held her hot tea cup. "Wonderful. I promise if we invite some people to your place tomorrow, we won't get in Harlan's way. Hopefully, what we find will help him."

Already kicking herself for being played into whatever underlying plan Anne had, Sarah slipped her hand from Anne's grasp and put it in her lap. "My place? Why not yours?"

"Because you're centrally located and everyone already knows where the carriage house is."

Sarah leaned back. "Who do you propose we invite to my house?"

Anne reached into her purse and pulled out two slips of paper. She glanced at them and laid one on the table in front of Sarah. "I divided the people I think we should invite into two lists for us to call. There aren't a lot."

From the way she held it, Sarah was able to see the list Anne retained for herself had a few more names on it than the list Anne handed her.

"We both better call our lists as soon as possible," Anne said, "because some of them are riding tomorrow morning. To catch them, let's set our meeting for noon and tell everyone we'll serve lunch."

"Lunch?"

"Definitely. From my years in politics, I've discovered people tend to come if they know there's going to be free food." Grabbing her purse and coat, Anne rose in a practiced motion. "Why don't you get Emily or Marcus to whip up something for a light lunch? You're lucky to have professional chefs who can help you." She was gone before Sarah could utter the word "no."

CHAPTER TWENTY-THREE

Hoodwinked. Bamboozled. Used. Gullible. Stupid. Sarah didn't know which word, if not all, she should apply to herself now that she finally could get words out of her mouth. She wasn't quite sure how she'd managed to go from agreeing to being part of a simple conversation to hosting a luncheon, for which she not only had to handle the food but had to invite almost half of the guests. The adage "Fool me once, shame on you; fool me twice, shame on me" ran through her mind.

Sarah calculated she was far beyond shame, considering how many times Anne had fooled or taken advantage of her. After the most recent time, when Anne assumed the spotlight for the YipYeow Day event Sarah was running to raise money for the animal shelter, Sarah had promised herself never to be manipulated by Anne again. At least, Sarah told herself, this might help Jacob.

Opening the house wasn't a big deal. There was

plenty of room for everyone in the carriage house's living room. If everyone came, she could always bring in a few extra chairs from the dining room. The problem was the food.

How could she have agreed, or let herself seem to agree, to put out a light lunch for all these people? To Sarah, the kitchen was a foreign country. If Riley hadn't been recently murdered, Sarah would be telling anyone who would listen that she thought cooking was a fate worse than death.

Unfortunately, Riley had been killed, so that kind of crack didn't seem funny today. It also wasn't funny that Sarah didn't have any of her go-to people available. With Emily and Marcus juggling their time between the Southwind Pub and Southwind, she simply couldn't ask them for help with less than a day's notice. Her favorite backup cooks were also out of pocket. Grace was up to her ears at Southwind, and Sarah doubted, even if he was up to cooking, that Anne wanted Jacob anywhere around this lunch meeting.

Perhaps she could get away with a deli tray, chips, and brownies from the grocery. Everyone could make their own sandwich, much like a make-your-own-sundae party. Then again, even on her list, there were people who didn't eat meat or cheese. A deli tray, like a pizza party, was a no-go.

Calling Anne back and giving her the option of no meal or helping pay for someone to cater lunch was probably the most logical thing Sarah could do, but she decided it was her last option. She wasn't going to crawl to Anne. She'd figure out a way to pull it together by herself. If she made it clear as each person came in that she'd prepared lunch, they'd know they weren't getting a gourmet meal. But, what to serve?

Maybe she could make a casserole or an all-in-one-pot meal. Or, come to think of it, she could go to her own freezer. She had two small vegetable lasagnas Emily had made and frozen for their mother for when she hosted her two mah jongg groups at the end of the month. Maybelle hadn't taken them home when she and Mr. Rogers visited on Wednesday. Because her mother didn't need them for a few weeks, Sarah was sure Emily could find the time to whip up two more lasagnas.

If Sarah took them out of the freezer the minute she got home, they would be perfect to serve tomorrow as her main dish. Surely, there were some other recipes in one of her favorite cookbooks that would work for the rest of the meal. A plan of action formed, Sarah rose and tossed her empty cup into the trash can before heading home. She could do this—would do this—for Jacob.

Besides, she might be a noncook, but she had quite a collection of cookbooks to work with. There had to be some recipes in them she could handle. Emily always laughed at her and asked her, "Why," when she regularly perused Sarah's ever-growing shelf of cookbooks. This was why. Sarah had these cookbooks for situations like this.

Once home, Sarah was greeted by RahRah and Fluffy. She gave Fluffy a hurried walk and then went into the kitchen and moved the lasagnas from the freezer to the refrigerator. Before selecting four cookbooks from her collection, Sarah took a moment to turn on some music.

She spread the books across her kitchen table. Staring at the slow cooker on the cover of the first one, she immediately knew she would make her sister's gluten-free squash soup. That would hit the spot for the riders who'd been out in the wind, give the gluten-challenged eaters something they could make a main course out of, and delight almost everyone else. It didn't hurt that it wasn't difficult to make.

She pushed the cookbook aside and opened a different one to try to get ideas for something else to serve. While she flipped through the recipes, RahRah plopped himself onto the tops of her feet. When Sarah tried to extricate a foot before it fell asleep, RahRah stirred only long enough to situate himself in a more firmly attached position. Amused, Sarah shifted her attention from the cookbooks to her cat.

"Are you comfortable? Did you miss me?"

An answering throaty purr warmed Sarah's heart. Her cat asked so little from her but gave her so much joy. There were lots of times, like today, when Sarah questioned what life would have been like if her late mother-in-law hadn't pulled RahRah from Katrina's swirling hurricane waters and if Bill hadn't come into her life. If Sarah forgot about the bad aspects of her marriage—and with the rat there had been plenty—there was much, like RahRah, the carriage house, and her dear mother-in-law, to be thankful for. Remembering the warmth of Mother Blair, Sarah couldn't imagine how such a caring person had ever raised a son like Bill.

Thinking of being thankful and of her ex brought Thanksgiving to mind, including the big salad Emily and their mother always prepared. It was an orange almond salad they'd left the almonds out of during the years she was married to Bill because of his extreme nut allergies. If she remembered correctly, the recipe and picture of that salad were in the third cookbook she'd put on the table. Excited, she accidentally dislodged RahRah from his comfortable perch.

He walked out from under the table, stopped, and sniffed.

Sarah didn't know if he wanted her to laugh, cry, or simply feel guilty for disturbing him. For the moment, though, she ignored him as she searched for the recipe. Finding it, she skimmed the ingredients and directions and was thrilled to see it would be a cinch, even for her. The prep time would be short because she'd substitute bagged, pretorn greens for the required heads of lettuce, canned mandarin oranges for orange sections, and precut bits and slices of almonds rather than cutting and dicing them herself. The salad, lasagnas, soup, and her grocery's brownies, cookies, and premade orange rolls would do the trick for tomorrow.

Satisfied that her menu necessitated only a quick trip to the store, she turned her attention back to RahRah, who still stood in the middle of the kitchen, giving her a look that made her feel guilty. "I'm sorry. I got excited. I think I've actually put together a meal to serve tomorrow."

RahRah sniffed again. He obviously wasn't impressed with her success. Maybe if Sarah changed her tactics, he'd be a little warmer.

"Would you like a treat?" She walked to the cupboard where she kept his and Fluffy's treats, noting from the corner of her eye that RahRah followed.

Apparently, she was back in his good graces. As Sarah placed a treat in his bowl, he purred and immediately went for it. Typical man. The way to his heart was through his stomach.

Then again, the same could be said of her female puppy. Usually at the word "treat," Fluffy came running. She'd skid to a stop just short of sliding into Sarah, wagging her tail nonstop until she was given her treat. Although she rustled the bag, Fluffy was nowhere to be seen. Looking around the kitchen, Sarah saw Fluffy hadn't finished the food she'd put in her bowl before Sarah had left to do her stint at the animal shelter. Maybe she was sleeping and hadn't heard the magic word?

Sarah repeated it more loudly this time. Except for a contented sound from RahRah, the house was silent. Too silent. "You've had your treat. I'm going to go make sure everything is okay with Fluffy."

Fluffy obviously wasn't in the kitchen. When she once again didn't respond when Sarah emphasized "treat," Sarah's level of concern rose. She quickly checked her bedroom, dining room, and living room, but there was no dog in any of them. In the front hall, near the door, Sarah found a small mess, but no puppy. Fluffy apparently had either wanted to go out before she got sick or avoided the carpeted areas of the house.

Because the hallway was pristine when Sarah came in through the front door, it was obvious Fluffy had gotten sick since Sarah saw her when she got home.

With butterflies in her own stomach, Sarah noticed the door to the half bath off the entryway was partially open. She pushed it the rest of the way. A pathetic-looking puppy lay curled on the cool tile floor.

"Fluffy!"

Fluffy whimpered.

Sarah picked her up. Fluffy clung to her like a baby, shivering.

"It's going to be okay. I promise."

Seeing the watch on her arm, Sarah realized the veterinarian clinic across the street was scheduled to close in less than ten minutes. Rather than taking the time to call them, Sarah, still juggling Fluffy, patted the phone in her back pocket, grabbed her keys from the bowl in the entryway, and, with a yell to RahRah in the kitchen, took off down the driveway, forgetting about tomorrow's lunch.

CHAPTER TWENTY-FOUR

Sarah wasn't sure how she got from the carriage house to the clinic. She knew there was a specific door for Cats and Dogs, but she didn't take the time to read the word above the first door she came to. Instead, she flung it open.

Inside, a woman wearing an animal clinic T-shirt with a big paw symbol on it was behind the reception counter. She looked up from what she was doing as Sarah barreled through the doorway.

"Help me, please. My dog is sick. I don't know what's wrong. I don't have an appointment and you're about to close, but, please, is there a veterinarian on duty who could see her. She's so pitiful. I didn't want to wait until Monday. Fluffy usually sees Dr. Tonya or Dr. Vera, but I'll be glad to let her see Dr. Glenn, too."

"You did the right thing," the woman assured her. "I'm not sure Dr. Tonya is still here. She was finishing up in the cat room and then leaving, but I know Dr. Glenn is. Tell me what's wrong with Fluffy." She bent across the counter toward Sarah and Fluffy with a concerned look.

"She threw up and she can't stop shivering."

Straightening up, the woman pointed toward where, on the dog side, wooden benches were built into wherever there was a wall. "If you'll sit over there and put one of the leashes from those hooks on Fluffy, I'll come back for you in a few minutes." Before she disappeared through a door off the reception area, the woman, who Sarah realized looked familiar, but she didn't think it was from here at the clinic, paused and smiled. "Don't worry. Dr. Glenn will take good care of both of you."

Sarah, still clutching Fluffy to her chest, did as she was told. Whispering to Fluffy that "Everything will be all right" and "I'm sorry I didn't hear you being sick over my music," Sarah leaned back against the wall, which served as the back of her bench. Looking more closely at the bench, she saw it was shellacked with a finish she bet was easy to clean and was deep enough for pet owners to easily sit and hold their pets on their laps or let them lie on the bench next to them.

Not putting Fluffy down, Sarah pulled one of the nearby throw pillows strategically interspersed on the benches to soften the harshness of the wood and pushed it behind her. Never having been on the dog side of the waiting room before, she glanced across the big room, beyond the reception desk, to the cat side, where she usually brought RahRah. It was half the size of the dog area. She wondered why she'd never noticed that before. Probably because she never looked beyond the gigantic horseshoe-shaped reception desk that divided the two sides and dominated the room. Sitting there, Sarah thought the desk was exactly like the reception desk used for checking humans in and out at Birmingham's University Hospital.

Fluffy shivered more.

Sarah shifted her arms to hold the puppy tighter. "It's going to be okay," she whispered.

As Fluffy laid her head on Sarah's shoulder, Sarah tried distracting herself by looking at the different heartworm and flea medications on display.

After what seemed like an eternity but really wasn't more than a few minutes, the same woman opened the rear dog-treatment door and motioned for Sarah and Fluffy to follow her. Introducing herself as Carole, which didn't help Sarah place her, she took them into a hall longer than the one Sarah usually went down when she brought RahRah in. Carole directed them into the first little room on the right. Except for a chair, exam table, and a small cabinet on which a few instruments lay on a paper mat, the room was bare of decoration.

"Why don't you put Fluffy on this table and tell me in detail what's wrong with her?" Sarah did what Carole told her but kept her hands on Fluffy while Carole, who Sarah now realized was a vet tech, listened to Sarah as she took Fluffy's temperature.

"Fluffy was fine when I walked her and left this morning. When I got home, I was busy and didn't realize she wasn't her active self or that she hadn't finished her breakfast."

The tech petted Fluffy while, Sarah realized, using

her hands to check the little dog. "Did you take her out when you got home?"

"Yes. I was thinking about something else, so I only took her for a quick walk. When we came back in, I went right to the kitchen. She didn't follow me, but I thought it was because she was getting one of her toys. Maybe she was lethargic and I didn't notice."

"What alerted you to know she didn't feel well?"

"She didn't come for a treat."

Carole peered at Sarah, her eyes narrowed into a quizzical look.

"No matter what Fluffy's doing, she always comes if I offer RahRah, my cat, and her treats. I had some music on and got involved in what I was doing, but about fifteen or twenty minutes after I got home, I called her to come get a treat because I was giving one to RahRah. When she didn't react, I went looking for her. Fluffy wasn't in any of her usual spots, but I found a small mess in the front hall that wasn't there when I came home. She was in the half bath off that hall, lying on the tile floor, shivering and whimpering."

"Probably trying to cool off. This little one has a slight temperature. We'll have Dr. Glenn look at her. I'll be back in a moment."

When Carole left, Sarah moved closer to the table. Perhaps instinctively, Fluffy and she leaned into each other for comfort. As Sarah whispered that everything would be all right because the doctor would make her feel better, the veterinarian came through the door, almost as if her reference to him was his entrance cue. Sarah took a step backward, closer to the one chair in the room, as Carole followed behind him. Moving to a spot out of his way, Carole positioned herself near the end of the table.

Dr. Glenn focused his attention exclusively on Fluffy. "Not feeling too well?" He bent over Fluffy, letting the puppy get to know him. Still talking softly, but nonstop, he examined Fluffy before he looked up to where owners, like Sarah, apparently waited. When his gaze met hers, Sarah saw recognition in it. "Sarah?"

"Hi, again." Realizing he might think Fluffy was a dog from the shelter, she quickly added, "This is Fluffy. She's mine. When she didn't come for her treat, I realized she hadn't eaten the food I left for her this morning. Looking for her, I discovered a pile of vomit in my hallway and then found Fluffy lying lethargically, except for shivering and whimpering, on the tile in my bathroom."

"Did you see anything in her throw-up? Anything she might have gotten into like dental floss, tissue, or something else from a trash can?"

"No."

"Well, we'll see if we can make her feel a little less pitiful. We're going to take her back to our main treatment room so we can do a few blood tests, get a stool sample, and check her over in more detail. If you'll wait here, I'll be back in a few minutes."

"Oh." She hadn't expected them to take Fluffy away from her. When she brought RahRah in, everything was done with Sarah present in the little cat exam room. Then again, she couldn't think of a time when RahRah visited a vet for anything but healthy maintenance visits.

Sarah stepped up to the table and placed her hand on Fluffy. As she petted her, she assured her everything would be okay. "Dr. Glenn and Carole will take good care of you, and I'll be right here waiting for you."

After Dr. Glenn and Carole left with Fluffy, Sarah sat in the chair. She hadn't really comprehended how stark the exam room was while Fluffy and the others were in it. Unlike the cat examination room that had equipment, including a mini pressure cuff in it, this dog room apparently was used only for simple exams and triage.

Worried and anxious for a distraction, she pulled her cell phone from her purse and tapped her local news app to see if there was anything new reported on the investigation into Riley's death. Not seeing anything, she wondered where the police were in their investigation and whether, as Anne believed, Jacob would be arrested.

Glancing at the clock on the wall, Sarah couldn't believe Fluffy and she already had been at the vet's office for almost an hour. Sarah wondered how much longer it would be before she knew what was wrong with her. Hopefully, because she didn't have pet insurance, whatever the problem was wasn't serious and wouldn't require a lot of expensive testing to diagnose.

Not that she begrudged doing whatever was necessary for Fluffy, but Sarah wasn't made of money. One of Harlan's clients, killing time waiting for him, had once told her how much an echo and another test for his dog had cost him. Although Sarah was no longer living paycheck to paycheck, she still carefully budgeted everything. If Fluffy needed tests like that other dog, it would make a big dent in the little bit of savings she hoped to use to go back to school. This time, she wanted to get the degree she hadn't thought was as important as marrying Bill. Still, whatever Fluffy needed, Fluffy would get.

Sarah might not have had Fluffy as long as Rah-Rah, but the dog was hers. Thinking of her two pets, Sarah promised herself that on Monday, the first thing on her to-do list would be looking into the cost of buying pet insurance. Having made that decision, she wondered if she was too late. What if something horrible was wrong with Fluffy? If she was found to have hypertension, a heart problem, or something more serious, would she be uninsurable because of a preexisting condition? Sarah's worries were interrupted by Dr. Glenn's return.

"Fluffy is going to be fine. It's nothing serious."

Sarah barely heard what the veterinarian said next. She was so relieved that Fluffy was going to be okay and it wasn't some terminal problem. "Excuse me, what did you say?"

Dr. Glenn smiled at Sarah as he repeated himself. "We got Fluffy's blood work back, and there's no bacterial infection. She's simply got a virus and is dehydrated. I'm giving her an IV now, but as late in the day as it is, I'd like to keep her overnight for observation in case she has any problem staying hydrated."

"But I thought, from something Dr. Tonya once said, animals needing observation are transferred to the emergency clinic on Spring Street when you close for the weekend."

"Normally, that's true, but I live upstairs, and I'm

keeping an eye on another dog tonight, so it isn't a big deal for me to check in on Fluffy, too. Besides, we're still boarding dogs that need to be allowed out in the run." Perhaps he sensed her fear. "Don't worry. I'm not going to charge you to board her—we're neighbors."

Remembering Cliff had told her he'd remodeled the upstairs of the animal clinic as a living area she almost didn't listen to the rest of what he was saying. "I'd just feel better about keeping Fluffy tonight. You can give me a call around seven tomorrow morning. If everything goes like I think it will, you can pick her up first thing in the morning. Fluids, a little food I'll give you, and plenty of rest, and she'll be the Fluffy of old in a day or two."

"That's wonderful." Sarah's moment of relief passed when she thought about RahRah at home. Could he be sick, too? What if he was and she didn't know it because she'd been here at the clinic with Fluffy? "This virus?"

"Don't worry, it's not one you're going to get. Fluffy probably has more to worry about catching a cold from you."

"I wasn't worrying about that. What about Rah-Rah, my cat? They're inseparable. Could he be sick, too?"

"Inseparable? That's unusual. Because they generally don't care for the smell of each other is one of the main reasons we use two different entrances and have a dedicated cat examination room. Unless we're swamped with cats, we keep all of their treatment and boarding areas separate from the dogs."

"RahRah and Fluffy started off skittish with each

other, but I guess they never figured out they weren't supposed to like each other. They are the best of buddies, though RahRah is the alpha male in their relationship. He could be home sick now. Do I need to bring him in?"

"No. I don't think this is a bug RahRah will catch. We've only been seeing it in dogs, but Fluffy isn't going to feel much like playing for a few days. If RahRah tries bossing her into playing, separate them. I want Fluffy to rest."

"I will."

"Good." He looked at his watch. "It will probably take another half hour for the IV to finish. I've got it going slow. We're officially closed, so most of the staff has left. I'm sure you want to see Fluffy, so rather than waiting here for the IV to finish, why don't you come in back with me, and I'll give you the grand tour before you say good night to her."

Relieved, Sarah almost gushed her appreciation that she could see Fluffy before she went back to the carriage house. "That would be great, Dr. Amos. I've never been beyond this kind of exam room on the cat side."

"Well, I think you'll be pleasantly surprised by our facility. By the way, as I told you earlier, around here and everywhere, for you, it's Glenn."

"Sarah."

He grinned. "Yes, I know. I think we had this discussion at the shelter."

Flustered, Sarah's face warmed. "Having Fluffy sick seems to have wiped everything else out of my mind. Plus, seeing you in your white coat examining her, 'Dr. Amos' seemed more appropriate."

"Well, how about I take my white coat off." He proceeded to remove his coat. "Does that make it easier for you to call me Glenn?"

Sarah laughed. "Yes, it does." She put her hand in her pocket and touched the list Anne had given her. In her panic over Fluffy, she'd completely forgotten about it. She pulled the paper from her pocket and glanced at it. Dr. Amos was on her list. She held the piece of paper up with the names facing her. "Glenn, this may seem like it's coming out of the blue, but Anne Hightower and I want to invite you to a lunch we're having tomorrow at my carriage house to brainstorm about things related to her brother, Jacob, and Riley. Anne hopes getting people together, comparing their memories, might trigger something we can use to help Jacob. You know Jacob, don't you?"

"I know him because he helped me get some tax credits when we renovated this place, plus we occasionally ride together when I find time to join in on one of the Wildcat excursions."

"Oh, you must have known Riley, may she rest in peace, too, through the Wildcats?"

"She rode with me a couple of times long ago, but I don't really like taking a passenger. When I let her know that, she steered clear of me. Almost as if I didn't and hadn't ever existed."

"With her working at Jane's Place and you sharing parking with Jane's Place, I'm surprised you didn't run into each other."

"I occasionally saw her dumpster dumping, but if I walked anywhere near her, she slammed the dumpster cover down and hightailed it away from me. I don't think I can add much, but I'll be glad to come tomorrow. Jacob's a good guy. I find it hard to believe he killed Riley. Without Cliff and him, I could never have gotten everything approved to change my grandmother's house into this clinic and make a home for Carole and me upstairs."

He opened the door he'd entered from for her. "Come on. I have a patient who will be very happy to see you."

CHAPTER TWENTY-FIVE

Looking around the hallway Glenn led her into, Sarah saw most of the doors they passed opened into doggy exam rooms. She never realized how much of the practice must be devoted to dogs or how big the clinic was. Through the one door that wasn't closed, Sarah could see a giant room, which she assumed was their destination when she spotted Carole sitting on the floor in front of a wall of cages, cuddling a more animated Fluffy. An IV tube connected to a digital monitor and a fluid bag was being used to hydrate Fluffy.

Instead of looking at Fluffy's leg and paw, where she was sure the IV needle was, Sarah concentrated her gaze on Carole's face, while Glenn went to check on the other dog the clinic was monitoring. Now Sarah recognized where she had seen Carole before. Carole was the woman who held the break room door for her at the shelter this morning. The vet tech must have been part of the meeting with the vets,

Harlan, and Phyllis that was wrapping up when Sarah arrived.

Fluffy looked very comfortable in Carole's lap. "She was feeling a little skittish, so I thought, because we're officially closed for the day, I'd hold her until the drip finished."

"Thank you." Sarah instinctively said, her mind wandering to what kind of couple Carole and Glenn made. Although Carole was at least six to eight inches shorter than Glenn, they were both fair-haired, tanned, and athletically built. Sarah could easily picture them running into the surf or sipping drinks from coconuts. She bet they both belonged to the Wildcats.

"It's nothing. She's a real sweetie."

Sarah agreed. As Carole stroked Fluffy's head, Sarah felt a pang of jealousy at how easily the puppy seemed to change her allegiance, but then Sarah decided she'd like anyone who hugged her while she had a needle and IV running into her.

Wanting Carole to know about Fluffy's background, Sarah proceeded to tell her the entire story of how Fluffy, after being abandoned by someone, spent weeks running wild and neglected through their neighborhood until Mr. Rogers, who used to own the house next door, where Jane's Place now was, made the puppy feel safe enough to trust him. She wrapped up her story by explaining how, when Mr. Rogers was injured, Sarah took Fluffy in for what was going to be a temporary stay but ended up being permanent when Mr. Rogers moved into an assisted living retirement facility that didn't allow pets.

She'd just finished telling Carole Fluffy's story when Glenn reappeared.

He casually placed a hand on Carole's shoulder. "See, I told you Fluffy would be fine. She's in good hands. Carole adores dogs, especially when they need a little extra tender loving care."

"I can see that."

"You should see her at the shelter. No matter how many times I tell her not to play favorites, she does."

"Hey, you two, I'm sitting here. I can hear you."

While Sarah said, "And I bet your ears are burning," Glenn simultaneously noted, "And loving everything you're hearing."

All three laughed. "Sarah, while Carole is otherwise occupied, let me show you around the treatment room." He pointed toward the far wall of the room, where a whiteboard was prominently positioned next to several affixed wooden holders that charts or papers could be slipped into. "Let's start over there."

Getting closer to it, Sarah saw the whiteboard was broken into categories, like the ones she'd seen in hospitals or on her favorite medical TV shows. With a glance, one could see the patient's name, where the patient was, who was assigned to the patient, and any special notes related to the patient. There were two names on the board, one of which was Fluffy's. Two charts stuck out of the wooden holders, one of which Sarah assumed also had Fluffy's name on it.

"The most important person in this office is our receptionist or, in the busiest part of each day, our two or three receptionists. They prepare the dog or cat's chart, communicate with owners, and notate if it's a regular appointment, it's an emergency, or if there are special concerns, and tell us, back here, what the owner says is going on."

"Sort of a triage system?"

"Exactly. You've already been through our initial exam system, but when we bring your pet back here, we keep a careful charting of who and what we're doing. Here in the center of the room, arranged in an X configuration, is where we treat animals. We have two exam tables, which we can raise and lower, a wet sink table, and the open area. The open floor space near the cages against the wall is for when we need more space for treatments, like the one Fluffy is getting."

"The exam tables look to me like they function the same way those in the other rooms do, but the wet sink? I've never seen one like that."

"It's about the same length and width as an exam table, roughly four feet by two feet, but it has an open grille system, instead of a flat solid top. We use it primarily for dental cleanings because we need to be able to anesthetize and monitor the animal during the entire procedure. Once the animal is asleep, we clean the teeth using pretty much the same equipment as your dentist. The only difference is where you spit into a basin, we have water constantly dripping and going down the drain."

Sarah glanced at the cages near where Carole sat with Fluffy. "So you do everything in this one room?"

"Oh, no. We have two full surgical dog suites, X-ray and sonar machine areas, and a complete lab.

When we take a blood test, like I did with Fluffy, we get most of the results back in-house within thirty minutes. A great bit of my ability to diagnose is tied to lab work, but there's so much more to it than that."

"Like what?"

"Well, for example, an owner came in recently for her dog's annual physical and shots. She happened to mention he seemed to be having blank staring moments. During my exam, I heard a heart murmur. We did blood work and an echo and discovered a heart irregularity precluding blood getting to the brain at times. Because we figured it out and caught it early, it was easily treatable with medication. If I hadn't listened to the owner and only had stayed within the boundaries of her dog's annual physical, we might have missed an early intervention because the owner didn't think the staring symptom was a big deal."

"It could have been." Sarah involuntarily shuddered.

"Sarah, are you okay?"

"The story about your patient, and what happened to Riley this week, made me think how precious and fragile life is for humans and animals. Thank you for the tour and taking care of Fluffy tonight. I'd better be going. I have to get ready for lunch tomorrow."

"Is there something I can bring?" He held up his hands. "I'm pretty good in the kitchen."

Considering the delicacy of his work, Sarah was tempted to assign him the salad but felt funny asking someone she barely knew to make something for tomorrow. "That's okay. I've got this under control. I know exactly what I'm making."

"Jell-O in a Can? I understand it's one of your specialties."

Sarah was taken aback. "How did you know about that?"

"When I was in town checking out whether this house or another location was best for my practice, the Food Expo was going on. I thought attending it would be a good way to check out my potential customer base. You did your demonstration of Jell-O in a Can while I was at the civic center."

"Who knew my demonstration could be a tool for our chamber of commerce? What other places did I help beat out?"

"There were two locations in Birmingham, plus this house. Carole was in favor of Wheaton from day one, but it was Jacob who convinced me I could have a good practice and a good life here. He shared his dream for the entertainment district and introduced me to Cliff."

Glenn waved his hand around the room. "As you can see, it all came together perfectly—or at least it did while Mr. Rogers was our neighbor. Since Jane bought his house and opened Jane's Place, her constant complaints about our animals making too much noise or smelling, which they don't, and this unfortunate incident with Riley are impacting business."

Sarah stared at Glenn. All the warm and fuzzy feelings toward animals and people she'd been attributing to him evaporated in the face of his selfish and callous remark. After tomorrow, she'd make sure

Fluffy and RahRah saw Dr. Vera or Dr. Tonya because it was obvious that, for Dr. Glenn, the bottom line of his practice was what mattered.

Back at the carriage house, even though Glenn had assured her RahRah should be okay, she needed to see for herself. In the kitchen, her cookbooks were untouched on the table and RahRah's food bowl was empty, but RahRah wasn't in his usual place stretched out on the linoleum. True, the sun wasn't shining on RahRah's claimed spot, but, still, he rarely lay anywhere else. "RahRah!"

A soft meow from under the kitchen table caught Sarah's ear. Relieved, Sarah braced herself with one hand on the edge of the table and bent to RahRah's level. She reached out to stroke the stretching cat. He didn't pull away. Instead, he shook his body and inched closer to her. When Sarah let herself drop completely to the floor, he leaped into her lap.

Using her as his new floor, RahRah proceeded to reach back and clean himself. Sarah didn't care. She was only glad to see her precious cat in one piece. "I missed you. I'm sorry I left so suddenly, but Fluffy wasn't feeling well."

When RahRah stopped cleaning himself and raised his head as if peering around the room for Fluffy, Sarah couldn't help wondering how much he really understood. She knew cats and dogs weren't supposed to have the same intellect as humans, but there were times she really felt that assumption was flawed. This moment was just such an instance. Anyone, including Glenn Amos, would be hard-pressed to sway Sarah's belief that RahRah didn't sense something was wrong with his beloved Fluffy.

Gingerly, Sarah put RahRah back on the floor. "I hate to leave you again, but I have to run to the store to get a few things—okay, almost everything—to make tomorrow's lunch."

RahRah stared at her for a few seconds before he resumed cleaning himself.

With her knees creaking more than they did even a year earlier, Sarah stood by the side of the table. She sorted through the recipes she planned to serve tomorrow. On a pad, she wrote the ingredients she needed for each. If the recipe had a picture she couldn't carry to the store with her, she took a photo of it with her phone. This way, she knew she'd buy the right squash or whatever the recipe called for. Not being a cook, Sarah found the variety of items, like the different types of squash, overwhelmed her when she went shopping. Over time, she'd found that for the few times she cooked, the picture method kept her from having to make multiple trips to the store to correct her mistakes.

Astounded at how anyone could get so confused in a neighborhood supermarket, Emily thought Sarah's system was a hoot. For Emily, recognition and understanding of food, even the most exotic, came naturally. Not for Sarah.

She glanced over to where RahRah lay on the floor. "Don't look at me like that. Either come help me find pictures to take to the grocery store or keep cleaning yourself, but don't you dare laugh. I'm doing the best I can."

CHAPTER TWENTY-SIX

Sunday morning, Sarah took one more look at her dining and living rooms and decided everything was as ready as it was going to be. Maybe not for Anne, but at least for the guests. Disposable bowls, plates, silverware, and cups were all strategically placed next to trivets or spaces on the table, where moments earlier pieces of paper marked the location of the dishes she now placed on them. Everything was pushed back far enough so she didn't have to worry about RahRah or Fluffy getting into the food.

Normally, she would have locked her pets in her bedroom while the guests were here, but knowing Fluffy had been caged all night and would be somewhat subdued, while RahRah would put his nose up and leave the crowd alone, she'd opted to let them run free. Besides, it was cool enough that most people would be wearing jackets. Rather than trying to hang them all in her small entry closet, she'd made her bed and was going to let the guests pile them on there. Hopefully, no one would mind a little pet hair or a cat curled up on the coat pile when they retrieved their coat.

"Okay, guys, best behavior. The first guest should be here any minute." The doorbell ringing underscored her point. Sarah walked to the front door, RahRah and Fluffy behind her. "Want to bet it's Anne?" She reached for the doorknob.

"Harlan!" She stepped back to let him in. "I didn't expect to see you here today."

He looked back at her from where, bending on one knee, he petted both animals. "Did you think I'd skip your little 'find the clue' party or the free lunch?"

The free lunch comment tipped Sarah off as to who told Harlan about today's get-together. "You've been talking to Anne. This is her idea, you know."

"She made that perfectly clear. After all, you would never do anything when I specifically asked you not to, would you?"

Sarah swallowed hard. "Never."

Anne arriving saved Sarah from making further apologies or putting her foot in her mouth any deeper than it was. "Harlan, I'm glad to see you. Isn't it nice of Sarah to open her house today? I'm hoping someone will remember something that will be helpful to your defense of Jacob. Are there any specific questions or areas I should delve into?"

Harlan rose. He brushed his hands off on his pants. "Nothing I can think of. I wish you'd trusted me to develop the evidence in the way I saw best. Trust is important in lawyer-client relationships. Because you obviously don't have it in my abilities, I won't be able to represent you going forward. Of course, I will continue to represent Jacob, unless he decides to discharge my services."

"I hired you to represent both of us." The timbre of Anne's clipped words reminded Sarah of the first time she'd felt a piece of steel.

"No, you hired me to go with you to the police station, which I did. In the parking lot, Jacob asked me to represent him in this entire matter."

"But . . ."

"Anne, there isn't a 'but.' My clients either trust me or they don't." He nodded toward Sarah. "Tomorrow, Sarah will send you a formal letter informing you of the need for you to obtain other representation for the future."

Responding to the doorbell ringing, Sarah missed Anne's retort. At least, Sarah thought as she opened the door, Harlan was keeping her onboard to type the letter to Anne. She didn't relish the discussion they'd have at work tomorrow. She only hoped it ended without her typing herself a letter, too.

More people arriving necessitated Sarah showing them where to put their coats and directing them to help themselves to lunch. It also served as a means for her to avoid what looked like a heated conversation Harlan and Anne continued in the far corner of the entryway.

From the flurry of arrivals, either Anne invited more people, like she had Harlan, or word had spread there was a free lunch to be had. Glad she'd cut the lasagnas into small squares, Sarah hoped there would be enough food for everyone, especially when the bikers eventually came.

On one of her many trips to her bedroom with coats, Sarah noticed little paws barely visible under her bed. As she dropped her armload of coats on her bed, she had to give RahRah and Fluffy credit. They'd figured out a much better place to be during the next few hours than she had.

"So this is what you use this room for?"

Sarah spun around to see a grinning Cliff. She ignored his question. "Other than Harlan, Anne, and Jane, you're the first familiar face I've seen in a while." She pointed to where RahRah's paw still showed. "Do you think, with this crowd, anyone would notice if I squeezed under there next to RahRah?"

"I would." Cliff put his arm around her and pecked her on the head.

Uncomfortable someone might walk in if their public display of affection intensified, Sarah pulled away.

Dropping his shoulders, Cliff pouted but stopped when someone brought in a pile of coats. He didn't speak again until the person had left the bedroom. "Does Anne really think anything will come out of this session?"

Sarah sighed. "Other than people getting a free lunch? When she proposed getting a small group together, she made me think we might, but with this crowd, I doubt it. I guess I better get back out and help Anne with the guests."

"And not take advantage of this quiet moment in your bedroom?" He laughed at the semi-scowl she threw in his direction. Together, they exited the room, almost bumping into Glenn and Carole carrying their coats in.

The contrast between the two men was striking. Although both were tall, Cliff's huskier build and ruddier coloring made him more a cross between Paul Bunyan and a surfer dude while Glenn's blonder, muscular look seemed more suited for a tennis court. Forgetting Cliff and Glenn already knew each other, she hastened to make introductions, but they cut her off.

"This lunch really has you overwrought if you forgot I was the one to remodel Glenn's building."

"It really is amazing how well Cliff was able to take that old house and not only bring it up to code for Glenn's practice but for living quarters for Glenn and a guest attic apartment for me," Carole observed.

"Guest?" The looks Carole shot Glenn were adoring, Sarah realized, but not romantic.

"Yes, when I came here, I needed a little time and space to get myself back together. My big brother gave me that chance with a place to live and on-the-job vet-tech training."

Glenn blushed. "Any brother would have done the same." He threw his jacket on the bed. "Hey, I'm dying to try your food. Did you make Jell-O in a Can again?"

"Dying to try her food isn't always the best line if you're near anything made by Sarah," Cliff said.

Sarah gave Cliff a little shove, but he ignored her.

"She even has an 'Eat at Your Own Risk' apron."

"Oh, I'd love to see that. Come show it to me while they talk about their bikes. Glenn already rode this morning." Carole linked her arm through Sarah's. "I can tell this is going to be the beginning of a fast friendship."

Back in the main guest area, Sarah checked to make sure there was still enough food if the bikers who hadn't arrived yet, like Eloise, Botts, and Drs. Vera and Tonya, ever got there. She also wanted to ensure everyone had what they needed before Anne and she ushered them into the living room for Anne's disguised interrogation.

Working her way around the room, Sarah was delighted to receive compliments on her squash soup, which she told everyone and anyone who listened was a gluten-free recipe from Emily's Southwind repertoire. Of course, Jane, overhearing her remark about the soup, chimed in that the one served at Jane's Place was even tastier because it wasn't gluten-free. It was all Sarah could do not to suggest Jane leave if the cuisine of the Chef of Convenience failed to please her.

Glancing at the clock on her living room mantel, Sarah realized they couldn't wait much longer for the missing riders.

Anne apparently had the same thought as she strode to the archway between the living and dining rooms and loudly said, "Everyone, we're going to begin the meeting in five minutes, so please raid the table for one last bite and find a seat. There should be plenty of seats because we're still missing a few Wildcats. Hopefully, they'll join us shortly."

As if validating Anne's words, the door opened and in walked Drs. Tonya and Vera, both dressed in boots, jeans, and leather jackets covered with various insignia. One of their more prominent badges was what Sarah now knew marked them as belonging to the Wildcats.

"I'm so glad you could come. May I take your jackets?"

"We'll hold on to them," Dr. Tonya answered. "There was quite a chill out there when we were riding."

"Grab some soup, then. A mug to warm your hands or a bowl to send it directly to your innards."

Dr. Vera's giggle at Sarah's comment was almost enough impetus for Sarah to make another joke about convenience cooking, but the unamused look Dr. Tonya shot in her direction silenced her. Sarah decided talking about the animal clinic to her would be a safer topic.

"Although I think you were either leaving or had left when I ran in with Fluffy yesterday, I can't tell you how glad I was at how close your clinic is." As she went on to tell them what had happened and how well Fluffy was doing now that she was home, whatever was bothering Dr. Tonya evaporated with her interest in Fluffy.

Dr. Vera glanced around the room. "Where is Fluffy? We'd be glad to take a quick look at her."

"She's under my bed. RahRah and she were smart enough to avoid this crowd, but they refused to let me join them."

This time Sarah's comment was better received by Dr. Tonya. "That makes two of us. This isn't my kind of scene today. Tell you what, why don't you guide me toward where Fluffy is and I'll make a quick house call. After all, we need her to be healthy for you to bring her in for her last round of shots."

Sarah pointed in the direction of her bedroom, and Dr. Tonya immediately went that way. Although Dr.

Vera didn't physically follow her, there was no question in Sarah's mind that her gaze did.

"Don't you want to go, too?"

Dr. Vera hesitated then pointed to the front of the room where Anne was getting ready to speak. "Between you and me, the answer is yes, but I can't right now. Glenn will be annoyed if we aren't front and center when Anne speaks. With all the noise-related complaints Jane lodged with Chief Gerard and everything else happening in our own backyard, he seems to think it's important we grease the political wheel wherever possible."

"You don't?"

"I think we can work things out without going overboard." She held her hands up and made her fingers into quotation marks. "I'm not a 'master politician.'"

"Is he?"

"Both he and Tonya are. It's something they learned in the military. I keep telling them to let Carole and me mind the clinic while they get out there and do what they think is necessary, and we'll have a perfect arrangement. So far, though, neither has agreed with me."

"Dr. Tonya doesn't seem like a politician. From her scowl, I'd have said she didn't hide the fact she wasn't too happy with my soup joke."

"Oh, it wasn't you she was irritated with. Mandy Davis, who Tonya despises, was standing a few feet behind you. Don't let what you saw of Tonya's demeanor a few minutes ago influence you. This morning, Tonya got in the middle of a disagreement among some of the Wildcats whether to do a scenic ride or focus on more off-roading and stunts. Seeing Mandy here merely topped off an already lousy morning."

"Does Dr. Tonya know Mandy from the Wildcats, too?"

Dr. Vera waved her hand. "No. They go back years. Glenn's looking in my direction. I guess I better mingle."

"One thing before you go. A number of Wildcats haven't gotten here yet. Does that have anything to do with this morning's dispute?"

"Possibly. Our group rode out to Millerpond Bridge. Botts's group opted for back-road riding and stunts, so they may have been gone longer." Her sunny expression darkened.

"I gather neither of you were too thrilled with what he wanted to do."

"We rarely are. That man gets in everyone's face and wants everything his way. This time, he got some new equipment on his bike that he wanted to show off."

"So?"

"He claimed he didn't want to try it out alone. Because of the two opinions where to ride, we all got off to a late start this morning. Tonya has no patience for him or his shenanigans. Once she spends a little time with your pets, she'll be back out here raring to go."

"You mentioned Tonya was annoyed with Botts causing a delay. How did everyone else feel?"

"The same as usual. Annoyed. How well do you know Botts?"

"Pretty much only in his professional capacity."

"Well, whatever you've heard, believe that and ten percent more."

"Even about Riley?"

Dr. Vera clamped her lips tightly. "Maybe add twenty percent there, from both sides. I shouldn't speak ill of the dead, but talk to any Wildcat and you'll probably get a similar opinion of both."

"What do the Wildcats think of Jacob?"

"That's he's a naive sweetheart. Otherwise, we wouldn't all be here."

Before Sarah could figure out a way to ask without seeming too nosy, Dr. Vera pointed down the hall. "There's Tonya. I think playing with RahRah and Fluffy did the trick."

Sarah agreed. The emerging Dr. Tonya had a different walk and look than the one who'd disappeared into Sarah's bedroom.

With everyone assembled in the living room, Anne began with a brief overview of why she'd invited them to come. Sarah was glad, especially with Harlan standing in the back of the room, that Anne took full credit for today's gathering. In fact, Anne went so far as to thank Sarah for opening her house, which was centrally located, without acknowledging any more of a role for her.

"I'd like you to think back to the night Jane's Place opened. Remember how we were all having a wonderful time tasting Jane and Riley's specialties."

"Not to mention sampling the open bar," someone yelled, breaking Anne's almost-hypnotic rhythm.

With what Sarah recognized as Anne's pasted-on politician's grin, Anne continued, "That's right. We sampled Jane and Riley's specialties and the open bar. All of us were having a good time. Even when we had to wait in line, we were appreciative of Riley cheerfully explaining her vegan dishes, until Jane beckoned her over so the two of them could properly welcome us . . ."

Anne's voice trailed off as Eloise burst into the room, clutching her motorcycle helmet. Her usual perfectly lacquered coiffure was beyond helmet hair. The pale hue of her skin made Sarah think Eloise was ill. Her voice quavered as she caught her breath. When everything horrific had gone down at the bank, Eloise had kept it together for the other employees and customers. Right now, Sarah couldn't tell if Eloise was on the edge of losing it or simply disheveled from riding. She rushed to the older woman's side. Out of the corner of her eye, she saw Harlan doing the same.

"Eloise, what is it?" Harlan asked.

"I tried calling you, but you didn't answer. That's why I came here. There's been a horrible accident."

CHAPTER TWENTY-SEVEN

Eloise wordlessly stared at Anne.

"Is it Jacob? Is he hurt?"

Eloise shook her head. "He's with Chief Gerard."

Impatient, Anne raised her voice, demanding more details. "At the hospital?"

"Jacob isn't hurt. Chief Gerard took him to the station house. Harlan, I didn't know if he would let Jacob call you right away, so I tried calling you, but my call went to voice mail."

Harlan put his arm on Eloise's shoulder and drew her toward him. He spoke directly to her. "Eloise, who is hurt and what happened?"

"It's Louis Botts. He's dead."

"What?"

"How does that involve my brother?" asked Anne.

"Jacob and Botts got into another shouting match before this morning's ride, near where all the bikes are parked outside the veterinary clinic." She pointed at the veterinarians and some of the people they were sitting with. "Botts and Jacob were about to come to blows, but others broke up the fight. Botts and Jacob stalked off in opposite directions, but, like everyone else, they came back to get their bikes ready to ride. Because of their disagreement and a split of opinion where we should ride, things got off to a late start. Jacob went with the group on the highway, while Botts and I joined those who opted to go off-road stunting."

Sarah couldn't get her head around Eloise doing stunts. "You do wheelies?"

"Oh, no. I just enjoy watching them. When it was Botts's turn, he did a showy, but easy, stunt. He was just about through a twisty spin when his engine stalled and he flipped over the handlebars. The bike fell and pinned him. Between the bike's weight, the heat, and his helmet blowing apart . . ."

Harlan hugged Eloise closer.

She accepted his embrace and then pulled back, looking him in the face. "I knew Anne would be here. I wasn't sure you would, but I thought you both needed to know Jacob is at the police station."

"You're right."

If the situation hadn't been so serious, Sarah might have found humor in the taller woman towering over Harlan's shoulder, but the moment wasn't funny. "Eloise, if the accident happened well after their fight, why did Chief Gerard take Jacob to the station?"

"He wanted to question him while the bike is being checked out. I heard that someone said they thought they saw Jacob tinker with it, but I don't see how. There wouldn't have been enough time."

Having caught her breath, Eloise regained her

usual authoritative manner. "Harlan, I know Chief Gerard can't officially talk to Jacob because he has legal representation, but I don't trust Jacob to remember he shouldn't say anything until you're there. That's why, Harlan and Anne, I think Jacob needs you. You'd better go."

Harlan released Eloise. "Are you going to be okay?"

Sarah stepped forward. "I'll make sure she is, Harlan. Go on."

Not even trying to argue with Sarah, Harlan and Anne left immediately. They were followed by several of the other guests, including the veterinarians and Carole. Before he went, Cliff took a moment to tell Sarah he was going to go see if there was anything he could do for Jacob, and he'd call her if he found out anything more.

Settling Eloise in one of her oversized living room chairs with a scotch on the rocks, Sarah joined the few people who remained clustered around the food table. She was immediately glad she had. As they finished off the remnants of her food, they were discussing Botts's accident and Riley's death. When one mentioned how good the vegan dishes still were at Jane's Place, but that it was a shame Riley was gone, Sarah interjected a question about Riley and her involvement with the Wildcats.

"She was a flirt in a cute way," one said, "but she always, or at least until Botts came on the scene, reciprocated through her cooking."

"To the person who gave her a ride?"

"Usually, but not only then. When she rode with Jacob or even was a random rider, we could always count on her for one of her vegan specialties as a main dish for our potlucks. She wasn't as reliable when she started riding with Botts."

"Why was that?"

"Probably because he thought he was too good for everyone."

Responding to the cold flatness of the voice, Sarah jerked her head around to see who had made the comment. It was Mandy.

"What makes you say that? Are you a Wildcat?"

"Not me, but I've known Botts for a long time. If they find his bike was sabotaged, I won't be surprised. Only that it didn't happen sooner."

Mandy's comment was like a floodgate for those standing around the table. No one spoke up in his defense. Rather, most either couldn't stand him as a person or made references to the rumors about his hands not being clean. The key question lingering on everyone's lips was whether Botts's death was another murder.

CHAPTER TWENTY-EIGHT

As the remaining guests left, Sarah made a point of grabbing Mandy before she could get out the door. "I was hoping we could have a minute to talk."

"About what? I think I made my position on Botts clear."

"Oh, no. Not that. Considering the circumstances under which we met the other day—we were all so shocked by Riley's death—we didn't have a chance to be properly introduced."

For a moment, the two women sized each other up. Sarah remembered the bright green shade of Mandy's eyes and how they sparkled in contrast to her pale skin and auburn hair. Staring at her now, Sarah realized Mandy was older than she'd thought. The lines etched into her face and forehead weren't all from smiling.

"Obviously, you know I'm Emily's sister and, I hope, one of Grace's friends."

"Yes. Grace thinks very highly of your sister and you."

"The feeling is mutual."

Mandy leaned her head back and laughed. "And you don't know what to say or ask me at this moment, right?"

Sarah nodded.

"Grace and I met last year when she took and then volunteered with a self-defense class I teach once a month for low-income women. We've been together ever since. Does that answer your question?"

"At least one of them."

"What else do you want to know?"

"The standard stuff like what is your full name, occupation, and have you ever studied martial arts?"

"Sarah Blair, you're a strange woman, but I'll bite. Mandy Davis, paralegal, and, yes, I've taken martial arts courses. Why?"

"Because I didn't know your last name, and Chief Gerard thinks someone who is familiar with martial arts killed Riley. I'm trying to find everyone who might have a background that Harlan can use to cast doubt if a case is brought against Jacob."

"Don't trouble your head. Harlan already knows my background and that he can cast aspersions against me if Botts was murdered, but I don't provide Jacob with any help when it comes to Riley."

"What about the fact that Grace thinks you have her back?"

"I do, but I'm not an idiot." Mandy pulled the door open. "Do you really think I'd cross that line even for her?"

CHAPTER TWENTY-NINE

Sarah walked back into her living room, where Eloise still sat. "Are you all right?"

"Of course, dear. Once I caught my breath from running from the parking pad up your driveway, I was fine. I've been sitting here replaying what happened this morning in my mind. Do you need any help cleaning up before I leave?"

"Thanks, but it will only take me a few minutes. I used disposable everything. Do you have your car across the street?"

"No, I walked this morning."

"Well, you're not going to walk home. I'll drive you."

"That's not necessary."

"You're probably more shook up than you realize. Besides, can't you just hear my mother now if anything happens to you?" Dragging her own name into four syllables, Sarah did an imitation of her mother that made Eloise smile.

Although Eloise and Maybelle hadn't been close

friends for long, they'd known each other for years through various bank dealings. "I have to give it to you. You nailed your mother on that one."

"I know. I've had a lot of years of listening to be able to get it right. So no fighting. You'll let me take you home."

"Only if you pour me another drink and let me help you clean up."

"I'll take the pouring you another drink part of the deal."

Leaving Eloise in the living room, Sarah went to the kitchen, where she kept her liquor. Not expecting anyone to be in the kitchen, Sarah almost jumped a mile when she saw Jane rustling through the papers near her cookbooks and pressure cooker. "What do you think you're doing?"

Jane turned to face her, dropping the piece of paper she held. "I was looking for your squash soup recipe." She picked up the single sheet of paper again and held it out to Sarah, who didn't take it. "I found it right here by your pressure cooker."

"It isn't mine. It's Emily's."

"I know. You kept going on and on about how good it was and gluten-free, so I was interested in seeing how it differs from mine. Because you were busy with Eloise and your guests, I thought I'd take a peek around before I left."

"With the recipe in hand."

"Oh, no. I was simply going to compare them in my head." She pointed at the clock on the kitchen wall. "Oh my, look at the time. I've got to get ready for our dinner service." Jane started to leave, still clutching the recipe.

"I think you'd better leave that here."

Jane dropped the recipe back on the counter. "How silly of me. See, you got me flustered. I'll ask Emily about the spice she uses in her recipe the next time I see her."

"You do that."

Jane left. Sarah was confident the recipe would have gone with Jane if she hadn't come into the kitchen when she did. For a minute, Sarah felt pretty good. She might not be much of a cook, but she had to have done something right if Jane was so tempted to steal her recipe.

Remembering her initial purpose, Sarah poured Eloise a stiff scotch on the rocks. She thought about pouring one for herself but passed. Instead, she took Eloise her drink. Eloise took it gratefully and gulped a good-size swallow of the liquor. With a sound of approval, she sat back. "I was beginning to think you forgot me until I heard you talking with Jane."

"You heard everything?"

"I think so."

"What I don't understand is that it isn't a complicated or particularly secret recipe. I'm sure Jane could have found it in a dozen cookbooks without having to rifle through my kitchen."

"True, but the cookbooks don't have that something extra Emily adds that distinguishes her soup and other dishes from the ones in the books. Jane probably figured Emily notated the recipe with whatever she adds."

"But that's the point. She doesn't add anything to the soup that I know of."

"Then what she adds is skill and her love of cooking. Emily knows exactly how to mix the ingredients and when to take them off the heat. Apparently, you did today, too." She took another sip of her drink.

Sarah sighed. "When it comes to Jane, I think she scorches everything she touches."

At Sarah's dry observation, Eloise had to work to control herself from spitting out her mouthful of scotch. "Not when I'm drinking, please." She swallowed but started laughing again.

"What I said wasn't *that* funny." Perplexed at Eloise's continued reaction, Sarah narrowed her eyes, waiting for an explanation.

"It's not what you said. It's the context of it all. Your mother and I are meeting at Jane's Place tomorrow at noon. We're ostensibly celebrating my birthday. Why don't you join us?"

"Jane's Place rather than Southwind? When did Mother and you go over to the dark side?"

"Now, now, don't forget, your mother wants to be called Maybelle by all of us. That means Emily and you, too."

At this, Sarah opened her eyes wide open and rolled them until she was in danger of them becoming stuck in the back of her head.

"Sarah, it's simple. As a city councilor, I need to frequent all of Wheaton's restaurants and other businesses. Maybelle and I thought we'd have lunch, check out the competition, and do a little investigative work. Having you come along will be perfect. Not only are three snoops better than two, but, after today, Jane will be so skittish around you that you can be our perfect distraction while your mother and I look around."

"Promise me, if I do it, you'll taste all my food first to make sure I don't drop dead because she poisons me."

"You shouldn't say things like that. Considering Wheaton's recent history, that isn't particularly funny. Besides, Jane would probably mess up that recipe, too."

Realizing Eloise had drained her glass, Sarah offered to get her another.

Eloise declined and handed Sarah her glass. "I better be getting home. That is one more than I usually have, but I needed something to settle me down."

"The accident was that bad?"

"I've seen worse, but what I don't understand is how his helmet disintegrated the way it did. The weight of the bike crushing his chest is what probably caused his death, but his head injuries were far more severe than they should have been for the speed he was going. That helmet shouldn't have cracked through like it did."

"I don't understand."

"Helmets are all different, but something was wrong with that one. I'd say it was a cheapie, but all of Botts's equipment was over-the-top. I'm not up on all the different types of helmets, but the three vets are. They helped me pick out that one." She pointed to her helmet sitting in a chair across the room. "You ought to talk to them about what happened with his helmet."

After she took Eloise home, Sarah came back and quickly cleaned up. She was taking the last bag of garbage outside when her cell phone rang. Leaving the garbage bag by her back door, she grabbed her phone. Caller ID showed Cliff's name. She answered the call. "Hi."

"Everyone gone?"

"Finally. How are things with Jacob?"

"He's not in jail. That's the best I can say. I sat in the waiting room with Anne for an hour while Harlan was in an interrogation room with Jacob. When they came out, Harlan told Anne and me to go home. He and Jacob went back to Harlan's office."

"Anne must have been furious."

"She was, but Jacob politely told her to be quiet and get over it. He was meeting with his lawyer, not hers."

"And she shut up?"

"Snapped her mouth shut. I get the feeling Jacob rarely stands up to his big sister. Harlan had him out of the station before she recovered."

"I wish you had filmed that moment. We might have made a fortune selling it to our present mayor. Their campaign against each other promises to get low rather than sticking to the high ground. Don't you think?"

"Yeah. Speaking of campaigns, I'm still trying to win you over. Dinner this weekend?"

"Sounds good to me."

"I'll call you later. Maybe we'll go somewhere special for dinner."

"Surprise me."

CHAPTER THIRTY

The next morning Sarah tried to talk to Harlan about what had transpired the day before, but he was swamped. The only thing he could tell her was that Chief Gerard was convinced someone, whose name began with a *J*, had probably tampered with Botts's bike. Again, the chief wasn't going to arrest Jacob until he had forensic confirmation, but Harlan felt an arrest was only a matter of time.

As lunchtime approached, it felt treasonous to be going to Jane's Place, but the idea of reversing the snooping tables on Jane appealed to Sarah. Her thoughts were wicked, but, except for a few minutes in their entire relationship, Jane, her ex-husband's bimbo, had repeatedly been the source of enough grief for Sarah and her family that she couldn't imagine their relationship ever improving.

Her complicated relationship with Anne was different. Anne had traits Sarah admired, but these very traits often intimidated Sarah into giving in too easily or simply being silent. With the confidence she'd gained in herself during the past year, Sarah knew her days of being intimidated would lessen.

Because she didn't have to be at lunch until noon, Sarah decided to stop by the veterinarians' office to see if one of them might be taking a lunch break and would explain the difference in helmets to her as Eloise had suggested. She also wanted to find out more about the problems they were having with the shared parking area and if either Carole or Glenn's apartments gave them a view of the motorcycle and general parking areas.

Entering through the doorway on the dog side, she immediately realized from the number of dogs and owners waiting that nobody on the staff was probably at lunch. Three people, including Carole, were manning the reception desk. Standing where she was, Sarah could see the cat waiting room was equally full. Normally, she scheduled RahRah as the first appointment on a Wednesday or Thursday. She wondered if Mondays were always like this.

"Hey, Sarah," Carole called. "Is there anything I can do to help you?" She peered over the top of the desk. "Do you have RahRah or Fluffy with you to-day?"

Sarah walked quickly up to the desk. "No, I don't. Eloise suggested I ask one of the vets about motor-cycle helmets, but I gather they're backed up today."

Carole nodded in agreement. "Mondays are crazy around here. I wish I could help you, but that's a hobby my brother and I don't share. Motorcycles scare me."

"Me too. Is there a good time to come back, or would any of the vets be interested in a drink after work today or tomorrow to answer my questions?"

"I don't know, but I'll check. Be back in a second." Without waiting for a reaction from Sarah, Carole disappeared into the treatment area. She quickly returned. "If you're free tonight at seven, all three of them and I will meet you for a drink at the Southwind Pub."

"Perfect, but tell me, how did you get all three of them to agree so quickly?"

Carole smiled, a dimple showing. "That was the easy part. I told them you were buying."

"Apparently, buying a round is as good as a free lunch."

"Oh, no. It's better."

"See you at the Southwind Pub at seven." Sarah turned to leave, but as she neared the door, commotion between a large German shepherd not wanting to enter the building and the person holding its leash broke out. The more the owner pulled, the more the dog dug in. He sat in place, his giant body blocking any possibility of entrance or exit. Whether the owner pulled on the leash or alternatively soothed the animal, it snapped and snarled. His bark excited the other dogs in the waiting room and started a round of barking even louder than Sarah had heard in the parking lot.

"Sarah, come back this way." Carole turned her attention to speaking into an intercom. "General Beau is out here and he's quite agitated."

Sarah couldn't make out the reply, but Carole barely flipped the intercom switch when all three vets flew out from the back. General Beau growled at them and then, just as quickly, relaxed at whatever they said. Slowly, they approached General Beau.

Sarah stared at the transformation until Carole said, "Sarah, follow me. Let me get you out of here the back way. It's going to take a few more minutes for them to completely calm General Beau."

Carole led her through the treatment area she'd previously toured. Today, different vet techs were holding leashes, talking to the dogs, and moving them up and down on the hydraulic-lift tables. The room and the whiteboard were full, and it looked like even the sink table was being used as a normal treatment table.

Sarah hurried to keep up with Carole as she took Sarah down a hall on the far side of the treatment room, past the surgery rooms. "How did the vets calm General Beau down so quickly when the General's owner couldn't?"

"Oh, he's not the General's owner. He's fostering General Beau on a long-term basis."

"Carole, when we have such a good shelter, why is Beau being fostered long-term privately?"

"Beau's a little too skittish with loud noises and unfamiliar settings to be in the general shelter population. His foster parents usually can easily bring him here because he trusts all three of our doctors. They either served with him or knew his handler in the military."

"The dog was military?"

"General Beau was a land mine sniffer. Thanks to him, lots of lives were saved, but the posttraumatic stress aftereffects of being too close to an exploding bomb necessitated his retirement. Our vets arranged for General Beau to be fostered in Wheaton because he needed special care. When his handler is discharged, they'll be reunited." Carole opened a door at the end of the hallway. "Here you go. This will bring you out in the parking lot."

"Thanks." Glancing through the doorway, Sarah could see the motorcycle pad and the place at the edge of the parking lot where she'd stood with Jane after Riley was found dead. She tried to orient herself to how the building twisted from the point she'd entered to this door because she realized it wasn't a straight path. Either parts of the house had been added on after it originally was built or Cliff had done some clever remodeling to most effectively utilize the space for the clinic and the living quarters.

Sarah was about to ask Carole whether her apartment overlooked this area, but Carole had already pivoted to return to the treatment and reception areas. Better to ask her tonight over their planned drink than to try delaying her when she obviously was in a rush to get back to business.

Outside, Sarah crossed over a small patch of grass to where at least ten motorcycles were parked on a cement pad under one of those prefab metal roofed open shelters. At first glance, she thought the bikes were simply crammed together, but, looking more closely, she realized there was a rhyme and reason to the parking system. It dawned on her that each bike was in an assigned space. Some were on blocks, but most were parked so they could easily be rolled or ridden from the pad without disturbing any of the other motorcycles. Although every bike had the Wildcat insignia somewhere on its rear fender, each was individually decorated.

Some had streamers coming from the handlebars, while others were covered with stickers. Sarah examined two of the heavily stickered motorcycles more closely. One probably belonged to a member of the summer retiree group because the stickers were from the different places in the United States its owner must have visited. Because of the preponderance of national park stickers, Sarah wondered if the owner was attempting to check off all the national parks by a certain time.

The candidate- and issue-oriented stickers covering the second bike reminded her of the back of an older car whose owner constantly added bumper stickers with every election or issue without ever removing any from prior campaigns. Whoever owned this bike was no youngster, judging by some of the campaigns represented.

Sarah looked around to see if she could pick out the silver motorcycle Jacob said he'd seen the night Riley died. At least five of the ten could have been the one he saw. She had the feeling silver was a popular color. Although she didn't know what color Jacob's bike was, Sarah bet it was silver, too. She'd have to come up with another way to identify Riley's killer.

Parked on the far side of the path, Sarah recognized Eloise's pristine gold-with-lavender-accents saddlebags and handlebars, from her description of them. Examining it closer, she saw it was lower than many of the other cycles and its seat appeared to be more cushioned. Sarah had had trouble imagining a leather-jacketed Eloise wearing red lipstick and a crossbones-decorated helmet over her hair, riding into the sunset on a heavy, metal bike. Seeing the comfort of this ride, Sarah's mental picture of Eloise softened to pink lipstick and a lavender helmet and jacket.

Rather than walking all the way back to Main Street, Sarah decided to cut through the parking lot and use the back entrance to Jane's Place. As she neared the open dumpster, she was almost overcome by the smell of rotten eggs. Why was the smell so bad? Deciding it would be better for the neighborhood if the dumpster was closed, she walked over to flip the door shut. Approaching the dumpster, she could see it was almost overflowing. Apparently, the sanitation department hadn't collected trash from the weekend, or possibly even before that. She wondered if the garbage service realized Jane's Place was now fully operational.

Sarah peeked inside. The source of the smell was obvious. Discarded plastic bags had burst open filling the dumpster with egg cartons. Some of the open cartons still had eggs in them, but from what she could see, most of the trash was discarded eggshells. Knowing the kind of garbage Southwind produced as a full-service restaurant, she couldn't understand how Jane's Place, which had a heavily vegan menu, could possibly use so many eggs. As she stared into the dumpster, the answer came to her—only if Jane put eggs in almost every dish.

Pulling her phone out of her pocket, Sarah quickly snapped pictures from every angle, but she knew that wasn't enough. She needed to share this information with someone before the dumpster was emptied, but who? Even before she finished formulating the question, the solution pulled into the parking lot in the form of a big white sedan that whipped into the middle of two spaces.

Despite the smell, Sarah stayed protected by the metal dumpster until she was sure the car was in park and the ignition turned off. With a wave, she approached the driver and her passenger as they extricated themselves from the car.

"Hi, Mom!" She waited for her mother to automatically correct her.

Once again, her mother didn't disappoint her. "It's Maybelle, please."

"Yes, ma'am—I mean Maybelle."

A suppressed snicker behind her mother made both Maybelle and Sarah focus on its source, Eloise.

"Was there something you wanted to say, Eloise?" Maybelle asked.

Eloise waved a hand in the air. "Not at all. I'm just here for a pleasant lunch." She stopped and sniffed the air. "What is that putrid smell?"

"Rotting eggs." Sarah pointed to the dumpster. "Apparently, they're from Jane's Place."

Eloise, her hand over her nose, peeked into the trash receptacle. Sarah could almost see the wheels turn as she viewed what Sarah had seen. Moving away from the dumpster, she grabbed her cell phone from her purse.

Uncertain if Eloise had come to the same conclusion she had, Sarah started to ask her, but Eloise hushed her with her free hand. Sarah didn't recognize the name Eloise said, but she understood when Eloise asked for inspectors to immediately be sent to

Jane's Place. "I don't care if they are on other jobs. Call them in and get them over here immediately. This is high priority. I'll be waiting for them."

Eloise hit the end button on her phone. "Sarah or Maybelle, if you know anyone at the newspaper, you might consider dialing them up and getting them out here, too."

Considering she was a competitor of Jane's, Sarah weighed the pros and cons of her calling in the media. "But what if we're wrong?"

"Then there's no story. If you can't think of anyone offhand, they have a confidential tip line you can use."

"But, Eloise," Maybelle said, "you probably have the best contacts of all of us. Why don't you call one of them?"

"Because I don't think it would be politically correct for me to leak this story. Of course, if a reporter finds me here, I'll spin it from the angle of me protecting the public's health and safety at all times."

Although that made sense to Sarah, she still worried about them being wrong. "Before we go crazy with this, shouldn't we find out if our presumption is correct by confronting Jane?"

Her mother rolled her eyes. "That liar? Besides, after as many dealings as your sister and you have had with that woman, do you think Jane would check with you first or simply act and apologize later if she was wrong?"

Maybelle rummaged in her pocketbook until she found her phone. "I wish I had a burner phone, but I guess it can't be helped. Eloise, do you know the confidential tip number?"

When she completed her call, Maybelle started walking toward the restaurant. "Well, are you two coming?"

Eloise shook her head. "I want to wait for the inspectors, but I think it might be a good idea for the two of you to go in and immediately order several of Jane's vegan dishes for the three of us. Hopefully, by the time I join you, we'll have a good sampling of the specialties Jane has been serving."

Chapter Thirty-One

"Come on, Sarah. We're going to go in the front door."

"But, Mom, your car is in the restaurant's parking lot. Most people who park in a restaurant's rear lot use the door near where they leave their car."

"True, but I want to give Eloise some time, so it makes it appear she arrived after us."

"But anyone could have looked outside and already seen the three of us out here."

Ignoring her daughter, Maybelle led Sarah around to the restaurant's main entrance. Greeting the hostess, she spoke loud enough that anyone in earshot could hear her. "There will be three of us for lunch. Our third person is running a little late, but we'd like to be seated so we can begin ordering."

When her mother finished talking, she shot a grin at Sarah as the hostess led them to a table that seated four. Sarah inwardly groaned. No one would ever call her mother subtle.

Without thinking, Sarah started to take the one

chair that faced a wall on which hung a large modernistic picture rather than one from which the entire dining room could be seen. Her mother stopped her.

"Sit over there. That chair has a better view."

Not thinking it worth arguing, Sarah acquiesced without asking what view her mother was referring to. Once she was seated, she realized she not only had a view of most of the guests in the dining room but also of the swinging kitchen door. Her mother slid into the seat next to Sarah. It essentially offered the same view as Sarah's. Apparently, her mother was expecting something to happen, so she wanted them positioned to watch. From the way her mother was perched on the edge of her chair, Sarah wondered if Maybelle would be able to contain her excitement until whatever she hoped for happened. Sarah was so focused on her mother that she didn't notice the waitress approach their table.

"Welcome to Jane's Place. I'm Karen and I'll be taking care of you today. May I get you something to drink while you look over our menu?"

"A sweet iced tea, please. What do you want, Sarah?"

"Unsweet tea."

Maybelle held up her menu. "I've heard your vegan dishes are delicious. People tell me they can't even tell they don't have eggs in them."

Sarah kicked her mother under the table.

"Ow." Maybelle scowled at Sarah but quickly turned her face back to the waitress. She pointed toward the menu. "I'd also like a glass of wine. What do you have by the glass that you'd recommend if we're going to order a few of the vegan dishes so the three of us can taste all of them?"

The waitress pointed to an entry near the bottom of the menu. "That one is a favorite because it complements all of our vegan choices."

"Good. I'll take that then. And because our friend is going to be under a time constraint, would you bring her a glass of water with a lemon and a straw and can you take our order now?"

"No problem. What can I get you?"

"We've never had the vegan dishes, so that's what we want. What do you like best?"

Sarah averted her gaze from her mother. She was afraid if she looked at her, she would break out laughing at Maybelle fawning over the waitress. Sarah had to admit her mother had the waitress engaged.

"Our best seller, and my favorite, is our spinach quiche. We also sell a lot of our banana chocolate chip pancakes and our Jane's Place Special French Toast."

"You have pancakes and French toast available after breakfast?"

"Yes, ma'am. Those two dishes are so popular we have them available all day long."

"Oh my. All three sound delicious. I'll tell you what. There are three of us, so why don't you give us one of each. Is that okay with you, dear?" Not waiting to see if Sarah nodded, Maybelle added an order of pumpkin quinoa muffins.

"I'll put your order right in."

After the waitress walked away, Sarah turned to her hummingbird-size mother. "Pray tell, where do you plan to put all the food you ordered. I'm a bulk eater, but there's no way the three of us can possibly eat everything you ordered."

Maybelle smiled. "That's why we'll need takeout boxes."

"I'm missing something."

"We're gathering evidence. Any good lab will be able to tell if there are eggs in the dishes. I only ordered the things that should be made with egg substitutes."

Elbow on the table, Sarah plopped her face onto the upended palm of her hand. She shook her head. "Mom—Maybelle, I know from Harlan there's such a thing as a chain of evidence. Once we get up from this table with those boxes, Jane's lawyer, if she has one, will argue we tampered with the food before it was tested."

"Nonsense. We're going to protect the chain of evidence." Maybelle searched her pocketbook until she held up a black marker and a partial roll of masking tape. "This will do the trick. We'll seal the boxes and initial them."

Sarah stared at the tape and pen in her mother's hand. "Why in the world do you have masking tape in your purse? What else do you have in there, the kitchen sink?"

Her mother frowned. "I left the sink home today. The guild had a planning meeting at the church yesterday, and because I knew we needed to hang sheets of paper from a big pad on the wall, I brought the tape. Luckily for us, I forgot to take it out of my pocketbook last night."

It wasn't worth arguing with her mother. If she believed they'd be able to take the leftovers to a lab, so be it. Hopefully, the professionals Eloise called would find something before she and her mother left the restaurant.

Eloise arrived at the same time their waitress served their drinks. It amused Sarah that, like her mother had done with her, Maybelle didn't give her friend a choice of seats, either. Once Eloise was settled, Maybelle leaned forward conspiratorially.

"Well?"

"Well what?" From the twinkle in Eloise's eye, Sarah knew she was having a good time pulling her mother's leg.

"Did your people arrive?"

"They did."

"And, well?"

"Well what?"

Sarah stifled a laugh. Eloise obviously was having a ball running a version of "Who's on First?" on her mother. It was equally clear Maybelle's patience was wearing thin.

Eloise must have sensed she'd pushed the game far enough, because her expression flattened. She glanced at the tables around them. "They're here. They took samples from the dumpster, but that still doesn't conclusively prove the eggs in there necessarily belong to Jane's Place."

Maybelle pointed to the door to the kitchen as their waitress came through it carrying a large tray. "We'll have more than enough evidence in a moment."

"What do you mean?"

Maybelle didn't answer while the waitress placed

her tray on a nearby serving caddy and began empty-
ing their order onto their table.

Eloise's eyes widened as the plates and muffin bas-
ket soon covered the tabletop.

"Mother couldn't decide which vegan dishes to
try, so she ordered all of them."

"That's not true. I only ordered the three main
dishes Karen here highly recommended."

At the compliment, their waitress blushed. "Is
there anything else I can get you?" When they indicated in unison there wasn't, she hoisted her empty
tray from the caddy and carried it back into the
kitchen.

As the three sorted out the plates of food so they
each got a taste of everything but, as Maybelle reminded them, left enough of each to be boxed for
testing purposes, Jane came out of the kitchen. She
began visiting each table in the dining room.

Knowing Marcus and Emily took turns doing the
same thing during meal services at their restaurants,
she assumed Jane was either welcoming each group
of guests or checking on how they were enjoying
their meals. Sarah didn't know about Jane, but if anything was reported amiss to Marcus or Emily, they
not only immediately made it right but often
comped the guest either that portion of their meal
or a dessert. When Sarah first filled in as a server at
the original Southwind restaurant, Emily had explained the goal was for guests to leave with a good
taste in their mouth. Knowing the restaurant cared
and the staff or owners would make it right usually

meant that, even if something had gone wrong, a person would try the restaurant again.

When Jane reached their table, she smiled broadly. Although Maybelle and Eloise managed to respond with Cheshire cat grins, Sarah couldn't, even when Jane went out of her way to pointedly welcome her to Jane's Place. "I see you're sampling our vegan specialties. I certainly hope you're enjoying them."

"I am. In fact, I've got to commend you. This food is almost too good for me to believe it's vegan." Sarah fixed her gaze on Jane's completely relaxed face, while pushing her plate slightly in Jane's direction. "If I didn't know better, I'd think there were eggs in these dishes."

Jane laughed, but Sarah noted the previously relaxed thin lines around her mouth and eyes had tightened. "But then they wouldn't be vegan."

Eloise agreed. "Plus, I'm sure many of your patrons would be furious."

"Not to mention Riley would probably roll over in her grave." Maybelle took another bite of the food in front of her.

"Mother!" Sarah couldn't believe her mother was invoking the late Riley's name while the three of them were in the midst of a sleuthing sting.

Maybelle swallowed and stabbed another forkful of food. "Don't get so huffy. There's nothing sacrilegious about telling the truth. Everyone knows Riley's vegan recipes are what draw people to Jane's Place. You agree with that, don't you, Jane?"

Jane's relaxed posture and genuine smile were

gone. Watching the transformation, Sarah wasn't sure what she would term Jane's current expression.

"Maybelle, Riley was a lovely girl and it may be true her recipes contributed to our initial success, but I've modified each one considerably," Jane said through clenched teeth. "If you're enjoying what you're eating, they're my recipes, not Riley's."

A loud commotion in the kitchen and one of the kitchen staff sticking his head out the swinging door and calling for "Ms. Jane" interrupted anything else she might have said. Abruptly leaving them, Jane headed for the kitchen. She shoved the swinging door so hard it stuck in its open position.

Eloise followed. Maybelle started to stand, but Sarah put her hand on her mother's arm to restrain her. She kept it firmly in place, even when Maybelle tried to pull away. "Let me go. This is going to be good."

"Which is why you need to stay here with me. We can watch through the doorway. From the look of things, whatever inspectors Eloise called in, they've taken control of the kitchen." For a moment, it appeared Sarah's suggestion would do the trick to satisfy her mother, but someone pushed the door closed, leaving Maybelle and Sarah without ringside seats.

Sarah suggested they leave, but her mother refused. Although they couldn't make out every word, because of their proximity to the kitchen, they heard voices rising. Sarah was sure she also heard repeated mention of the word "egg."

After about ten minutes, other patrons began to

become aware something was happening, because nothing was coming out of the kitchen. Some called their waiters or waitresses over to their tables. Finally, Karen, the waitress assigned to their table, went to the swinging kitchen door. As Karen pushed through it, Sarah felt like every eye in the restaurant was watching her disappear into the kitchen.

She didn't come back.

CHAPTER THIRTY-TWO

The few minutes the kitchen door was closed seemed far longer than they were. When it opened, instead of Karen, it was Jane who entered the dining room. Although there were other times Sarah had seen Jane when her face was a few shades lighter than her flaming red hair, this time the two were almost indistinguishable.

A few steps into the room, Jane stopped. "I'm terribly sorry to disturb your lunches, but due to a problem in the kitchen, I'm going to have to ask all of you to leave." As people started to react to her request, she put her hands up, gesturing for silence. "Everything you've eaten is perfectly safe, but due to a problem beyond our control, we're going to have to close for the remainder of the day. We anticipate Jane's Place will be back in operation tomorrow. Of course, there is no charge for today's lunch, and because of this unfortunate and unexpected occurrence, if you stop at the hostess desk as you leave, you will be handed a voucher for a free entrée for your next visit."

Jane pointed to the hostess desk, which Karen had slipped behind. She waved an order pad and a stamp in the air. Although some people continued grumbling, many grabbed their coats and hurried to get their entrée voucher before a line formed. Standing in front of where Sarah and Maybelle still were, Jane effectively blocked them from exiting from their table while she repeated her apology a few more times until the restaurant emptied. Once the last patron left, she turned toward where Sarah and Maybelle were putting on their coats.

"I'll get you for this."

Maybelle moved out from behind her chair and stood toe to toe with Jane. "Are you threatening us?"

"What if I am?"

Standing erect, the older woman eyed the younger one. "Young lady, I'd think about your words before you let your tongue wag any further. Whether it's within the confines of this restaurant or outside of these walls, integrity is important. What are you going to get us for? Telling the truth about the food you've been serving? That wouldn't be one of the more brilliant things you do, but then again, as we well know, your actions haven't always reflected good judgment or, for that matter, any judgment."

"Mom." Sarah pulled at her mother's sleeve, but Maybelle shook her off. Locked in her eye war with Jane, she apparently wasn't about to let Sarah distract her. "Mom," Sarah repeated. "She isn't worth getting upset over."

Jane turned her venom on Sarah. "Look who's talking. You couldn't even keep your husband happy."

"How dare you? Bill's affair with you was his and your doing, not mine. Unlike the two of you, I didn't lie to him or anyone else. How could you tell people who were depending upon you your meals were vegan? What if someone had an egg allergy and died on your watch?"

Jane's face paled and her mouth dropped open.

As Sarah turned to pick up her purse and collect her mother, she didn't see Jane sink into the chair Eloise had vacated.

"I didn't think about that."

"What?" Sarah turned to face Jane, who sat with her face hidden by her hands, her shoulders quaking.

An escaping sob from behind Jane's hands dissipated Sarah's anger. She didn't pity Jane. Her behavior was abominable, but there was something that every now and then, like this moment, was a chink in Jane's armor. Perhaps what softened Sarah in these few instances was her own identification with the fear or vulnerability she thought Jane held inside her. "What did you say?"

Jane kept her face down as she raised her eyes to look at Sarah. "I said I didn't think about it. Southwind is going to be a big success, and I only wanted to be successful, too."

"But Emily and Marcus are doing it by hard work, not cheating."

"I didn't mean to cheat. When I tasted Riley's vegan dishes, I realized how good they were, and you have to admit everyone else agreed once we opened."

Sarah nodded but kept quiet, hoping Jane would continue.

She did. "It was only after we were already serving meals that I discovered every now and then Riley cheated a little with her ingredients. It wasn't much, but like your sister, Riley knew how to give a recipe that little something extra with spices or salt."

"That's not cheating. Emily enhances dishes without changing, disguising, or lying about what they are. Riley had that ability, too."

The rebuke flew over Jane's head. "After Riley died, I tried making one of her recipes and it was terrible. I doctored the tofu in it with spices and other things, but it only tasted right when I added an egg. We were busy that night, and people seemed to like it. Well, I wanted Jane's Place to be a success, so I reworked more of the recipes. Once I added a little butter and a few eggs, I couldn't stop people from ordering them, and I couldn't go back to the original recipes without losing customers."

Observing Jane's earnest reaction to the dilemma she'd created, Sarah couldn't help but ask what should have been, she thought, the logical solution to Jane's problem. "Why didn't you just take the vegan dishes off your menu?"

The look Jane shot her was the irritated one an exasperated adult might give a child who asked "Why" once too many times. "Because the vegan dishes were key to our identity. Riley's dishes and our reputation were tied together. That's what people were coming for. After she died, I was hoping to come up with something different in the weeks before Southwind opened, but Botts signed off so Southwind could open almost the next day. Even doctoring your sign to buy a few more days, I ran out of time."

The logical illogic of Jane's explanation almost lulled Sarah into understanding her when Sarah was jarred back to reality by one of the things Jane had admitted. "Are you saying Botts deliberately delayed the final inspection of Southwind?"

Jane wrung her hands. "I don't want to speak ill of the dead. Let me just say he had his way of doing things that benefitted him and people he liked. Who knows what accelerated Southwind's inspection? The way Botts worked, I thought, considering the strained relationship between Marcus and him, it would be weeks before he did Southwind's final inspection." Jane's lips curled into a pout. "I swear. I can never catch a break. What with Riley's murder, my needing to rework her recipes, and any time I might have had to figure things out lost when Botts moved the South-wind inspection to the top of his list . . ."

Sarah flinched and, for the moment, tuned Jane out. Maybe she was ultimately to blame in more ways than today's fiasco for Jane's Place being in trouble. There was no question she was the reason Southwind was inspected when it was. If she hadn't sweet-talked Botts, maybe Jane would have had more time to avoid the mess she was now in.

Thinking through the timing of things since Riley's death, Sarah's old fears of inadequacy crept into her mind, but she pushed them away. She hadn't been the one to put eggs and other ingredients into dishes and call them vegan. She hadn't lied to the public. Sarah didn't know what was going to happen to Jane's Place. The city would eventually release a report that the media would surely pick up, if they didn't first jump on the story because of Maybelle's tip. Probably the city would do nothing more than slap Jane's hand with a fine and require removal of the faux vegan dishes from the menu, but the negative impact of the media coverage of Jane's deceit and endangerment of the public was where the fallout would be. It was doubtful a new restaurant like Jane's Place could survive the field day the Wheaton newspaper and television stations would have with this story.

In retrospect, considering how many people tried the doctored vegan dishes, including the local paper's food critic, Sarah wondered why none of them queried whether eggs and dairy or some other recipe deviation made the food taste so good. She remembered reading a food critique once of a delicatessen that explained it was good and served kosher brand meats, but because the restaurant also served ham, it couldn't call itself a kosher deli. Instead, it had had to term itself "kosher style."

Perhaps Jane should have branded Jane's Place as "vegan style." Much like Southwind was going to have a few specifically health-related treats for people whose diets necessitated low salt, gluten-free, or whatever, Jane could have included a few true vegan recipes and had the others billed as styled.

Thinking about the restaurant's menu and figuring out what made everything taste so good seemed simple and potentially obvious. Sarah wondered if she was missing something equally obvious tied to Riley and Botts's deaths that would clear Jacob.

CHAPTER THIRTY-THREE

Sarah wanted to talk to Harlan immediately about what had happened at Jane's Place during Sarah's extended lunch hour. Unfortunately, he'd already gone to the courthouse for a pre-trial conference. When he returned to the office, he had a steady stream of clients.

After the last client left, Sarah powered down her computer. Before she turned off the coffee machine and emptied the remaining coffee, she picked up the pot and stuck her head into Harlan's office. Open and closed law books were strewn across his desk. He was so engrossed in researching some legal question that he didn't look up until she said his name.

"Do you want a last cup of coffee before I dump it?"

"Please." Harlan held out his cup, and she topped it off. "Heard you were in the midst of some excitement this afternoon at Jane's Place."

"How did you find out? I've been trying to tell you

about it all afternoon, but there wasn't a moment you weren't swamped."

"I could say a little birdie told me, but the truth is my last client was having lunch when the kitchen was closed down. She was trying to see if I knew any more than she did."

"What did she think she knew?"

"Not much. Apparently, she was one of the last to leave the room but noticed that rather than exiting like she did, you were still there, and Jane and you seemed like you were tussling about something."

When Sarah didn't volunteer any further information, Harlan took a sip of his coffee and raised his eyebrows. "So, are you going to tell me?"

Sarah sat in one of his guest chairs.

"This has to be good if it necessitates sitting down."

Sarah laughed. "It's sad, not funny." She explained to him how, after going out the back way from the vet clinic to meet her mother and Eloise, she was overcome by the smell of rotten eggs. When she looked for the source, she discovered the dumpster was overflowing with egg products.

Harlan's mouth dropped open. "Are you saying Jane used eggs in the dishes she claimed were vegan?"

"Yes."

He let out a short whistle. "That's a lawsuit waiting to happen. If someone became ill from Jane's food, it would be right up the alley of the law firm Grace's partner, Mandy, works at. Seriously, if this is as widespread as you say, I would be surprised if they don't end up with some clients suing Jane."

"There were lots of eggs served at Jane's Place. Believe me, Emily and Marcus use eggs, but not in that quantity. When I saw what I thought were far more eggs in the trash than a normal restaurant, I figured Jane must be using them in the vegan dishes everyone's been ordering."

"That's pretty good detective work. I bet most people wouldn't have made the connection." He leaned back waiting to hear more of Sarah's story, but Sarah was too busy enjoying Harlan's compliment of her deductive-reasoning skills. After almost two years of second-guessing everything she did, especially in Harlan's office, his compliment was something she couldn't help savor.

Finally, she remembered what he'd said. "Believe me, anyone overpowered by the stench would have started asking questions."

"But they probably wouldn't have made the connections you did. I'm actually a bit shocked."

Sarah frowned. So much for being excited by his compliment. "Why is that? Don't you think I'm capable of figuring things out on my own?"

"You're more than capable," Harlan hastened to assure her. "I was merely surprised you turned your findings over to the experts rather than taking things into your own hands."

She hated to tell him the truth, but wouldn't lie. "It was Eloise. She insisted on calling in the appropriate inspectors. I'm really not sure who she called, but without her I probably would have confronted Jane, blowing things up even worse than they are."

Sarah glanced out the window of Harlan's office.

There wasn't anything particular to see. A patch of grass, part of the street, and a limited amount of cement walkway. She knew, at one time, before the neighborhood had become run-down and then commercialized with offices like Harlan's, it was the starting point for many families. These families worked for their dreams, in the same way Emily and Marcus started with what was now the strip center Southwind Pub before finally opening an elegant dining restaurant on Main Street. They'd done it with hard work—not by cheating. Thinking about the Southwind Pub reminded Sarah she'd better address her other office closing tasks if she was going to be on time to meet the veterinarians.

Still concerned she was missing something obvious that might help Jacob, she invited Harlan to join the group meeting at the Southwind Pub. He not only accepted but, without being prompted, offered to finish closing things down so she could run home for a moment to take care of RahRah and Fluffy.

"How did you know I was going to stop home first?"

Harlan held up his hands and did a little bow with his head. "There's no way you'd leave RahRah and Fluffy much longer than this without checking their food and water. Besides, knowing Fluffy was under the weather yesterday, I know you want to eyeball her for a moment before going out, in case this drink turns into dinner." Harlan tapped his watch. "If you hurry, you can give Fluffy a short walk and squeeze in a moment of play with RahRah."

Sarah cocked her head to the side, sizing him up.

For being her employer, it sometimes amazed and frightened her as to how well he knew her. Maybe it was an inner intuitive sense or well-honed observation skills. Whichever, she knew these traits made him the lawyer she admired.

"Go."

She did.

CHAPTER THIRTY-FOUR

The world was right. As if turning her key in the door was her cue, Fluffy sat by the door, a mixture of patience and excitement. The sitting proved the puppy was getting the message of not jumping on people coming through the front door, but the constant movement of her tail and her barely being able to stay in her spot indicated Fluffy was feeling back to normal.

After dropping her keys in the bowl, Sarah bent and rubbed Fluffy behind the ears. "Good girl. Did you miss me today?"

Fluffy answered Sarah's rhetorical question by planting a wet lick on her cheek.

Still petting the puppy with one hand, Sarah dried her cheek with the back of the other. "We need to work on that, Fluffy."

The beseeching look in the pup's eyes made Sarah run her hand more deeply through Fluffy's fur. Down the hall, Sarah caught a glimpse of tan slipping into the kitchen. "Jealous?" she called, as she gave Fluffy one more good pat before rising and heading for the kitchen.

As if he hadn't just made his presence known to Sarah, RahRah ignored her while focusing his attention on his scratching post. Considering how infrequently RahRah used the scratching post, Sarah was convinced his present behavior was his version of being spiteful for either neglecting him or playing with the dog first. For either, Sarah knew the way to bring him around quickly.

Keeping up a steady patter of conversation, Sarah didn't stop to pet the active cat. Instead she went to the cupboard where she kept their food. She took out a can of RahRah's favorite extra-fancy wet cat food and picked up the can opener that had been her mother's. Although there were plenty of more modern can openers to be had, Sarah felt a sense of loyalty to this one.

The bribe worked. It amused her how easily Rah-Rah's disposition and attitude turned sunny. He came up to her and rubbed his body slowly against her leg, extending himself to his fullest.

Sarah always loved these quiet moments with RahRah so much more than the times he made sure she knew he was the alpha male in her life. She didn't blame him for, pardon the pun, wanting to be top dog. He'd earned the right, though she sometimes wondered how many of his nine lives he'd used along the way.

Any cat who survived almost drowning during a hurricane had to have used one life. True, he'd been adopted by the most wonderful woman, Sarah's ex-mother-in-law, Mother Blair, but then he'd lost her, which even Sarah mourned as a life loss. Happily, Sarah and the cat had become one, but circumstances had challenged their union, too. While she couldn't count how many lives he might have used, Sarah was sure of one thing: RahRah and she were bound together for the long run now.

"Here you go." She placed RahRah's dinner on the floor. He circled his bowl, tail in the air, acting as if he was sniffing its contents before he approved it. "Go ahead. You know it's your favorite."

Once Sarah was certain RahRah was eating and enjoying his meal, she returned to the cabinet and scooped out Fluffy's dinner portion. She placed her bowl on the opposite side of the kitchen. The puppy, who had stayed quiet throughout the time she spent with RahRah, let out a yip and attacked her bowl.

"Hungry?"

Sarah checked both of her pets' water bowls and then turned on the night-light on the stove so she wouldn't forget it when she left. Although she didn't leave every light in the house on for RahRah and Fluffy, she hated the idea of leaving them in the dark. Consequently, besides the one she'd just turned on, she always tried to leave lights on in the laundry room and the front hall.

Knowing her pets were otherwise occupied, she went to her bedroom and changed from her work clothes to a pair of jeans, a nice sweater, and short boots. She ran a brush through her hair and checked her lipstick before returning to the kitchen.

Fluffy had gobbled her meal down while RahRah

was still picking at his dinner in between rest breaks. From his contented purr as he lay stretched across the kitchen floor, Sarah knew he'd happily nibble on and off while she was gone. She checked the time and was glad to see she could take Fluffy for a quick walk before meeting everyone at the Southwind Pub.

CHAPTER THIRTY-FIVE

Sarah arrived at the Southwind Pub exactly at seven. Harlan, Carole, and Dr. Vera were already seated at a large round table, each with a different drink in front of them. Harlan had his usual neat scotch, and she was sure Vera's was the Pub's specialty Long Island Tea, but Carole's stumped her. She would have guessed beer because it was in a frosted mug, but she doubted any beer was ever garnished with a cherry. Sarah deliberately took the seat next to Dr. Vera, hoping the drink would loosen her tongue and because it guaranteed one of the other doctors would have to sit on Sarah's other side.

Harlan caught the attention of their waiter and indicated refills for all, and that Sarah needed to place an order. When the waiter, whom Sarah knew from the days when this was still the original Southwind restaurant, approached her, she ordered a glass of the house sauvignon blanc. She quietly made it clear to him she was buying only the first round for everyone, so he would need to run different tabs.

"No problem. Before you got here, Mr. Endicott filled me in on your plans for the first round and that he would cover drinks thereafter."

"Did he now?" Sarah glanced at Harlan.

He grinned back at her impishly, making her suspect he guessed what the waiter and she were discussing.

"Yes, ma'am. He did. I'll be back with your wine and the other drinks in a minute."

"Thank you."

Although it was slightly longer than a minute, the waiter was true to his word about his speed. He placed Sarah's wine in front of her just as Drs. Tonya and Glenn arrived.

"Perfect timing." Sarah quickly assumed the hostess role as the doctors settled in at the table, Dr. Glenn next to her and Dr. Tonya in the remaining seat next to Dr Vera. "What would you like?"

After two beers were ordered, full greetings were exchanged. "And please," Dr. Glenn said, "let's forget about the use of the doctor title tonight. We get enough of that at the clinic, right?"

While his two colleagues made sounds and motions of agreement, Sarah took advantage of the reference to the clinic to confirm her understanding that all three had had training in combatives. "I didn't realize until today that the three of you served together. I wouldn't have thought three veterinarians would have been assigned to the same unit."

"We don't usually talk about our military service," Tonya said.

Carole quickly interjected, "My fault, Tonya. It came

up when Sarah was in the waiting area when General Beau got so upset."

"As agitated as the General was, I was very impressed with how the three of you calmed him down, and that's when Carole filled me in on his history."

Vera pulled the bowl of nuts closer to her. "There's no secret we all served our country, but we weren't in the same unit. I met Glenn in basic training, but while we didn't serve together as veterinarians we kept in touch. Tonya started out as an animal handler with a unit that was later combined with the one Glenn was in."

She stopped and drank more of her Long Island Tea. "My relationship with Tonya predates our active duty time. We went to vet school together, both on military scholarships. After graduation, we began paying back our obligations at the same time. Even though we were sent to different duty stations, we remained friends. It was only through references in her letters to me that I realized my two friends had become friends."

"It's a small world," Sarah noted.

"And getting smaller every day," Harlan observed.

The other two doctors nodded in agreement as Vera continued, "When it came time to be discharged, it was a no-brainer to practice together. We never made a big deal one way or the other of being vets because we decided when we established the clinic it would be better to be known by either our individual names or by the clinic's name, rather than constantly hearing jokes about our service and career."

Glenn accepted his drink from the waiter. "That's

what she says. I always thought Three Veteran Vets had a fun ring to it, but I was outvoted by my partners."

"And it's a good thing you were," Carole said. "Could you see what kind of sign my brother would have put up if his partners had let him have his way. Our grandmother would probably have rolled over in her grave."

"Or, in her own patriotic way, Granny might have sat straight up and saluted us." He held his glass up. "In fact, I'll offer a toast to Granny because without her generosity, there wouldn't be a clinic."

Everyone clinked their glasses against his, except Carole. Sarah was curious why that was. "You know, I met your grandmother shortly before she moved to the retirement home. Bill, my ex, and I were getting settled in the big house and she brought us a pie as a welcoming gift."

"That sounds like Granny."

Carole nodded. "She loved to bake. Was it a Granny Smith apple pie? They were her favorite. When we were kids, she supplied her own apples from a giant tree out back, where the parking lot is now."

Sarah could see the old lady delivering the pie in her mind, but she didn't recall anything except being in such a tizzy that she'd merely said thank you without inviting the woman in. She'd never had a chance to reciprocate because Glenn and Carole's granny moved to the retirement home a few days later.

"It might have been an apple pie, but I don't really remember. It was a long time ago now. Speaking of long ago, after she died, your house sat vacant for years. Although it was kept up well, it always looked so lonely. I'm glad the two of you decided to bring it back to life."

"That's all Glenn's doing. It's his house. I'm merely the beneficiary of my big brother's altruistic nature."

A hush fell over the table before Glenn, staring at his sister, picked up the conversation. "Granny did different things for each of us." He turned his attention back to everyone at the table. "When Granny died and left me the house, I was in vet school on a military scholarship. That meant I still had to finish school and give Uncle Sam back a few years. I guess I could have sold the house, but I'd always loved it. When I ran the numbers, I realized, other than taxes and maintenance, there were no big expenses associated with keeping the house vacant until I finished my commitment and could decide what I wanted to do with the rest of my life."

"Luckily," Tonya said, "Glenn became friends with Vera and me. We helped convince him Wheaton and his house would be the perfect location for our animal clinic."

"Once they had me convinced the house could work for what we wanted to do, things fell into place. I met Jacob, who helped us tremendously and who introduced me to Cliff."

"Of course, part of twisting Glenn's arm was that Tonya and I just happened to be available to staff the clinic with him." Vera winked. "We knew he couldn't do it without us."

Glenn rolled his eyes as he glanced at the ceiling. "What choice did I have? When these two decide on a course of action, beware!"

"I've learned how that goes." Harlan nodded toward Sarah.

This time, everyone, except Sarah, laughed. Instead, she bristled at his comment. She cut their merriment off by bringing up the more morbid subject of Botts's death. "I understand one of the reasons Botts died was his helmet didn't adequately protect his head. When I told Eloise I didn't understand why his helmet didn't work, she suggested I ask the three of you about the Wildcats and the different types of helmets people wear."

The three vets looked at one another before Tonya finally spoke. "We really don't like to speak ill of the dead."

Recognizing this as a similar theme when it came to anyone talking about Botts or Riley, Sarah hastened to reassure the veterinarians. "Oh, I'm not asking you to. I want to help Jacob if possible, but I don't know anything about motorcycles or motorcycle gear. Eloise calls herself a retiree Wildcat, who only knows enough to have fun. She said the three of you are more hardcore riders who can explain bikes and helmets better."

Trying to read each of their faces and body language, Sarah decided Tonya's serious expression and clasped hands still meant she didn't want to talk about this subject, whereas Glenn didn't really seem to mind. He made it clear however his interest was in eating when he signaled the waiter back to their table and asked for a menu.

"I hope you don't mind. I was so busy today I didn't have time for lunch. The Southwind Pub has such great burgers I figured I'd kill two birds with one stone. Anyone else hungry?" He offered the menu to the rest of the table. After everyone placed an order and the waiter left with the menu, Glenn turned back to Sarah. "I don't know that I'd call any of us hardcore riders, but ask away."

"Okay, let's start with his helmet? Was it like the ones you wear?"

Tonya snorted. "Not in the slightest. I wouldn't be caught dead in a pudding bowl helmet."

When no one else laughed at the description of his helmet as a pudding bowl, Sarah stifled her inclination to giggle at the image. Maybe, except for her, they'd all already heard the joking reference and it was no longer funny to them.

"Botts liked looking fashionable. Safety wasn't always his top priority." Vera stopped talking when Tonya cleared her throat.

Sarah wondered what the dynamics were between the two of them. It also dawned on her that the pudding bowl description might not have been a bad joke. "I don't think I understand. Is pudding bowl an actual type of helmet?"

"Yes," Vera said. "Helmets come in all sizes and shapes. Glenn and Tonya wear full face helmets, which are designed to give the maximum protection. Their helmets cover their entire heads. They have immovable pieces that protect the skull and chin. In order to talk or eat, they take their helmets off. I prefer a little more flexibility but still want safety, so I use a flip-up or modular helmet. It comes down and covers my skull the same way as theirs, but my chin bar can be flipped up or removed." She pantomimed flipping up her chin bar.

"Botts was one of the riders who went crazy on the aftermarket stuff. Because he liked to go more for show. He preferred the look of a pudding bowl helmet that was open in the front and didn't come down far in the back." Vera traced the shape in the air with a long, thin finger. "It has good lines, doesn't mess the hair quite as badly, and is showier than ours. The pudding bowl helmet also doesn't have a chin piece. Basically, it doesn't cover more than the top of the head, ears, and cheeks. Botts was a top-of-the-line, showy-versus-safety guy."

"I ride a pretty well-outfitted Harley," Glenn said, "but Botts's Mercedes was as decked out with aftermarket stuff as he could get. If that wasn't enough, he dressed to match his bike."

"What do you mean?"

"If you looked closely at his handlebars and grips on any given day, you'd notice there was a stripe of the same color on the side of his pants and jacket. He also had coordinated blue, black, and red pairs of gloves."

"Did he have different helmets to match his outfits?"

"No, only one, but he used different colored stickers on it so it would coordinate, too. There's no guarantee our type of helmet would have protected him the way his bike fell, especially if the gossip that his helmet had a split in it before the accident is true, but there is no question the design of his helmet didn't serve the purpose he needed when he hit. Whether or not his helmet was already damaged is meaningless. It was the chest injury he sustained from the handlebar or whatever hit him rather than bashing the back of the head, where he had no helmet protection, that was fatal."

"How horrible." Sarah shuddered.

Carole echoed her sentiments. "No matter what we thought about him as a person"—her voice trailed off but then picked up again—"at least he died doing something he truly enjoyed."

So far, other than superficial "Bless his heart" comments, like Carole's, no one had really said anything nice about Botts. Even though she'd previously said she wasn't interested in what they thought of him, Sarah decided to try to find out. "You've all mentioned knowing Botts in different ways. Would you help me get a picture of him for Jacob or Riley's sake?"

It seemed like it was the mention of Jacob's name that melted them because they all started talking at once until Harlan raised his hand and, in a voice between a schoolteacher's and a litigator's, said, "One at a time, please. Let's go around the table. Glenn, why don't you start."

As Glenn shifted position in his chair and played with his drink, Sarah wished Harlan had started with one of the women. Sarah had a feeling something important was bubbling right below the surface with them. Because she was afraid Glenn's reluctance to talk might affect the others, she intervened and pointed to the women sitting at the table. "Now, Harlan. You can't ask Glenn to go first on a night he's outnumbered. Ladies first, please."

"I'll start, but realize I can't speak for the experiences everyone had." Tonya gestured with her hand to include everyone at the table. "The one thing all of us have in common when it comes to Botts is that at some point in time we went out with him."

"Whoa," Glenn said. "Don't count me in there. I rode with Botts a few times, but I never dated him. In fact, I wasn't too thrilled when my sister went out with him."

Sarah wondered when Carole went out with Botts, but she wanted to keep Glenn's train of thought going. "What did you have against him?"

Glenn paused before answering. He looked at Carole, but rather than meeting his gaze, she concentrated on a spot on the table. "Botts was a narcissistic show-off. Whether it was his ride, his gear, or simply himself, he had an attitude of entitlement. There were times he reminded me of an impulsive eighteen-year-old strung out on steroids. Guys like that don't necessarily tend to be safe riders or nice human beings."

Sarah was confused. She understood his feelings for Botts were negative, but she didn't understand if Glenn's reference to steroids was his way of saying Botts had been doing drugs or something that wasn't on the up-and-up. "What do you think he was doing?"

Glenn squirmed in his seat. "It's not like I really know. He always gave me the feeling he was slimy and holding his hand out for something, so I tried to avoid the guy. What I couldn't avoid were the rumors circulating about how he scheduled and conducted city inspections."

Harlan leaned across the table. "Glenn, was he taking bribes?"

"I can't say. That's what I heard, but he never outright asked me for money. Still, there was something tied to his last inspection of the clinic that didn't sit right with me."

"Was that the only reason you didn't want to ride with him?" Harlan asked.

For a moment, Glenn sucked his cheeks in and pressed his lips together. "No, that was only part of why I stopped signing up for rides with him."

"What was the rest?" Harlan kept the timbre of his voice strong.

"I didn't like the way he treated the female members of the Wildcats. He was dismissive, rude, and patronizing."

This was one of those times when Sarah wanted to say, "Tell me what you really think," but she bit her tongue. Better to let him keep rambling or have one of the others disagree with him. Only, no one did.

CHAPTER THIRTY-SIX

"We don't want to come across as unfeeling about Botts's death," Carole said. "Although we all appreciate the round of free drinks, I think I can speak for all of us. We're here this evening because of Jacob. We're afraid he's being railroaded for something none of us believe he could possibly have done. When it comes to Botts, to steal an idea from an old song, he basically done us all wrong."

"In what way?"

"In every way, but it didn't seem that way in the beginning." Carole glanced at the two female doctors, who both nodded. She swallowed, but instead of speaking, Carole plucked the cherry from her glass. She examined it and dropped it back into her drink.

Tonya rested her hand on Carole's arm but stared at Vera, who nodded.

"Carole," Sarah said, "you were saying something about how Botts was in the beginning?"

"When I dated him." She paused and took a deep breath before letting her words tumble out. "Let me back up. I was, I guess, the first one to have any kind of relationship with Louis. We met at a party when I was a freshman in college. I could tell he was older than me, but I thought he was another student. It wasn't until after we started dating that I learned not only was he charming, kind, and handsome, he was closer to my brother's age and, as he called it, taking a sabbatical that focused on yoga, Wing Chun, and getting high. He didn't have the swagger he developed later, but he was demanding. I fell quickly. To accommodate him and the activities he loved, I moved in with him and stopped going to classes."

This time, when Carole paused, she looked at her brother. "Unfortunately, by the end of the year, when he dropped me for someone else, I'd flunked out, developed a nasty habit, and was bouncing around from place to place because I was homeless. Glenn and Granny picked up the pieces. They got me into rehab and supported me while I got clean." Carole held up her glass. "It may not seem like a lot when I toast Granny each day with a glass of soda, but it's another milestone for both of us."

Vera picked up the conversation's thread. "I got to know Botts shortly after we opened our clinic. Being new to Wheaton, I thought joining the Wildcats would be a good way to meet people, especially other veterans. Botts was on one of my first rides with the group, and he invited me to join him and a few of the riders for a bite after we rode. I had a pleasant time, and when he asked me to dinner that weekend, I accepted. During dinner, when I clarified where I'd seen active duty, he told me he'd been in the military, too. Out of the blue, he asked if I was familiar with Rolling Thunder. When I said yes, he implied he took part in it."

Sarah couldn't remember what Rolling Thunder was, so she interrupted Vera to ask as the waiter put their meals on the table.

"Rolling Thunder has been a special ride in DC from the Pentagon to the Vietnam Memorial Wall to commemorate veterans missing in action. It started out as a fairly small rally in 1987, but grew to over three hundred fifty thousand veterans and others participating."

Tonya lifted her glass, signaling the waiter for a re-fill. "Even though it's been a fixture for years, it may be discontinued."

Harlan swallowed a bite of his bacon cheese-burger. "I hadn't heard anything about that."

"Everything I know is secondhand, so I'm not wholly sure of the details or if it's simply a rumor. What I understand is, despite it bringing in plenty of people staying overnight in hotels, spending money, and respecting our veterans, the security and other considerations involving the Pentagon since nine-eleven have made the costs higher and the logistics more difficult. It looks like money is going to out-weigh respect."

Sarah could see how the thought of the DC rally being canceled could upset Tonya, but she was curi-ous how the rally tied in with Botts and the other doctors. "Did any of you ever ride in Rolling Thun-der?"

"Tonya did it first," Vera said. "When she de-scribed how meaningful it was for her to be with so many other vets, I joined her the following year. Considering its mission is bringing attention and accountability to our prisoners of war and soldiers from all wars who are lost in action, Botts's outrageous boasting irked me. While he made a big deal of having been part of it, things he said showed me he'd obviously never done more than read about the rally. His lack of credibility completely turned me off. There were other things that evening, but let's just say after that date, our only other interaction was when we passed at Wildcat rides and when he got mad when some of us tried to warn Riley about him."

Hearing there was a possibility of a direct connection with Riley caught Sarah's attention. Not wanting to act too excited, she picked up a french fry and nibbled at it while she tried to figure out how to succinctly ask the journalists' Five Ws questions. "Who was trying to warn Riley and about what?"

Tonya tapped her fingers against her empty glass. "Vera and I tried to warn Riley about what a scuzzbag Botts was when we saw she was begging rides from him. She refused to listen to us. In fact, Riley accused us of being jealous of the attention he was paying her."

Once again, Harlan quietly cut into the conversation. "Were you?"

Sarah glanced from Tonya to Harlan. As tightly wound as Tonya appeared, Harlan seemed as interested in eating his cheeseburger as he was in waiting for her answer.

"Of course not. We hated seeing him take advantage of her."

Vera took over the conversation. "Being older, if not wiser, we simply wanted to share the wisdom from our encounters with him, but she was having none of it. We can't imagine what he planted in her head about us, but she was head over heels for him."

"Are you sure she wasn't taking advantage of him?" After she posed her question, Sarah was sure she saw a look exchanged between Vera and Tonya, but she couldn't read it. She decided to take a stab in the dark. "Tonya, Carole told us what he did to her. Did he do something to you, too."

"Sorry. Ours was more of a metaphysical relationship while we served together, but it was over by the time we were both in Wheaton. I can safely say he wouldn't have dared treat me like he did Carole."

"Why not?" Shocked that the words slipped out with such force, Sarah clapped her hand over her mouth.

Tonya laughed. "I'd heard others say you were the curious one, but in all the times I've seen you with RahRah, I never realized how much so."

Sarah's face warmed at the rebuke "That's because when I see you professionally, my worry level overtakes my normally inquisitive nature. I stand in your office, in my own zone, in awe of how all of you interact with RahRah and make him relax. Plus, no matter how worried I am about RahRah, you have a knack for calming me, too." She reached for another french fry, but instead of eating it, she held it in mid-air. Remembering how well distracting Dr. Tonya with Fluffy had worked at Sarah's house, Sarah thought maybe another animal distraction would help now.

"I know this is a little off subject, but there's one dog at the shelter I wish you could help find a home.

He's been there the longest, but Buddy is so sweet I hate to see him not having a forever home."

"The dog with only three good legs who's losing his sight?" Carole asked.

"Yes. You know him, too?" Sarah hoped Carole's knowledge of Buddy was from her being at the shelter rather than the clinic having to treat him. "Is he okay? Did something happen that Phyllis brought him to the clinic since I walked him Saturday?"

"Oh, no. He's fine. We all know Buddy from our work at the shelter."

Sarah relaxed at Carole's assurance, almost not hearing Glenn explaining in more detail how the clinic staff interacted with the shelter.

"Because it's important to keep an eye on things when you've got a lot of animals in close quarters, one of us visits the shelter at least once a week for what you might describe as well-animal visits. Carole accompanies whoever goes. My sister claims she plays no favorites, but she always seems to have a few treats for her special friend, Buddy. I keep waiting for her to bring him home. I've even told her we have a run she could dedicate with his name."

Carole threw her napkin at her brother, which he successfully ducked. "Buddy needs a forever home, not one with a person who doesn't know how long she'll be staying in Wheaton."

Afraid Glenn might return fire and she'd lose total control of this session, Sarah quickly brought everyone's attention back to Tonya and Botts. Instead of seeming as edgy as she had only a few moments earlier, Tonya smiled.

"Okay, I guess it's still my turn on the hot seat."

Saying he hoped it would make Tonya's hot seat easier to tolerate, Harlan ordered another round for the table.

"There really isn't much to tell. Except for a few periods of leave, the three of us designed our Wheaton clinic through letters and e-mails to each other, sent from our various duty stations. We were able to figure out what we needed in the clinic and exactly where things should be placed by using a computer modeling program. The only thing left was putting it all together. Because I was mustered out first, I got the short straw of moving here and implementing our plans. The remodeling with Cliff and ordering the equipment went smoothly. The only rough spot was Botts. He tried to strong-arm me in different ways, but I wasn't having any of it. I didn't take that kind of thing from anyone when I was in the service, and I certainly wasn't going to put up with his nonsense when I had a mission to accomplish."

Thinking of the problems getting him to perform Southwind's inspection, Sarah asked if he'd delayed things for the clinic.

"He tried, but I called him out on it."

"And that worked?"

"No. What worked was showing him a new catalog of aftermarket motorcycle parts and accessories and telling him I had a credit and a forty percent customer satisfaction discount to use on my next order. Although I wouldn't buy anything for him, I offered to include anything he wanted to purchase to what I was getting. Of course, I explained, I couldn't put the order in until I knew the clinic would be completed on schedule because if there were overruns from things being delayed, I might not be able to afford to make an order. Botts showed up the next morning and did our final inspection. I put the order in, with what he wanted. Once the merchandise arrived, I didn't want anything more to do with that slimeball."

"How did Riley fit in?"

"Remember, because of Jacob's interest in economic development and Main Street, Glenn had met Jacob, who'd introduced him to Cliff. I don't know if the chicken or the egg came first, but when I was overseeing the remodeling job, the three of us started having drinks together and became friends. When Jacob invited me to go with Cliff and him to a student culinary exhibition that a friend of theirs was a part of, I accepted. That's when I met Riley."

Listening to Tonya, Sarah wondered if Cliff had ever had an interest in her. If he had, she doubted he'd done anything about it. As professional as he was, she didn't think he'd date anyone while he was remodeling their home.

"Anyway, Riley had me at the first bite. Her food was delicious. I hung around after the exhibition and complimented her on her food. She was gracious, but, in retrospect, her attitude was that it was almost her due."

"That's how she was when I joined the Wildcats," Vera said. "Did you find that there, too, Tonya?"

"I did. By now, Sarah, you know not all Wildcats ride together. It depends on interest, distance to be ridden, and even by friendships. When I joined the

Wildcats, because I knew Jacob and Cliff, I usually rode with their group. Riley was a regular on the back of Jacob's bike, so we saw each other every week. We became friends. Once Vera started riding with us, she, Riley, and I became the female threesome in the group until Riley took up with Botts instead of Jacob. When we told her what we thought of Botts, she stopped riding and hanging out with us."

Sarah thought their story sounded much like the break in Riley and Grace's relationship. "Do you know of any other friendships, like yours with Riley, that she ended in a similar way or that might have made her some enemies?"

Tonya tightened her lips. "Riley was a user. Once you were used up, like us, that was it, unless she held you in limbo in case she needed something more, like Jacob."

"Were there others like Jacob?"

Although Tonya couldn't come up with any other names, Vera did. "She once introduced us to her apartment manager. I think his name began with a 'D.' After he walked away, she boasted to us how the building had two rent-controlled apartments for lower-income individuals, and he'd managed to do something with the paperwork to get her place designated as one."

"I know you all are partial to Jacob, but were Riley and Botts a good match?"

"If you ask me, they suited each other perfectly." Tonya clammed up when the waiter reached in front of her to remove her plate. While he cleared the table and handed out their checks, Tonya and Vera retrieved their helmets from the floor. Afraid they would leave, and her moment lost, Sarah put a charge card, rather than cash, in the check holder's credit card pocket. She hoped it might increase the time the waiter needed to close the table out.

"Tonya, why did they suit each other perfectly?"

"Because both were snakes."

"Do you think Botts might have killed Riley and then had an unrelated accident?"

Vera stood. "Tonya and I have talked about that very question, but we don't think so. Riley cared about Botts, but he wasn't that into her. She was more of a passing fancy that he would simply have walked away from rather than physically harming. It wouldn't have been his style. Right, Tonya?"

Tonya bobbed her head in agreement.

As the waiter returned, Sarah addressed a final question to everyone at the table before they had an opportunity to leave. "If we rule out Botts as her killer, can you think of any enemies Riley had or anyone she'd had a falling out with?"

"Not really," Vera said. "Both Botts and Riley irritated a lot of people with their mouths and how they treated others, but not enough for anyone to kill either of them."

Sarah didn't have any follow-up to Vera's comment, nor did anyone else at the table. Instead, everyone stood, gathered their belongings, and said their farewells. Dr. Vera reminded Sarah to bring Fluffy, now that she was feeling better, in for her booster vaccine as soon as possible.

As the two female doctors walked toward the rear of the restaurant, where the restrooms were, Carole cut off the continuing idle chatter Sarah and she were having about Fluffy and her vaccines. Carole kept her voice low, but there was no mistaking the urgency in it. "I think Vera drank too much to safely drive her bike. Glenn can hold a second rider on the back of his, but it would be safer if Harlan would take her home, too. He brought me tonight. Vera's place might be a bit out of his way, but he's already taking me home, so maybe he wouldn't be too inconvenienced. Will you help me convince her she should pick up her bike in the morning?"

"Of course." Sarah had lost count of how many Long Island Teas Vera had had, but the number didn't matter as much as their potency. Although Vera seemed like she hadn't reached a point the Southwind Pub should have cut her off, she trusted Carole knew Vera's tolerance and might be aware of Vera's level of expertise with a motorcycle.

It was obvious to Sarah, from the sudden droop in Carole's shoulders, that she relaxed immediately once Sarah agreed to help convince Dr. Vera she'd had one Long Island Tea too many to drive. Sarah prayed it wouldn't be a hard sell.

Sarah glanced in Harlan's direction to enlist his help, but he was talking to Glenn. She had hoped to have an opportunity to talk with him after everyone else left the pub, but as he had at least one passenger, that would have to wait until tomorrow. Hopefully, he'd heard something helpful this evening, because she didn't think she had.

Apparently, Carole felt the same way. "I hope we helped in some way tonight, but nothing jumped out at me."

Sarah decided to be positive, even if she didn't feel they'd accomplished anything.

"Who knows when something will make a connection? I've read that sometimes things come together subliminally."

"Then, for Jacob's sake, I hope something one of us said or did will help you have a lightbulb moment. Oh, here come the doctors."

Tonya strode quickly through the restaurant. An ashen Vera followed a few steps behind her. "Vera's not feeling too well. We all rode our bikes, but she's willing to leave hers here if someone can give her a ride home."

"Harlan?"

Harlan stopped talking with Glenn and turned toward the sound of Sarah's voice.

"Vera is feeling ill. You drove. Would you give her a lift home?"

Sarah could almost see the wheels turning in Harlan's head as he took in her words, Vera's washed-out complexion, and the concerned looks on Carole's and Tonya's faces. "Certainly." He offered his arm to Vera, who took it. "Sarah, I'm driving Carole back to the clinic. Do you want a ride, too?"

"No thanks. It's only a couple of blocks, and I need the exercise."

CHAPTER THIRTY-SEVEN

Sarah stopped by the side of the hostess stand while she zipped up her jacket and put on her gloves. She was delighted at how quickly the waiter and busboy cleaned the round table her group had vacated, followed by the hostess immediately seating another large group. She scanned the restaurant. Every Southwind Pub table was full of food and, more important, from a profitability standpoint, alcohol or other drinks. Sarah might not understand how the food served was prepared, or, truth be told, care, but the need for customers, what they ordered, and how often tables flipped was something she easily comprehended.

Outside, the air was crisp, the kind where the fall cold snuck up on a person. She flexed her hands in her gloves, glad to have them on. She couldn't count on her fingers and toes how many times she'd stuffed her hands in her pockets because her gloves were at home. After one time too many, she now opted to keep them in her coat pocket until needed, rather than in a drawer in her bedroom.

Cutting back to the quiet of Main Street, she tried to process tonight's get-together in her mind. She wasn't sure she'd discovered anything that necessarily helped Jacob, but she'd learned a lot in the past few days. It nagged at her that she was missing a clue that was in plain sight.

When it came to Botts and Riley, Sarah concluded there was no question people had intense negative feelings about both. If Riley was killed by someone with military or martial arts experience, it seemed that included everyone, even a dog. Thinking about General Beau, she wondered what therapy worked against doggy PTSD. Buddy might have an uneven gait, but his personality was so easygoing compared to the General's.

Hypothetically, only because she didn't think he'd killed himself, if she eliminated Botts as responsible for Riley's death, she still had plenty of suspects she couldn't fully rule out.

Chief Gerard's focus was on Jacob because of Jacob's relationship with Riley, his angry outbursts with other people she dated, his being the only one on the scene when Riley was found dead, and his having a fight with Botts at the parking pad the morning Botts died. Stacked up against many of the other suspects, Jacob, Sarah had to admit, provided Chief Gerard with several reasons to view him as the killer. The problem was that the crime didn't fit Jacob's nature. It was obvious that even if one test came back that could be tied to a circumstantial case against Jacob, there would be an immediate arrest.

There were many people who had military or defensive training. Although their line of work would have given them the knowledge necessary to kill Riley, she ruled out Chief Gerard, Officer Robinson, and Dr. Smith as not having a motive. For reasons far more personal than analytical, she also felt safe taking Cliff off her suspect list. At the same time, because they'd all dated Botts or been used by Riley, she didn't think she could remove Tonya, Vera, Glenn, or Carole. Tonya and Vera seemed to have fared better in their relationships with Botts than Carole, but Sarah realized she needed more information about their interactions with Riley.

She hated to think it, but Glenn probably had one of the best motives for killing Botts. He obviously loved his sister, and Botts had almost destroyed her. Glenn seemed caring and generous, but she'd also seen his greedy business side. Could the crowd coming to Jane's Place for Riley's dishes and the complaints Jane filed have been a problem for him? Could Botts have been holding something over him relating to licensing or zoning that might have impacted his finances?

What about Jane? She had access to the motorcycle pad, and she certainly hated the barking dogs. But why would she kill the goose that was laying her golden egg? Perhaps a fit of jealousy? Maybe Riley, who had also tinkered with the vegan dishes, was blackmailing Jane that she'd reveal the truth. Jane would have known that would be the end of her restaurant.

Jacob wasn't the only person who'd dated or was rejected by Riley. Sarah was already aware of ties to Botts, Glenn, the apartment manager—Daniel, that was his name—and even Cliff, but from what Grace said, there were plenty of names Sarah didn't know. She wasn't even sure how to discover everyone who had been part of Riley's revolving door of adoring men.

What about Grace and Mandy? As much as Sarah cared for Grace, there was no way she wanted to think of her as a possible murder suspect, but her motive to kill Riley also was one of the greatest. Not only had Riley interfered with her getting jobs out of school, Riley had taken the job she beat Grace out for and had become a star at Jane's Place. In the meantime, Grace was working long hours for a restaurant that might or might not get off the ground. With Riley out of the way, the path was open for Grace to become Jane's executive chef. Sure, Grace had turned the recent offer down, but she also said Jane hadn't closed the door on the discussion. Grace, once things calmed down, could accept the job and end up far ahead careerwise from the point Emily and Marcus could offer her. Sarah paused. Grace was a friend. Could Sarah be so wrong about someone?

And what about Mandy? Grace herself said Mandy had her back. Maybe Grace had the motive, but, in her love for Grace, perhaps Mandy was the one who did the dastardly deed to achieve Grace's goals. She certainly had a hard enough edge.

Although more scrupulous in her interpretation of vegan recipes than Jane, Riley still doctored her recipes. That also translated into her interactions with other people. There was no question her friendships with Tonya, Vera, and Jacob took a hit when Botts came into the picture, but what about with some of the other Wildcats or, for that matter, the people where Riley lived? If Sarah added in Riley's apartment manager and neighbors, that also made Grace a suspect. No, that couldn't be.

If it turned out Botts's bike was tinkered with, Jacob wasn't the only one who could have done it. There were plenty of Wildcats who easily had the same access to the motorcycles parked on the pad as Jacob on the day of their fight. For that matter, what if whatever went wrong with his motorcycle was done earlier? How many movies had Sarah seen where brake lines were tampered with but the accident didn't happen for hours or days? There was no telling how many people had access to his cycle when it was parked near Jane's Place or anywhere else Botts left it unattended before his fateful ride. She needed to check with Harlan to find out if Chief Gerard had a report back and if the police had retraced Botts's steps over the past few days.

Were Riley and Botts's murders done by the same person or were there different motives involved? For example, did Botts murder Riley out of anger? What if Chief Gerard was right about Jacob? That couldn't be, but what if? Could someone have taken advantage of Jacob's jealous rage with anyone tied to Riley and used it as a cover for killing Botts? There were plenty of people who had motives: For Glenn and Carole, it might have been the drugs; for Carole, Vera, and Tonya, it might have been tied to their dating relationships; perhaps the apartment manager was as jealous as Jacob was when Botts moved in on his "Riley territory"; maybe Botts's behavior about his military service ticked someone off; perhaps Botts irked the more hardcore Wildcats with his showboating and rude ways; or, the most likely—what if Botts's apparently shady dealings as the city's building inspector caused someone major delays and economic losses like it did with Marcus and Emily. Any of these scenarios was possible, but one thing Sarah was certain about, everyone, including her, had a different opinion of Botts, and none were flattering.

What about the silver motorcycle Sarah and Jacob saw? Was it one or two motorcycles? Did they see the same person riding it? This lead didn't look promising. It appeared that at least half the suspects and an infinite number of Wildcats rode silver motorcycles. Just from those on the parking pad, she wondered how many silver ones had been in the buy Glenn negotiated.

Finally, what was she missing? Something still nagged at the back of Sarah's mind, but she couldn't grasp it. Maybe when she talked to Harlan, something he picked up on would help her find her missing link.

CHAPTER THIRTY-EIGHT

When Sarah reached the new Southwind restaurant's driveway, she paused and looked across Main Street at Jane's Place and the edge of its parking lot. Jane's Place was open for dinner, but unlike the past few weeks, the parking lot was empty. She bet the word about Jane and her recipes was out on the street or had appeared either online or in a print news article.

As Sarah walked up Southwind's driveway, she saw its parking lot was full. She was delighted Southwind was doing so well. Although she knew she should continue up the driveway to the carriage house because RahRah and Fluffy were home alone, she decided to stick her head into Southwind and say hello to her twin.

Inside, Southwind felt even busier than its parking lot suggested. Tables were full, waiters and waitresses were moving swiftly with trays of food and drinks, and the noise level reflected a satisfied group of guests. Through the open kitchen, Sarah spotted Marcus and Grace respectively expediting and working with the chefs on the line. It was obvious the kitchen staff was hopping.

Sarah scanned the restaurant for Emily until she saw her, a pile of menus in her hands, seating some guests. Tonight, rather than her white chef's coat, Emily was wearing a black dress. Either the hostess hadn't shown or Emily and Marcus thought it best Emily ensured table seating flowed, problems were immediately addressed, and customers felt welcome. They were big believers that even the best food coming out of the kitchen didn't matter if a diner's experience was ruined by poor management of the front of the house.

When Emily returned to the hostess station, Sarah sidled up to it as if she were adding her name to the waitlist. "Whew! You are busy!"

"It's been like this since we opened our doors tonight. We've been running a fifteen-to-thirty-minute wait time since seven."

"I better get out of the way before someone thinks I'm cutting in line."

"That's okay. We've got a few minutes until a table opens and I can seat anyone else. How did tonight's drink go?"

"The quick answer is I don't think it produced any new information, but it sure added to my list of questions. Speaking of those, how did you know about tonight's drink? I don't remember mentioning it to you."

"I may be busy here tonight, but I'm keeping my finger on the pulse of the Southwind Pub, too. My manager told me you were there buying a round for a group. He wanted to know if he should comp the round and any of the subsequent drinks or meals."

"They billed my credit card, so I gather you told him no."

"I did. I didn't want to give him the impression it's okay to play favorites if I'm not around or haven't approved the person."

Sarah wondered how much closer than a sister one had to be for preapproval by Emily. "Thanks."

As Emily turned to greet new customers coming to the stand to add their names to the wait list, she laughed. "Don't worry, I'll pull the slip and credit you tomorrow. By the way, Anne and Jacob are at table sixteen, by the windows."

With the numbering system revised after Southwind's two days of soft openings, "table sixteen" meant nothing to Sarah, but she didn't want to interrupt Emily to ask her to point it out. Emily was already busy chatting up the customers who had approached the hostess station. For a moment, Sarah watched Emily juggle writing down names, taking cell phone numbers or giving out electronic beepers, and notifying and seating a group when their table was ready. This was the epitome of multitasking, and, as always, Emily made it look easy.

Thinking about how chaotic it would be if she were the one working the hostess desk tonight, Sarah went to what they called the window side of the dining room. Pairs of lead-glass windows set off a bay window area that was large enough for two tables or one large party. The view of a small wooded area, which backed up to a similar one on her neighbor's property, was quite peaceful. Sarah especially loved it in the spring and summer when birds often nibbled at feeders Sarah and her neighbor had interspersed in their trees. Sarah hoped her neighbor never moved, but if he did, she prayed anyone buying the property would agree to keep the buffer zone between them.

Anne and Jacob weren't seated in the bay window area, but they were a twosome eating at a table for four near one of the lead windows. As Sarah made her way to their table, Anne waved for her to join them. Knowing her sister's menu, she recognized the few remnants on Anne's plate as the last of a vegetable plate dinner. Jacob's meal took no guessing as his steak and potatoes were barely touched.

"I don't want to disturb your meal. I simply wanted to say hello. Jacob, I'm glad to see you out and about."

"Yeah, but I don't know how much longer that's going to last. Harlan tells me it's only a matter of time before Chief Gerard arrests me."

"Maybe the chief is looking at somebody else. If he wanted you, surely he could have arrested you by now."

"No, he's waiting to get his ducks in a row so my big sister doesn't kill him."

"I don't understand." Sarah looked at Anne for clarification.

"Chief Gerard is waiting for the lab and forensic reports to come back. He doesn't want to jump the gun and make a mistake arresting Jacob, because he's afraid of the scene I'll make—and what I might do to him if I win the mayoral election."

"Is that a veiled threat about his job?"

Anne steadily met Sarah's gaze. "No threat. I'm

simply telling you what Chief Gerard is afraid of. He obviously doesn't know me well, because no matter how the chips fall, that won't influence my decisions for Wheaton."

Taking in Anne's determination, Sarah realized Anne was telling the truth. She wouldn't like it, but she'd sacrifice her brother if that was how the cards played out. Considering Anne had already dealt with difficult issues and accusations involving her family, Anne had the backbone to do whatever was necessary.

"Sarah, join me. Once the waitress clears our plates, I'm having dessert and coffee. Please keep me company or order something. Jacob is leaving."

Jacob stammered a "Wha—." Without another word, agreeing or objecting to his sister's declaration, he stood, said goodbye, and left.

Sarah's mouth was partially open at what had transpired, but she couldn't close it. She would never order Emily around in that manner.

"Don't worry. Once he cools down, he'll realize he got a free dinner tonight. Besides, I'll talk to him later to make sure everything is okay between us and explain I really needed to talk with you now. Please sit down." She gestured toward Jacob's empty seat.

Sarah slid into it. She gazed into Anne's eyes and again read them as having the flinty, cold-blooded aspect that always made her uncomfortable in Anne's presence. Thinking about how their last conversation had resulted in Sarah ending up in the kitchen, she promised herself that this time Anne wouldn't get the best of her.

"Are you paying attention to me?"

"I'm sorry," Sarah said. "I was distracted watching the waitress clear Jacob and your dishes. His plate looked like he never touched it."

"He barely did. This whole thing is eating him up." She glanced at the dessert menu the waitress had left on the table after wiping up the crumbs and handed it to Sarah. Sarah dropped it back on the table. Thanks to being Emily's dessert taster, she knew the menu items by heart.

"Jacob is barely functioning. That's why I'm doing the thinking for him."

"Maybe that's what's keeping him from moving on and handling things for himself." She waited for Anne's response.

When Anne opened her mouth, Sarah expected Anne to criticize her, but the return of the waitress interrupted whatever Anne was going to say. Instead, Anne shut her mouth and pressed her lips so tightly together that Sarah thought they looked like a white gash in Anne's face.

"Dessert?" the waitress asked.

"Apple pie à la mode and a cup of decaf for me. What would you like, Sarah?"

"A slice of carrot cake and regular coffee, please."

"Got it." The waitress retrieved the dessert menu.

"Won't the coffee keep you awake?" Anne asked. "I can't touch caffeine after six or I'm never going to fall asleep."

"It's no problem for me. Once my head touches the pillow, I'm out cold until RahRah or Fluffy wakes me."

As they continued to make small talk, waiting for their desserts, Sarah felt herself letting down her guard, but she also thought from the relaxation of the lines in Anne's face that she was, too. When the desserts came, they both dug in with gusto.

Anne was the first to put down her fork. "I'm sorry if I irritated you earlier. I'm simply worried about my brother."

Sarah didn't acknowledge her apology.

"Whether you believe me or not, I'm not your enemy."

"You've certainly had a funny way of showing that to my family and me."

"What do you mean?"

"I know you didn't want to see Main Street developed into an entertainment district and you delayed as much as possible until the council majority voted for the rezoning. Are you going to tell me you didn't have any role in Southwind not being able to open as quickly as Jane's Place? In fact, isn't it a little two-faced for you to be eating here this evening? We don't comp politicians."

Anne took a deep breath and avoided Sarah's gaze as she spoke with an evenly measured tone that reminded Sarah of a robot. "Sarah, we've had this conversation before. I've never denied being against the zoning of Main Street for entertainment purposes without a concrete plan. Part of my job is policing the health, safety, and welfare of my constituents. Letting people get rich from rezoning without thinking of the consequences isn't doing my job. This is a fine neighborhood, but without comprehensive zoning, the house next door could become a multi-dwelling residence or a house of ill repute. We could have restaurants and clinics, or these homes could have been a mishmash of high-end and lowbrow stores.

This is a neighborhood that has always been safe for our children to walk and play. I want to keep it that way. That means regulating businesses, addressing permitting, establishing a park, providing for traffic control, and a million other little things. Jane lucked out. Once the zoning passed, like at the Southwind Pub, the stars fell in line for her in terms of delivery and inspections. I'm looking into what Botts may have been doing. I won't have enough information to go public with it for a few days, but I assure you I had nothing to do with Southwind's final inspection delay. The only time issue you can blame me for was dragging my feet until the zoning for this area was established correctly."

Sarah sat back. "But what about the disagreements you had with Marcus?"

"Marcus wants everything done yesterday. Zoning takes time and so do permits. You know his former partners in the strip center restaurant were impulsive, made promises, and didn't always follow the process in the right order. Once Emily came back to town and Harlan became involved, things may not have happened as quickly as Marcus wanted, and there may truly have been an issue with Botts, but overall, things progressed. We've rezoned the area and established a designated set of streets to be an entertainment district."

Thinking of Marcus's short fuse, orange clogs, giant presence, and balloon pants, Sarah had to admit what Anne was saying made sense. She'd seen the side Anne was describing many times since she'd met Marcus, and she was also aware how Emily's presence and cool logic tamed him. Maybe, like Marcus, she'd

overreacted to Anne. Then again, there was no denying Anne took over the two meetings they'd been involved with together, and she'd conned Sarah into
providing food for each of the meetings. She could
agree to give Anne some leeway but not to step down
her guard entirely.

"Sarah, you don't have to like me, nor do you have
to fully trust me, but as we discussed last time, we
need to work together for Jacob's sake. Do you still
agree?"

"I do." As a sign of good faith, Sarah felt she
should tell Anne about her activities from the past
few hours, but she didn't want to mention Harlan.
Without anything positive, she feared Anne would
again think Harlan was wasting time rather than
working in a manner most beneficial to Jacob. "In
fact, I spent the last few hours having drinks with
people who might shed some light on Riley and
Botts's deaths."

"Did they?"

"Not really. They raised more questions that I'm
trying to work out in my mind."

"Well, maybe some of the things I've discovered
will help." Anne pulled a pair of reading glasses, a xe-
roxed map of downtown, and a short legal pad from
her oversized purse. "I had Botts's inspection reports
and files pulled for the past two years. I've been
going through them with a fine-tooth comb. Although I'm not positive I've caught everything, I'm
ninety-nine percent sure Botts began doing something fishy recently."

Anne cleared a space in the middle of the table

and spread the map out in front of Sarah. Sarah bent over it, noting it ran from just beyond her house on Main Street all the way to the strip center where the Southwind Pub was. Widthwise, it encompassed the streets that mixed residential homes with homes now being used for offices, like Harlan's building. Pools of red marks made the map look bloodstained.

"My assistant and I focused our attention on the lots or houses marked with a red 'X' that were reno-vated. For those properties, we made a timeline of when they were sold renovated. We paid particular attention to when the permits for construction were filed and when the final inspection was signed off."

"That sounds comprehensive. What did you find?"

Using her index finger, Anne tapped the shop-ping strip center where the Southwind Pub was lo-cated. "This was the first area renovated. The strip center had been there, but a group of investors bought it and updated it cosmetically. These same in-vestors joined together to build out the space that was designated as the original Southwind restaurant. From what we see from the permits and timeline we've created, there didn't seem to be any problems or irregularities with Southwind coming online the first time."

"Did something change after the original South-wind and part of the shopping center burned down?"

"Yes." Anne consulted her pad. "Post fire, Cliff was hired to rebuild or repair the strip center. He also separately contracted to build out what is now the Southwind Pub and several other spaces damaged by the fire. Most of the timelines for each of the buildouts were similar. The Southwind Pub and one other location took a few days longer because of the time lag before Botts gave them final approval."

"So he was delaying?"

"Not necessarily. He signed off on specific inspections of a few of the locations on Main Street, like Jane's Place, during the same time period. We know he was working alone, so it's possible his workload accounted for the delays. At the same time, some places took less time than comparable locations."

"Like Jane's Place?"

"Exactly. That made us look at everything from a different viewpoint."

"What was that?"

"We added to our analysis the owners' names, who did the remodeling or renovation work, and then cross-checked the time it took for Botts's approval based upon the project itself and who was involved. That's when we started seeing some interesting patterns. Three years ago, things were simple and didn't seem problematic. About two years ago, Cliff began landing a lot of the jobs. At first, there was no difference in the timelines, but if you look closely, you'll see several of the jobs where he was the contractor during the past year started taking extra time."

Sarah hated to think Cliff was dirty. Her hand fluttered to her hair and pushed back a strand that wasn't loose. She swallowed hard. "Could you tell if Cliff charged or was paid more by the owners for the days the job dragged on?"

"Just the opposite. He was losing money when the job dragged on because his fees were based upon set timelines. In one instance, he paid a penalty for the two extra days it took to complete the project."

Sarah sighed. "If he lost money or paid a penalty, surely Cliff's hands were clean."

"It would appear so, but in this last year, he had a lot of Botts-inspected projects under his belt. Some whizzed to completion quickly while others dragged, so we looked for another common denominator."

"Did you find one?"

"I didn't, but my assistant thinks she has. She went through all the old papers and noticed that whenever a new business or building that was finished on time opened, the *Wheaton Gazette*'s online social column ran a picture of Botts and the owner. The *Gazette* didn't do that for jobs that had major delays."

"Does that mean someone from the *Gazette* is in on the take, too?"

"That was our first thought. Then my assistant observed online pictures and articles are submitted or posted by private citizens. Most are disguised announcements about fundraisers and pictures taken at the fundraiser or opening. In Botts's case, he's usually with the owner and Cliff. That's why I didn't take Cliff off my suspect list."

"I think I can."

Anne peered over her glasses. Sarah was sure Anne knew from either the public grapevine or Jacob that Cliff and she had been on a few dates.

"Let me explain. The group I just met with, the three veterinarians, Drs. Tonya, Vera, and Glenn, and Glenn's sister, Carole, all had dealings at some point with Botts. Dr. Tonya handled the renovation dealings with Cliff and Botts. She told me Botts tried to strong-arm her over some of the permitting and inspections. When she called him out on trying to hold her hostage, she showed him an aftermarket motorcycle-goods catalog and told him she had a credit and forty-percent-off coupon he could use. Her only caveat for placing the order, including what he wanted to purchase, was that the project must come in on time. Botts took her up on the offer and performed his inspection. Surprise, the clinic's remodeling got back on schedule and finished on time. Cliff didn't have anything to do with Botts's attempted extortion. If it's true this time, I bet it's true across the board."

"Glad that lets Cliff off the hook, but it sounds like a bribe made and accepted in my book. Neither of which should be tolerated."

Sarah flinched at Anne's harsh tone. She kicked herself for telling Anne the names of the people involved. She'd forgotten Anne's penchant for being law-abiding. "Anne, this wasn't really a bribe. The doctor refused to pay Botts anything."

Anne frowned and turned her head to the side. "But, even though he paid for what he wanted, she let him use something that had monetary worth, and in turn he finished his inspection in a timely manner. I may not be a lawyer, but that sounds like an offer and acceptance or quid pro quo to me. We can't have things like that going on in Wheaton."

Sarah spread her hands across the map. "Botts is dead. Even if you could get some of the bribe money he received back using a lien or going after his estate, it's too late to make him serve time. I think we need to go forward, making sure this doesn't happen again. Besides, Chief Gerard doesn't have the manpower to investigate all the potential cases that might have already happened. How would you distinguish whether to punish someone who let Botts use a coupon and discount, someone who paid him cash, or, for that matter, someone who got him to act by sweet-talking and flattering him?"

With the last example barely out of her mouth, Sarah felt like she should kick herself. "I might have done some sweet-talking myself to urge Botts to do the final Southwind inspection." Sarah swallowed, afraid of Anne's response.

"There's nothing wrong with appealing to someone's good side to get them to do their job. I do it all the time. That isn't a bribe."

Sarah exhaled deeply. She waved her hands over the papers on the table. "I realize this is a far more detailed analysis than you usually do, but I know you've been on top of the different remodeling projects and proposed changes for the entertainment district. How, with as much scrutiny as you've given, did you miss that the delays might be tied to nefarious behavior?"

"That's not exactly fair. First, Botts reported directly to the mayor, not the council. So, I wasn't privy to the intricate everyday details of the jobs, only the bigger picture as it relates to Wheaton and the more mundane things like permitting. Second, the council is only a part-time position. My primary job is super soccer mom with two on the traveling teams. If you forgot, during the past year, I've been running everything with the kids by myself." She removed her glasses.

"The boys are doing well, but considering everything, they had to be my first priority."

"I know you're doing the best you can, but I'm still trying to wrap my head around how Botts got away with putting pressure on so many people without a red flag going up from any of them."

"Probably because he targeted his prey carefully and didn't delay a job so long that it seemed impossible. Look at the situation you've described with South-wind. If we were told a piece of equipment hadn't come in, a delivery was late, or an executed document hadn't been filed timely enough for the council to consider a permit or liquor license this week, we'd put it over onto the following week's city council agenda. To us, these delays were part of the normal course of business. To Marcus, Emily, and you, they were excruciating and felt like years, not days. And maybe my own prejudice about some of the projects on Main Street kept me from wanting to see or accept that the delays were targeted. Now, for Jacob's sake, I'm trying to put everything except him aside."

Under other circumstances, or with someone else, Sarah might have comforted the other person with a hug, but this was Anne. Instead, once again, they both agreed to keep working to find the real killer or killers.

Sarah left Anne gathering up her papers while she went back to the hostess station to say goodbye to Emily. Seeing her sister was still busy, Sarah merely waved. As she left the restaurant through the Main Street entrance, she couldn't get the "targeted" concept out of her mind. She knew Botts's targeted scheme might explain his death, but she wasn't sure how it related to Riley's.

As she walked toward the carriage house's driveway, her attention was caught by dogs barking in the outdoor runs and she noticed the outdoor clinic lights were on. Normally, they were turned off at night. Seeing movement by the dog entrance, she strained to see who it was. From the diminutive but athletic build and the light shining on the person's face as she put her key in the door, Sarah realized it was Dr. Vera. Why she was going in through one of the animal entrances instead of the staff's rear private entrance seemed weird until Sarah remembered Vera's motorcycle was parked for the night at the Southwind Pub rather than behind the clinic. Based on how much time had elapsed, Harlan must have taken Dr. Vera home and she walked back. Why?

CHAPTER THIRTY-NINE

Something didn't feel right. Sarah figured it would come to her, but what was important now were the cat and dog waiting inside the carriage house.

She knew she'd been gone too long when both met her in the front hall, the sound of the key in the lock calling them. Fluffy sat, showing off her new skill of not jumping on people. Almost as if to tempt Fluffy, RahRah walked up to Sarah and rubbed himself against her leg. He purred, daring Sarah to ignore him.

Of course, she couldn't. Sarah sat on the entryway floor. She gave Fluffy permission to move but focused her attention on giving RahRah lots of love. Fluffy seemed to understand. She lay by Sarah's side, barely touching her hip, while Sarah concentrated on RahRah until he stretched himself out, crossing his paws. Only then did Sarah pet both animals, each with one hand.

As much comfort as they got from being petted, Sarah knew her sensation of peace and joy was greater.

She could have continued running her hands through their fur indefinitely, but RahRah, with a shake, stood, let out a throaty sound, and strolled to the kitchen.

"I guess that leaves only us. Want to take a walk?"

Fluffy wagged her tail at the offer. Sarah leashed Fluffy and yelled a "Be back in a few minutes" to RahRah. Normally, the length of the driveway between the carriage house and Main Street sufficed to walk Fluffy. Tonight, Sarah urged Fluffy not to mark every tree on her property. She was on a mission to extend their walk across Main Street to the vet clinic.

The closer she got to the clinic, the more the hairs on the back of her neck tingled. She had the same feeling when she watched scenes on *Perry Mason* where Perry suspected something was amiss at an apartment or house he shouldn't be at. Usually, Perry walked up to the door and either pushed it open if it was ajar or rang the doorbell, only to have it opened by his client. Either way, there would be a dead body on the floor. Sarah decided to pull a Perry Mason to calm the queasy feeling she had. She only hoped she didn't stumble over a dead body.

Sarah picked Fluffy up and walked to the dog entrance she'd seen Dr. Vera use. "We still can turn around," she whispered to Fluffy. But they didn't. She rang the doorbell and waited. No one answered, so she rang it again. This time, leaving her finger on the bell a smidgen too long. Off-balance because her finger was still on the buzzer, she almost fell when the door was yanked open by Dr. Tonya. She steadied herself, while trying to hold the squirming puppy excited to see her favorite veterinarian.

"What is it?"

"Oh, I didn't expect to see you." She held Fluffy up like a shield between Tonya and her as she babbled the first things that came into her mind. "I was walking Fluffy and I noticed Dr. Vera letting herself into the clinic. She made me feel so guilty about not getting Fluffy's last shot, even though my days have been so crazy, what with working for Harlan and helping Marcus and Emily at their restaurant, that I hoped, if possible, I could get Fluffy's vaccination now. I also wanted to check how Dr. Vera was feeling."

"Unless it's an emergency, we don't treat pets after hours."

Sarah cast her eyes down. "I know, but you both made me feel so horrible for lagging on giving Fluffy the last shot of the vaccine, I thought now that Fluffy is healthy again, I should make sure she stays that way. I'm sorry if I intruded on your private time."

When Dr. Tonya reached out and calmed Fluffy by petting her, Sarah sensed she might be softening, and hastened to empathize with the other woman's position. "Working for Harlan, I know how valuable and rare downtime can be."

It apparently was the wrong thing to say because Dr. Tonya pulled her hand back. Fluffy immediately fought against Sarah restraining her. The dog's excited yipping made Sarah look beyond Dr. Tonya to the darkened reception area. A slight movement in the shadows caught her eye. Someone else was there who could hear them.

"That's why we insist on keeping regular hours."

"I understand. I didn't know you were here, and I

shouldn't have presumed Dr. Vera would see Fluffy on her free time."

Coming out of the shadows to stand beside Dr. Tonya, Dr. Vera, looking at her taller partner, stared her down. "I'm fine and we can make an exception this once. Bring Fluffy in."

Glaring, without a trace of the smile she usually had, Dr. Tonya stepped aside to let Sarah and Fluffy into the dog waiting area. Dr. Vera led the way through the exam room hall directly to the big treatment room. "Put Fluffy on that table while I get the vaccine."

Apparently deciding to join them rather than fight them, Dr. Tonya took Fluffy from Sarah's arms and steadied her on one of the two black-topped hydraulic-lift tables in the center of the room. Stepping back so she was even with the medicine closet, Sarah watched Dr. Vera prepare the shot. She moved closer to the closet's door and thanked her again.

From the closet doorway, Sarah noticed a small safe, the kind often found in hotel rooms or that people add after construction but bolted into the floor or cement to make it near impossible to steal, was open. "Is that where you keep your boarding animals' valuables?"

Dr. Vera glanced at the open safe. "No, just like a hospital, we use a number of controlled substances in treating our patients. All controlled painkillers and other drugs, the same one's human patients often are prescribed, are kept in that safe. None of us can access them without going through a very rigid sign-in/sign-out procedure."

Sarah immediately thought of Carole and her past problem. How tempting would this safe be to a person like that? "Do all of your employees have access to the safe?"

"No." Dr. Vera tapped the liquid in the needle to make sure there were no air bubbles. Without elaborating further, she walked out of the closet to where Dr. Tonya was stroking the belly of a very relaxed Fluffy. The two doctors kept up a running dialogue as Dr. Vera, using an alcohol wipe, cleaned a spot, then administered the shot. Fluffy yipped and struggled for a moment before relaxing as the doctors made nice to her.

"I really appreciate you doing this tonight. Maybe you should consider having evening hours one night a week."

"You sound like Glenn. He's pushing for that. We teased him that he wouldn't mind because he lives in the building, but we feel like there are enough nights we end up back here. Right, Vera?"

"Definitely."

Dr. Tonya handed a more subdued Fluffy back to Sarah. This time the puppy snuggled close to her.

"Well, I'm appreciative you made an exception for Fluffy. After being at the Pub, what brought you back here tonight?"

They answered almost simultaneously. "An alarm signal went off on my phone," Dr. Vera said. "Our service informed me that we have an emergency patient coming in," Dr. Tonya said.

Dr. Tonya gave Sarah a nervous, tight-lipped smile. "Imagine, two different types of emergencies happening at once. Let me walk you out so Fluffy and you won't be in the way when my emergency case arrives."

"Of course." Sarah glanced back over her shoulder to thank Dr. Vera again. Unlike Dr. Tonya, whose normal smile was back on her face as she escorted Sarah and Fluffy from the treatment room, Dr. Vera was no longer looking at them. Instead, Sarah saw her eyes dart around the room until they rested on the big wall clock.

Chapter Forty

Outside, walking Fluffy home, Sarah felt even more disturbed than when she'd first rung the clinic's bell. Something wasn't right. Dr. Tonya said there was an emergency coming in, but earlier she said the practice didn't take cases after hours. Why would an emergency animal be coming to them now instead of going to the Pet Emergency Hospital?

Playing devil's advocate, Sarah answered her own question. Perhaps the animal was one belonging to a friend or one they had a special relationship with, like General Beau. Even so, why wouldn't Glenn and Carole handle it before one of the other vets was called in?

Again, Sarah reached for a plausible explanation. Perhaps Glenn hadn't come straight home from the Southwind Pub. Maybe he wasn't in the house or somewhere nearby, so they had a backup system. Perhaps Dr. Tonya was on call. And, where was Carole? She should be home because Harlan drove her there.

Relieved Dr. Tonya's story was plausible, Sarah relaxed, but only for a moment. Why was Dr. Vera's story different? Sarah had seen Dr. Vera let herself into the building. If she was responding to an alarm, shouldn't there have been blaring alarms needing silencing and the police checking the clinic? Why lie? Sarah felt a sinking feeling in the pit of her stomach. What about the open safe?

Maybe Carole's drug problem wasn't under control. Perhaps Sarah had stumbled onto an intervention or the doctors had caught their vet tech at the safe. If either was the case, Dr. Tonya's attitude and frowning face were justified by Sarah and Fluffy getting in the way, but why hadn't Dr. Vera reacted the same way? If anything, she ate up time they could have been dealing with Carole by giving Fluffy her shot.

Time. That was what still bothered Sarah. When Sarah glanced back to thank Dr. Vera again as she left the clinic, the vet was staring at the clock. Her expression was anything but happy. Sarah might be reading into it, but in retrospect Dr. Vera seemed fearful. Sarah didn't know what, but she knew something was happening and time was of the essence.

CHAPTER FORTY-ONE

Frightened something horrible was about to happen, Sarah hurried back to the carriage house and unceremoniously dumped Fluffy in the entry hall. Normally, she would check on RahRah, but she didn't think there was time. She decided to return to the clinic but was torn between needing to help in some way and Harlan's constant refrain of "Leave it to the experts."

With Harlan's words in her ears and her memories of some of her own recent experiences, she debated between calling 911 or checking if Officer Robinson was on duty at the police station by calling the station's nonemergency number. She decided on the latter. If she got lucky and he was there, it would be easier to explain her gut-level feeling to him rather than a 911 operator.

He was on duty. While she waited for him to come on the line, she felt like she'd hit a jackpot.

"Robinson, here."

"Officer Robinson. Sarah Blair. I don't know exactly what's going on, but I think you need to check the vet clinic out before something terrible happens."

"Whoa. Slow down, Sarah. What are you talking about?"

Sarah explained everything and how the players related to Jacob, Botts, and Riley. To his credit, even though she heard a phone ringing in the background, Officer Robinson listened until she finished.

"Sarah, I'll go over there and check things out. Where are you now?"

"Outside my house."

"I want you to listen to me. Go back inside and stay there. Leave this to me."

"But . . ."

"I'll let you know if I find anything."

She thanked him and asked him to please hurry because she felt the time before something happened was short. Hanging up, she pulled the key to the carriage house from her pocket. She knew from their past interactions Officer Robinson wouldn't think she was simply a crackpot making a report. He'd follow through on what he'd promised and expect her to do the same. The only problem was, she didn't know exactly how soon he'd get around to checking the clinic out. That was why she couldn't sit inside the carriage house and wait, but she'd make sure not to get in the middle of anything. She'd simply go across the street and observe until he got there.

Passing Southwind, she thought about enlisting Emily's help for her surveillance mission, but the parking lot was still full. As she crossed Main Street, she couldn't help but smile. Hopefully, the success

Marcus and Emily were having with the Southwind Pub and their new white-tablecloth restaurant would continue.

Afraid of being noticed if she stood in front of the clinic, in case anyone was looking out its windows, she decided to come at it through the rear parking lot by making it seem she was retrieving a car from Jane's Place. That way, she could watch the back door from the motorcycle parking pad. Although Jane's Place didn't have many customers, she hoped there was enough traffic in the parking lot that if the barking got louder when she approached the runs, it would be written off as her being an annoyance instead of a spy.

As she came around the back of the building, something again felt wrong. She listened, but all she heard was silence. That was what was wrong. There were no animals in the runs. Sarah looked at her watch. It was only ten. Even though Chief Gerard, Jane, and the neighbors had struck a truce for the core dinner hours, Jane had had to acquiesce to a reasonable evening time for the boarded animals to be allowed outside. Sarah didn't know the exact time they'd agreed to, but she knew it was for all days of the week, so it had to be after most of Jane's diners would be gone and those still drinking wouldn't care. Based on the customer traffic at Southwind, considering weekends, surely Jane wouldn't have agreed to anything before ten. But, Sarah had heard dogs barking when she brought Fluffy over.

Taking advantage of the silence, Sarah crossed the open parking lot and sidled up to the motorcycle parking pad. Her idea of seeing whether Drs. Glenn and Tonya's bikes were there went out the window when she realized half the parked bikes were silver Harleys and each had a Wildcats sticker on the back. Frustrated, she debated whether to continue snooping or wait for Officer Robinson. The problem, she feared, was he would ring the doorbell and whoever would answer would tell him everything was fine, so Officer Robinson would have nothing else to investigate.

Sarah felt her question was divinely answered when she tried the door near the parking pad. It opened. Almost on tiptoe, she snuck inside and listened. She wasn't really going to break her promise to Officer Robinson, but it couldn't hurt to try to hear more to help him out. She paused for a moment while she remembered which turns retraced the path Carole and she had taken earlier in the day.

Nearing the big treatment room, she heard voices and paused. Although Sarah couldn't make out how many voices were talking or most of the words being said, she was positive she heard Botts's name repeated several times. She needed to get a little closer. Surely, if Sarah didn't go into the room the people were in, there were enough nooks and crannies she could duck into if anyone came into the hall.

Inching forward, Sarah tested each footstep so nothing squeaked when she put her full weight on it. She crept closer but stopped when Dr. Tonya's voice seemed crystal clear. Looking ahead, Sarah saw the treatment room's door was partially open. Dr. Tonya was standing with her back to the doorway, while Dr.

Vera was nearer the water table used for dentistry. There was no sign of an animal being treated for an emergency.

Afraid to peek in any farther for fear of being seen, Sarah flattened herself against the hallway wall on the same side as the doorway. She waited and listened, clearly making out not only Dr. Tonya and Dr. Vera's voices but also Carole's.

As she strained to hear what they were saying, a sense of panic rose. Three to one wasn't good odds. Even she knew this was the time to back out graciously and let the experts handle the situation. Keeping herself flat against the wall and her gaze on the door of the treatment room, Sarah backed toward the clinic door she'd come in through. Passing the first cat exam room, her hands, tracking her movement on the plaster wall, she felt it change to a wooden door before the drywall began again.

Suddenly, Sarah's right arm was grabbed and twisted behind her back. She screamed in pain. No one came to help her. The pain intensified as she was pushed toward the main treatment room. She dug her heels in, trying to resist, but the pain was too great. As focused as she was on moving the way her attacker wanted her to, she almost didn't realize the person was speaking.

"Were you bringing your cat in this time?"

Sarah wished RahRah was with her, if only to scratch or hiss at Dr. Tonya.

"Move along."

Without arguing, Sarah did. She stumbled into the treatment room. Dr. Vera was in the same place she'd been earlier. Now, Sarah saw why. Dr. Vera's hands were tied flat to the grates of the wash table with animal restraints and the drill and water spigot were positioned right above her. Carole, her face wet with tears, sat in a heap on the floor, exactly where she'd held Fluffy during her IV treatment.

Tonya pushed Sarah nearer the hydraulic-lift table, where Fluffy had been just a little while ago. She grabbed one of the leashes hanging on the wall. "Put your arm around the column."

Sarah placed her free arm around the column that connected the tables together.

After a shove, Tonya released the arm she'd been holding behind Sarah's back. "This one, too."

Barely able to move her arm, Sarah willed her two hands to touch. Tonya tightly looped the leash around Sarah's wrists, binding her to the pole.

Sarah pulled against the leash. "This really isn't necessary."

Tonya glared at Sarah. She yanked the leash until the fabric cut into Sarah's skin.

Sarah looked at Dr. Vera, who shook her head. "Why did you come back, Sarah?"

"Because I sensed something was wrong."

Dr. Vera frowned. "You shouldn't have."

"That's an understatement," Dr. Tonya said. "It takes one Goody Two-shoes to know another one." She walked over to where Vera was tied and steadied the dental drill above her head. Tonya stepped on a button on the floor near the sink table, and the drill came to life. She moved it closer to Dr. Vera, who cowered as low as she could. Smiling, Dr. Tonya stepped off the button and returned the drill to its original position. Only when she walked away from the drill control did Dr. Vera, who had been bent over with her face almost touching the sink's metal grille, stand up again.

From the floor, Carole whimpered, "Tonya, stop. This isn't like you. He wouldn't like to see you like this."

"If anyone should know, it would be you, wouldn't it? Don't talk to me about him. Don't worry. You'll be with him soon enough."

Praying for Officer Robinson to come, Sarah tried to distract Tonya. "I felt something was wrong, but I don't understand, Tonya. What's going on? Can I help you?"

Dr. Tonya ignored Sarah's questions as she went to the open safe and removed three vials. She laid the vials and three needles on the black-topped table too far away for Sarah to knock off with a bent elbow or foot. Sarah couldn't bear to look at the vials, not wanting to think what possible use Tonya had in mind for them.

Sarah glanced at Dr. Vera. The doctor's gaze was focused on the vials.

"Why did you come back tonight?" Sarah asked Dr. Vera. "Was it something said at dinner about the payoffs or the dating?"

Dr. Vera's gaze never moved. "Yes. It was only tonight I learned how well Tonya knew Botts before she ran interference when Glenn made this house into an office. I always thought Tonya barely knew him before she came to Wheaton. At the Southwind Pub, Tonya not only said they'd served together, but she hinted at a deeper relationship."

Sarah didn't see the significance of what Dr. Tonya

had said over drinks about Botts and their military time, but apparently Dr. Vera had thought it important. Maybe this was the obvious thing Sarah and Harlan had missed. "What's important about them having served together?"

"I wasn't sure, but after all the talk about payoffs, I came back to see if I could find something irregular in the ledger."

"Was there?"

"No."

Dr. Tonya snorted. "Why should there be? I told you there wasn't a payoff, except for letting Botts use the credit and coupon. Why would I pay off my own husband?"

Sarah jerked her head in Dr. Tonya's direction. "Your husband? Louis Botts is—was—your husband?"

"In spirit only," Dr. Vera said. "Not legally. As Tonya said, they had a metaphysical relationship."

Sarah glanced at the clock on the wall. It was almost eleven. She didn't know if Officer Robinson was going to check the clinic before or after his shift, but either was cutting it close. She needed to stall. "I don't understand. How could Botts be your husband and play around with everyone else? You don't impress me as someone who would tolerate your husband stepping out on you."

Tonya rammed a needle into one of the vials and pulled back on the plunger. Sarah watched the syringe fill with a clear liquid.

"Our unit was a special one trained to sniff out land mines and bombs. Some, like Botts, were regular soldiers, but there was a group of animal handlers, and I was the veterinarian."

"That sounds like a really specialized unit."

"It was, but somehow instead of sending us into an area where we were needed, we were assigned to a remote village. There wasn't much to do there, except get to know each other. Botts was my soul mate, and he asked me to make it permanent. Because there was no minister there, we pledged ourselves to each other."

Wanting to keep Tonya in that overseas moment, Sarah prompted her to tell her more about their union. "Did you have a ceremony?"

"We did. We exchanged our vows on the most beautiful mountaintop. Above us the sky was blue, without a cloud to be seen, and below us was a gorgeous lake the same color as the sky. We were going to make everything legal when we got home."

Sarah tried to move her arms, but couldn't. "It must have been lovely, just the two of you."

Tonya smiled as she tapped an air bubble out of the syringe. "There were three of us. General Beau's handler was in our unit, but Botts and I had a special bond with Beau. We made the General our ring bearer."

"But I thought someone else than his trainer is fostering General Beau."

"They are until his official handler finishes his tour of duty. The night of our wedding, our base was attacked. We suffered lots of injuries and casualties."

"Were you hurt?"

"No, I was wide awake, so I'd taken a walk to the other side of camp, leaving Beau and Botts sleeping near Beau's handler. When the enemy hit, I was stuck where I was. Neither Beau's handler nor I got a scratch, but Botts was hit badly enough that when he recovered, he was discharged. The night of the attack did a number on General Beau, too."

The PTSD. That explained why Beau had PTSD.

"Loud noises, flashing lights, and strangers trigger a negative reaction in the General. It quickly became obvious he would have to be retired."

"So you made arrangements for him to be near you?"

"When a military dog is injured or sick and must be retired, it's best for him to be with his handler. In this case, that wasn't possible. His handler is career. I had a good-enough relationship with Beau to have been substituted as his handler, but because I was healthy and wasn't getting out of the service for a year, I couldn't be the one assigned to care for him in his retirement. It was a dilemma for everyone, but considering my relationship with Botts, who already was living in Wheaton, I suggested, and it was accepted, that because Beau knew Botts so well and I would be coming back here, General Beau would be put into retirement status in Wheaton."

"General Beau is lucky to have someone like you in his corner. It sounds like there was a lot of red tape, but you found a perfect solution for General Beau."

"It should have been. Except by the time the General got here, Botts didn't want him or me. He'd found a buddy with a farm who willingly took him in. Once we had the clinic, I tried bringing Beau to the office, but with his fears and aggression, I couldn't let him wander the office freely, and I didn't want to coop him up in a run all day, so I pay room and board for Beau to stay on the farm."

"I'm sorry," Sarah said.

"For what?" Dr. Tonya gritted her teeth. She laid the syringe on the counter as she double-checked that Dr. Vera and Sarah were still secured.

As Dr. Tonya again yanked the leash, Sarah tried to keep Dr. Tonya talking. She feared what might happen if she couldn't keep Dr. Tonya distracted. "I'm sorry for everything. It had to be tough coming home to a wounded dog and an ended relationship."

"Beau I could handle and help, but Botts was an absolute surprise. It shouldn't have been. We communicated regularly while he was hospitalized and when he first came home. He only stopped writing or Skyping at the end of my tour. I figured he was busy and we'd pick up and start over when I came home last year."

"He'd moved on?"

"He was seeing Riley then, but she was only one of many. The sweet, sensitive man I married on the mountain was now a showboating Mr. Big with a capital 'B.' When I tried to talk about us and what he was like now, he told me I was a pickle and he didn't like sour tastes."

"That's horrible, but killing all of us isn't going to change what's happened. Besides, no one will believe it if they find the three of us dead here together."

"They won't think anything if they find Vera and Carole together. And you, well I have all night to decide what to do with you."

Not exactly what Sarah wanted to hear. She tried a different tactic. "But why bother with any of us?"

"All of you are like Riley. You know too much."

"What do you mean?"

"One night, Botts and Riley's partying got out of hand and she told him she loved when pets were included in wedding ceremonies. He told her about our wedding and General Beau's involvement. Riley thought it was hilarious and teased me whenever she could."

Thinking of how she had characterized Riley as a dancing butterfly during the grand opening of Jane's Place, Sarah bet Riley's words could be piercing. "And she teased you one too many times in the parking lot?"

"Riley was upset when Botts drove off without looking back. I had been mounting my bike and saw the whole thing and laughed. She heard me and started yelling she'd created new menu items, including the General Beau Pickled Dog and the Botts Bye Bye Burger."

"Riley thought she could get those on the menu?"

"According to Riley, Jane would do anything to keep her. Riley taunted me with another menu item that was even more personal, and I lost it. I rushed her. I was only trying to make her hush, but she turned at the wrong moment and it became a choke hold."

"Botts figured out it was you?"

"Yes. He put together that the hold was a defensive one and I must have been outside when he raced off. Botts realized although he hadn't seen Riley follow him outside, I had. He asked me for money to keep quiet."

Tonya picked up the syringe again. Carole, who had been quietly sobbing, whimpered more loudly.

Tonya frowned at her but continued talking to Sarah. "The man who'd once pledged his love to me was blackmailing me. I couldn't tolerate that."

"No, you couldn't. So you decided to do something to his motorcycle?"

"Botts loved to rev up engines and take off flying, but he wasn't a great driver. It was predicted to rain the weekend he died, but I knew he still planned to do stunts on the gravel track and take one long ride over different types of terrain, so I tightened his front brake while he was in Jane's Place at the tasting party. The front brake is hard to control on a motorcycle, and with his skill level, I hoped he might wipe out and be out of circulation until I could think of a way to buy him off. He took care of the situation permanently for me."

Sarah didn't think a court would put the complete blame for his death on Botts's lack of riding skill when his brake was tampered with. It might not go down as murder one, but Sarah felt at least a charge of manslaughter could be made. The only thing Sarah was positive of was she didn't want to be the reason more charges eventually would be filed against Tonya.

"Why let Jacob be accused of everything you did?"

"I didn't mean to, but it worked well for me. Jacob couldn't control himself when it came to Riley. With a little prodding, Botts and he got into it just before Louis started doing his stunts, so everyone remembered their bitter exchange near Botts's motorcycle."

Carrying the syringe, Tonya walked toward Carole.

Vera called out, "Tonya, no! She didn't do anything."

"I have to. She's another loose end. She was supposed to bring the dogs in the night Riley died, but I did. Eventually, she'd connect Riley's death with me." Tonya bent near Carole. "It's going to be all right. Remember that good feeling Botts and you used to get? Well, that's the last thing you're going to remember."

Carole inched closer to the cages. Through sobs, she said, "No one will believe it. I've been clean for years."

Tonya smiled as she let Carole get farther away from her on the ground. Sarah felt sick. It was like watching a hunter toying with its prey before firing the kill shot. Only when Carole was penned in by the metal cages did Tonya grab Carole's arm and lift the needle above it.

Sarah called out before Tonya could administer the shot. "Tonya, look out!"

Instinctively, Tonya turned her head in response to her name. At that moment, Officer Robinson, followed by a slower Chief Gerard, sprang through the doorway and kicked the needle from Tonya's hand with his steel-toed boot. Officer Robinson grabbed Tonya. Despite her struggling, he finally pulled her arm behind her, much as she'd done to Sarah. The main difference was he exerted only enough pressure to handcuff her.

While Officer Robinson walked her out to his patrol car, Chief Gerard loosened the restraints binding Dr. Vera and Sarah. Holding the leash in his hand, he stood in front of Sarah. "What part of 'stay at the carriage house' didn't you understand? I'm tempted to put one of these on you to keep you out of trouble."

"I was afraid Officer Robinson wouldn't get here in time. When I didn't hear the dogs, I knew something was wrong."

"So did we. Officer Robinson hadn't seen anything when he walked around the front, but when he got to the back and it was quiet, he realized something was off. We worked so hard to iron out a schedule Jane and the clinic could live with, there should have been barking dogs. Luckily, Officer Robinson saw the unlocked back door and knew that wasn't the norm either, so he called me."

"How long were you in the hall?"

"Long enough to know Jacob may have been lovestruck and jealous, but he didn't kill Riley or Botts."

CHAPTER FORTY-TWO

"You realize, Sarah," Anne said the following Sunday, "that may have been your first and last ride with the Wildcats." She picked up a small plate from the Southwind buffet table and filled it with the brunch goodies she'd commissioned Emily and Marcus to make in celebration of finding the real killer, Sarah's sleuthing, the Wheaton police department, and the Wildcats. "Here come Jacob and Harlan. Jacob must have finished extricating your shoes from his bike. I think I'll leave the three of you alone while I go work the room. Looks like we have a good crowd of would-be voters here."

Sarah loved how Anne used every opportunity to politic. They might still not be bosom buddies, but they understood each other better now.

As Jacob and Harlan came up to her, both giving her a thumbs-up, her face warmed.

It had been scary and awfully freeing to ride on the back of Jacob's motorcycle, but she hadn't known what to do with her feet. She'd finally opted to rest the heels of her shoes in the opening between the tire and the exhaust pipe. Each time Jacob turned, she pushed her heels down farther to gain a better grip on the bike. It was only when they got back to the Southwind parking lot and she tried to dismount that she realized she was stuck. Jacob eased her feet out of her shoes, happy she hadn't burned herself. In order to avoid damaging his motorcycle, he'd spent the better part of an hour removing the pipes, pulling out the shoes, and rebuilding his bike.

Now, with an iced tea in one hand, Jacob made a show of wiping sweat from his brow with the back of the other. "Hardest work I've done today, but not as hard as what you did for me. Harlan and Sarah, I'm very grateful for everything you did to prove I was innocent, but, Sarah, based upon time and effort, I think we might now be even."

"No question. Is your motorcycle okay?"

"The bike survived, but I don't think I'll be inviting you back for another ride anytime soon. Still, I can't begin to tell the two of you how scared I was thinking things might never turn out the way they did."

Harlan clapped Jacob on the shoulder. "It worked out well for everyone, even Tonya. She may eventually stand trial for what she did, but at least for now, she's getting the medical treatment she desperately needs."

"I only wish she'd taken advantage of a VA or nonprofit counseling program before things ended the way they did."

"So do I. Jacob, if you'll excuse us, I want to show Sarah something."

"No problem." Jacob pointed across the room to where his sister was in full campaign mode. "I think it's time for me to have some fun being a pesky little brother."

As Jacob wandered off, Sarah was glad to see the bounce in his step was back, as was his penchant for annoying his sister.

"Sarah, come over to the front windows with me."

Curious, Sarah followed Harlan. Sarah knew Emily had crammed two small tables onto Southwind's porch, filling its limited space. If the numbers worked out and profits from Southwind and the Pub continued to flow, Emily planned to have Cliff build a bar and porch off the back of the building.

What could Harlan want to show her? She peered through the window, able to see Jane's Place. Sarah wasn't sure how Jane was managing to keep her restaurant open, considering how much her business had fallen off once the story of her vegan substitutions got around. Based on the number of cars parked at Jane's Place each night since the newspaper and the television stations reported on the scam, Sarah was positive Jane wasn't filling her tables even once. Unless Jane came up with a new concept soon, Sarah wondered how long it would be before Jane's Place closed.

Sarah cocked her head to the right and frowned. Grace was slowly walking up the walkway to Jane's Place. Sarah glanced toward Harlan. From where he was standing, she wasn't sure if he could see Grace. His jovial expression convinced Sarah that Grace's march wasn't what he wanted her to see. "Well?"

Harlan pointed outside to the table where Glenn,

Vera, Carole, and the animal shelter's Phyllis sat at a table. Buddy lay at Carole's feet. "I'd say most everything worked out well for everyone."

Sarah was stunned. "Buddy? And Carole?"

"That's right. Those four have met several times at the shelter, exploring how the clinic and shelter might become part of the animal rescue system. Phyllis deliberately brought Buddy to their meetings. You know Carole's always had a soft spot for Buddy but was afraid to take on the responsibility for a pet because of her substance abuse history. Well, whether it was what you did at the clinic or simply having more confidence in herself—because the last thing she wanted was the shot Tonya almost gave her—Carole recently asked to give Buddy a forever home, and Phyllis approved it. I think they'll be good together."

"I'm thrilled for both of them."

"I am, too, but you realize you'll have to pick a new pet to walk next Saturday."

"That's next week. Right now, I'm going back to the carriage house. I have a cat and dog who need a little loving."

RECIPES

E's Crock-Pot Butternut Squash Soup *(makes 10 servings)*

1–2 10-12 ounce bags of cut butternut squash

Chop an onion, an apple, and a red pepper (more if desired).

Put all in the Crock-Pot.

Add 1 box of vegetable stock.

When everything is soft, blend or puree.

Season with sage, garlic, cumin, salt, or pepper (whatever you prefer to your taste).
Add 1 can coconut milk into the Crock-Pot just before serving.

Jane's Chilled Zucchini Soup *(makes 6 servings)*

2 tablespoons extra-virgin olive oil
1 yellow onion, diced
¾ teaspoon sea salt (this can be increased to taste)
3½ pounds zucchini, quartered lengthwise, then cut
    crosswise into ½-inch pieces
2 chopped cloves garlic
¼ teaspoon freshly ground black pepper or red
    pepper flakes
6 cups chicken or vegetable stock
2 cups tightly packed baby spinach leaves
½ cup loosely packed fresh basil leaves
1 tablespoon freshly squeezed lemon juice (can be
    increased to taste)
2 tablespoons plain, full-fat Greek yogurt

In a large skillet, heat the olive oil over medium heat.

Add the onion and a pinch of the salt. Sauté about 6 minutes, until golden.

Add the zucchini, garlic, black pepper or red pepper flakes, and ¼ tablespoon salt. Sauté for 4 minutes.

Deglaze the pan by pouring in ½ cup of the stock. Stir to loosen any bits stuck to the bottom.

Cook until the liquid is reduced by half and then remove from the heat.

Pour ⅓ of the remaining stock into a blender. Add ⅓ of the zucchini sauté, ⅓ of the spinach, and ⅓ of the basil. Blend until smooth.

Transfer the mixture to a pot over low heat.

Repeat the above process twice more.

Stir the lemon juice and remaining salt into the soup.

Chill the soup in the refrigerator for 2–3 hours.

Serve garnished with a dollop of the yogurt.

The soup can be stored in an airtight container in the refrigerator for up to 5 days.

Emily's Lasagna Casserole

This can be made with store-bought sauce and noodles, but if you're willing to spend a little time on the sauce . . .

For the Sauce
2 28-ounce cans whole peeled tomatoes
3 tablespoons extra-virgin olive oil
4 garlic cloves, thinly sliced
1 teaspoon kosher salt
1 cup crème fraîche

In a large bowl, crush the tomatoes until pieces are bite-size.

In a large saucepan, warm the olive oil over medium heat. Add the garlic and cook, stirring, until the mixture sizzles (about 1 minute).

Add the tomatoes and 1 teaspoon salt and bring to a boil.

Lower the heat and let the sauce simmer, stirring often, about 30 minutes, until it is slightly reduced.

Whisk the crème fraîche into the sauce and season to taste with more salt, if desired.

Let the sauce cool to room temperature.

For the Lasagna
    Use a 9-by-13-inch baking dish.

tomato sauce, at room temperature
12 no-boil lasagna noodles
1 cup finely grated Parmesan cheese
1½ cups coarsely grated whole-milk mozzarella
    cheese
2 large handfuls fresh basil leaves torn into small
    pieces

Preheat oven to 400 degrees.

Ladle a thin layer of the room-temperature sauce
onto the bottom of the baking dish. Spread the sauce
to cover the surface of the dish using a spoon.

Add a layer of the noodles.

Spoon just enough tomato sauce to cover the pasta
and scatter some of the Parmesan, mozzarella, and
basil over the sauce. Repeat the layer process until all
ingredients are used.

Note: Make sure to end with sauce and cheese. Pasta
and basil burn if exposed, so they must be covered.

Bake 35–40 minutes until browned and the edges are
bubbling.

Rest at room temperature for fifteen minutes. Sprinkle some fresh basil over the top for garnish. Slice
and serve.

Pumpkin Quinoa Muffins (*makes 9 muffins*)

1 tablespoon flaxseed meal
3 tablespoons water
1¼ cup oat flour oats ground in a blender
½ cup quinoa flakes (plus extra for topping, optional)
½ cup blanched almond flour
¼ cup coconut sugar
2 teaspoons baking powder
1 teaspoon cinnamon
½ teaspoon vanilla bean powder or 1 teaspoon vanilla extract
½ teaspoon nutmeg
¼ teaspoon ginger
¼ teaspoon salt
¾ cup pumpkin puree
½ cup mashed banana (use either 1 large or 2 small)
¼ cup nondairy milk
¼ cup maple syrup
pumpkin seeds (optional)

Preheat oven to 350 degrees.

Grease a 12-cup muffin tin.

Combine the flaxseed meal and water. Set the mixture aside to gel while preparing the remaining ingredients. (This makes a flax egg, which is the vegan substitute for an egg.)

In a large bowl, whisk the remaining dry ingredients together (minus vanilla extract).

In a separate bowl, beat the pumpkin, milk, banana, and syrup together. Whisk in the wet flaxseed mixture and pour the wet ingredients into the dry. Stir to completely combine. Note: The batter will be thick but soft. It can still be stirred.

Fill each cup ¾ of the way full. Add water to the empty muffin holders (3). If desired, sprinkle the tops of the muffins with pumpkin seeds and quinoa flakes.

Bake on the center rack of the oven for 23–25 minutes. You should be able to insert a cake tester and have it come out clean.

Let muffins cool in the pan for 5 minutes.

Transfer to a wire rack and cool.

Acknowledgments

Authors have imaginations. By thinking outside the box, we create characters and plots for readers to enjoy. Still, we understand our stories must be anchored in fact. Several people were generous with their time and expertise when I wrote *Three Treats Too Many*. Of course, any errors are my own.

Sidney and Elenor Conn not only fed me a delicious lunch, but spent hours explaining motorcycles to me. Dr. Andy Sokol permitted me to shadow him at his veterinarian practice and patiently answered my questions. My thanks to the three of them.

I appreciate the editing Barb Goffman provided. Her suggestions and questions made me think, search for solutions, revise, and expand. Because of Barb's input, *Three Treats Too Many* is a better book. Thanks also to my agent, Dawn Dowdle, for her help and support.

There are no words to express the extent of my gratitude to Fran and Lee Godchaux. Without their input and help in so many ways, the final version of this book would not exist.

Connect with U(s)

Visit us online at
KensingtonBooks.com
to read more from your favorite authors, see books
by series, view reading group guides, and more.

for sneak peeks, chances to win books and prize packs,
and to share your thoughts with other readers.

facebook.com/kensingtonpublishing
twitter.com/kensingtonbooks

Tell us what you think!

To share your thoughts, submit a review,
or sign up for our eNewsletters, please visit:
KensingtonBooks.com/TellUs.